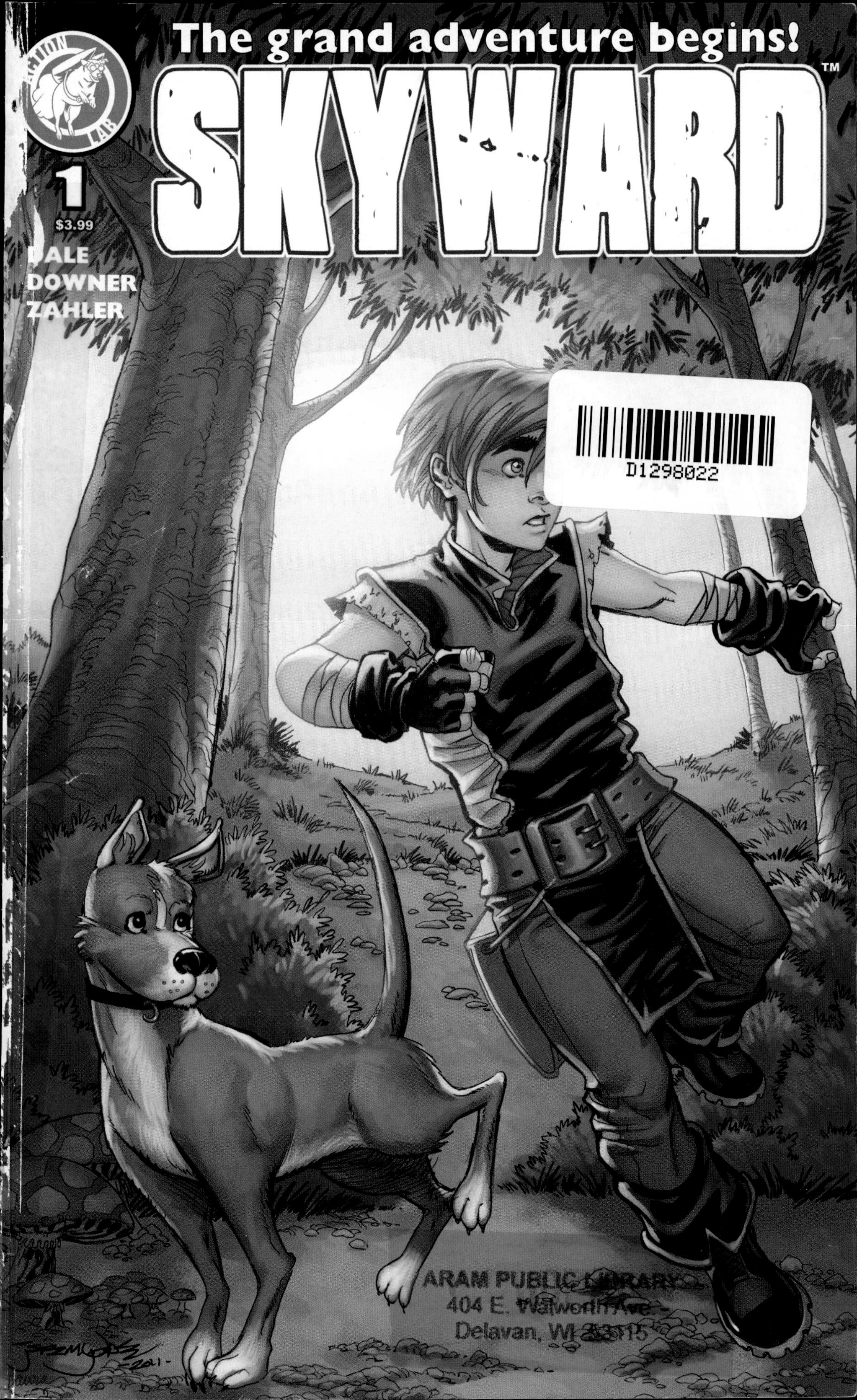
The grand adventure begins!
SKYWARD™
1
$3.99
DALE
DOWNER
ZAHLER

SKYWARD ™

1

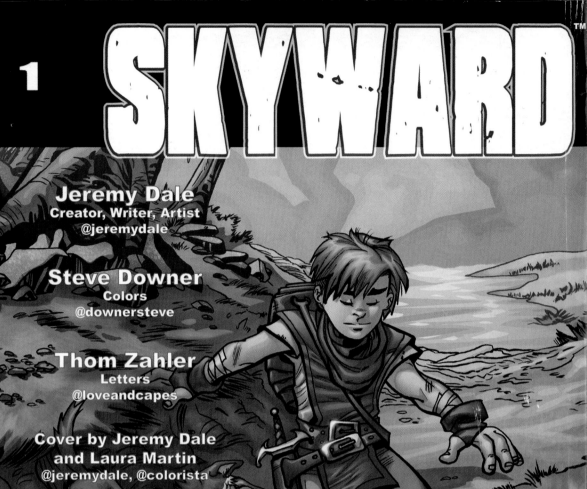

Jeremy Dale
Creator, Writer, Artist
@jeremydale

Steve Downer
Colors
@downersteve

Thom Zahler
Letters
@loveandcapes

**Cover by Jeremy Dale
and Laura Martin**
@jeremydale, @colorista

Kelly Dale
Editor
@kellyedale

KEVIN FREEMAN- PRESIDENT
SHAWN PRYOR- VP DIGITAL MEDIA
DAVE DWONCH- CREATIVE DIRECTOR
SHAWN GABBORIN- EDITOR IN CHIEF
JASON MARTIN- EDITOR
JEREMY WHITLEY- DIRECTOR OF MARKETING
CHAD CICCONI- LOOKING FOR PEACE IN A SAVAGE LAND
COLLEEN BOYD- ASSOCIATE EDITOR

Jeremy Dale
the talent

Kelly Dale
editor

Kirby
Canine Relations

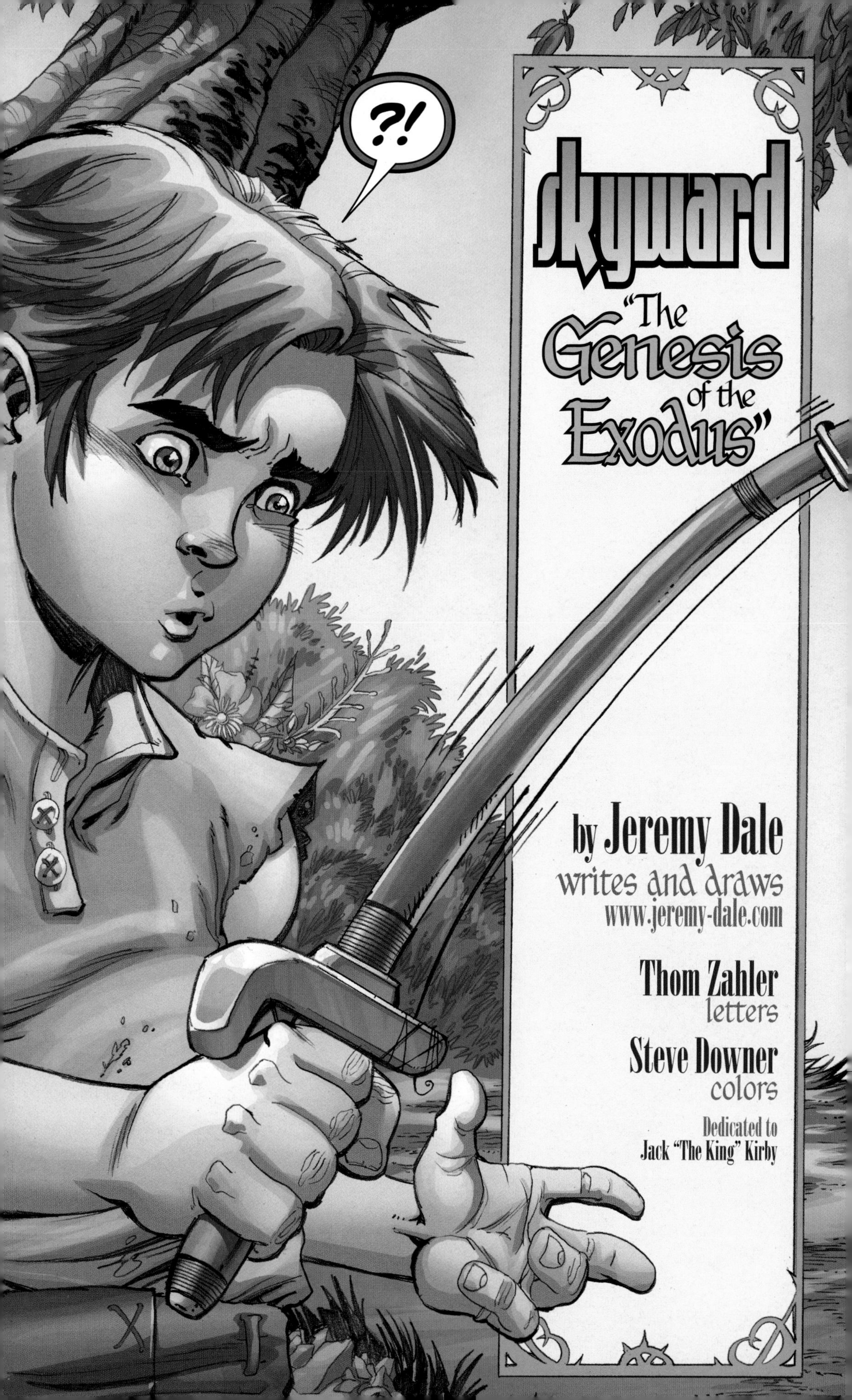
?!
skyward
"The Genesis of the Exodus"
by Jeremy Dale
writes and draws
www.jeremy-dale.com
Thom Zahler
letters
Steve Downer
colors
Dedicated to
Jack "The King" Kirby

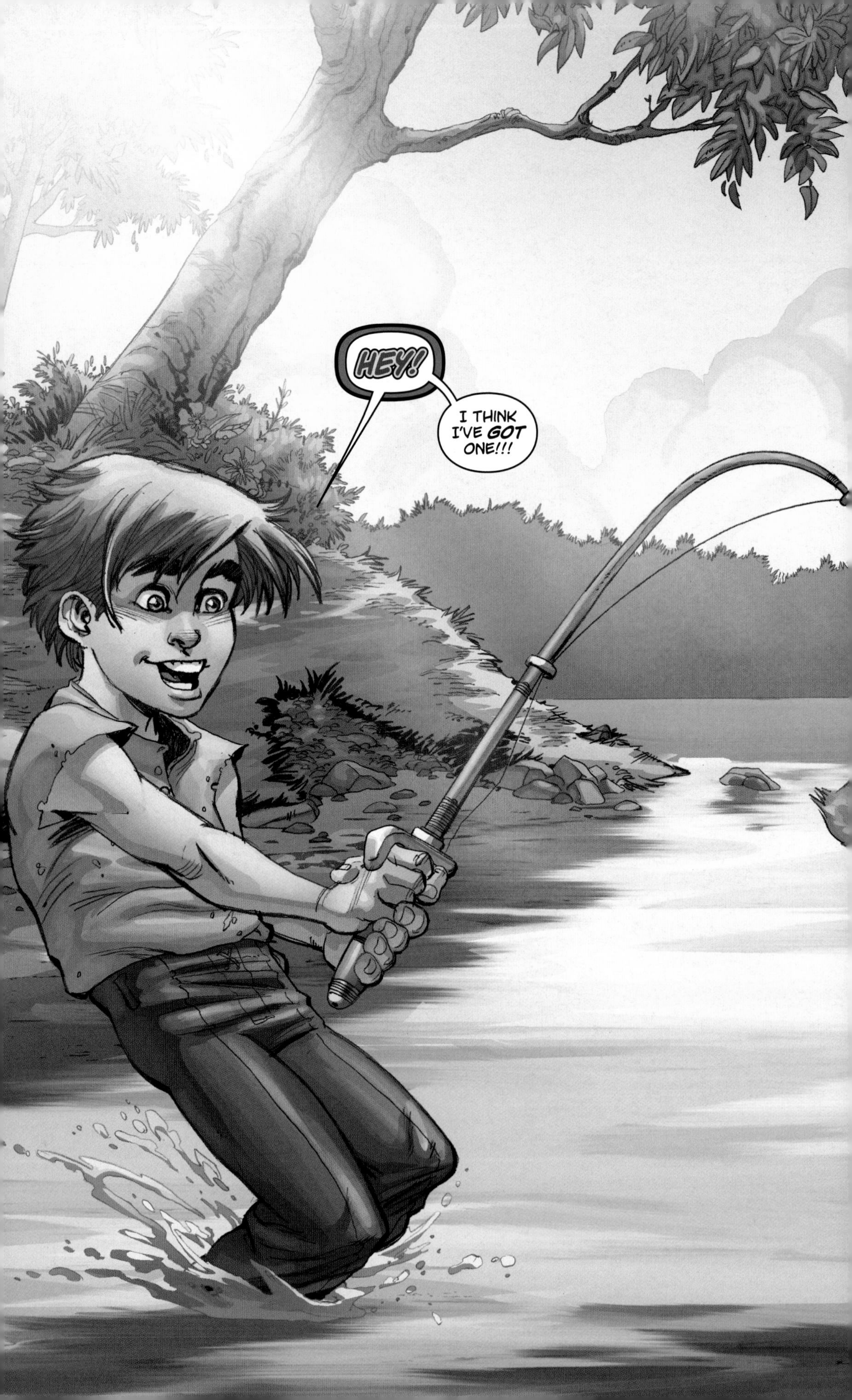
HEY!
I THINK I'VE GOT ONE!!!

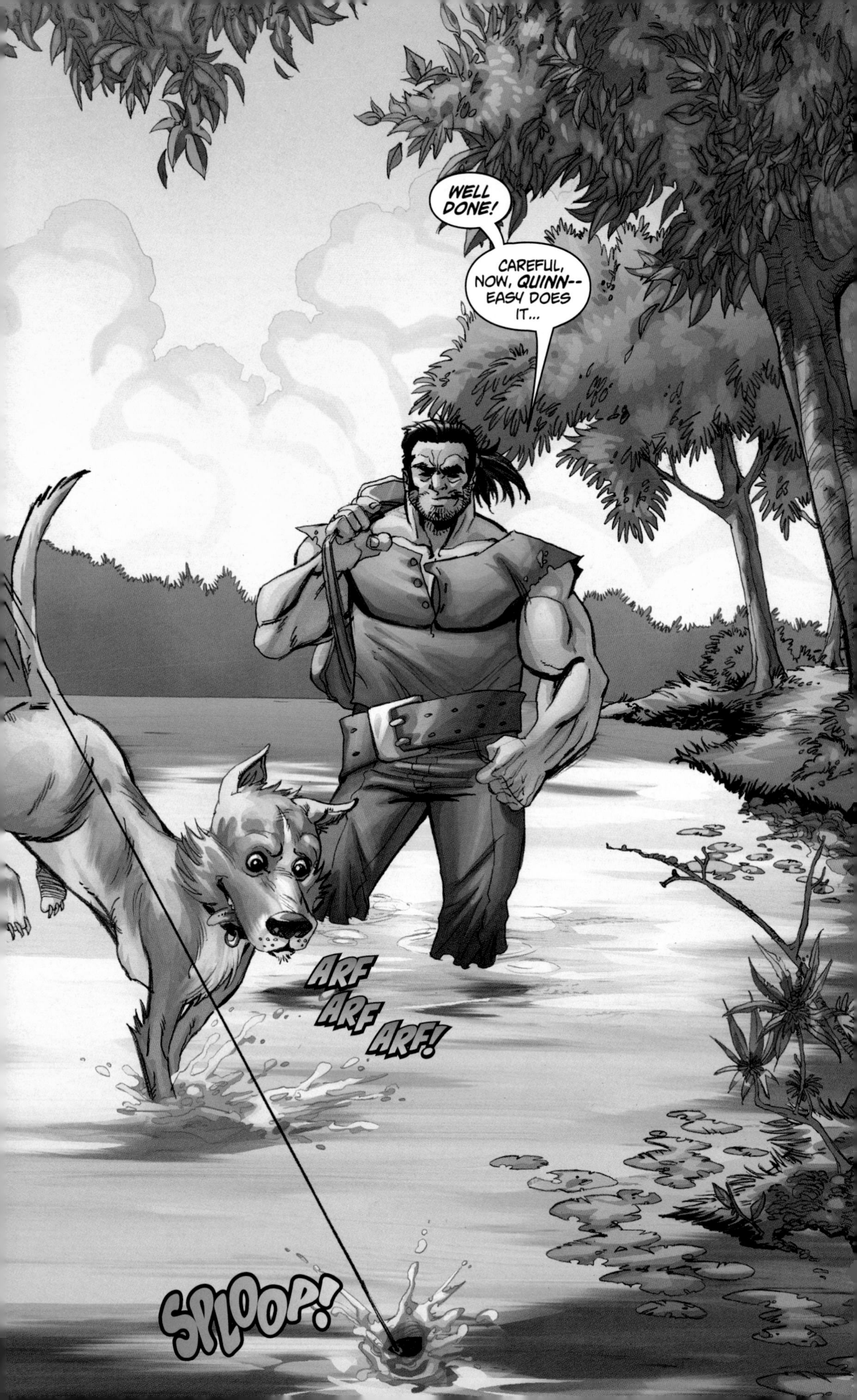
WELL DONE!
CAREFUL, NOW, QUINN-- EASY DOES IT...
ARF ARF ARF!
SPLOOP!

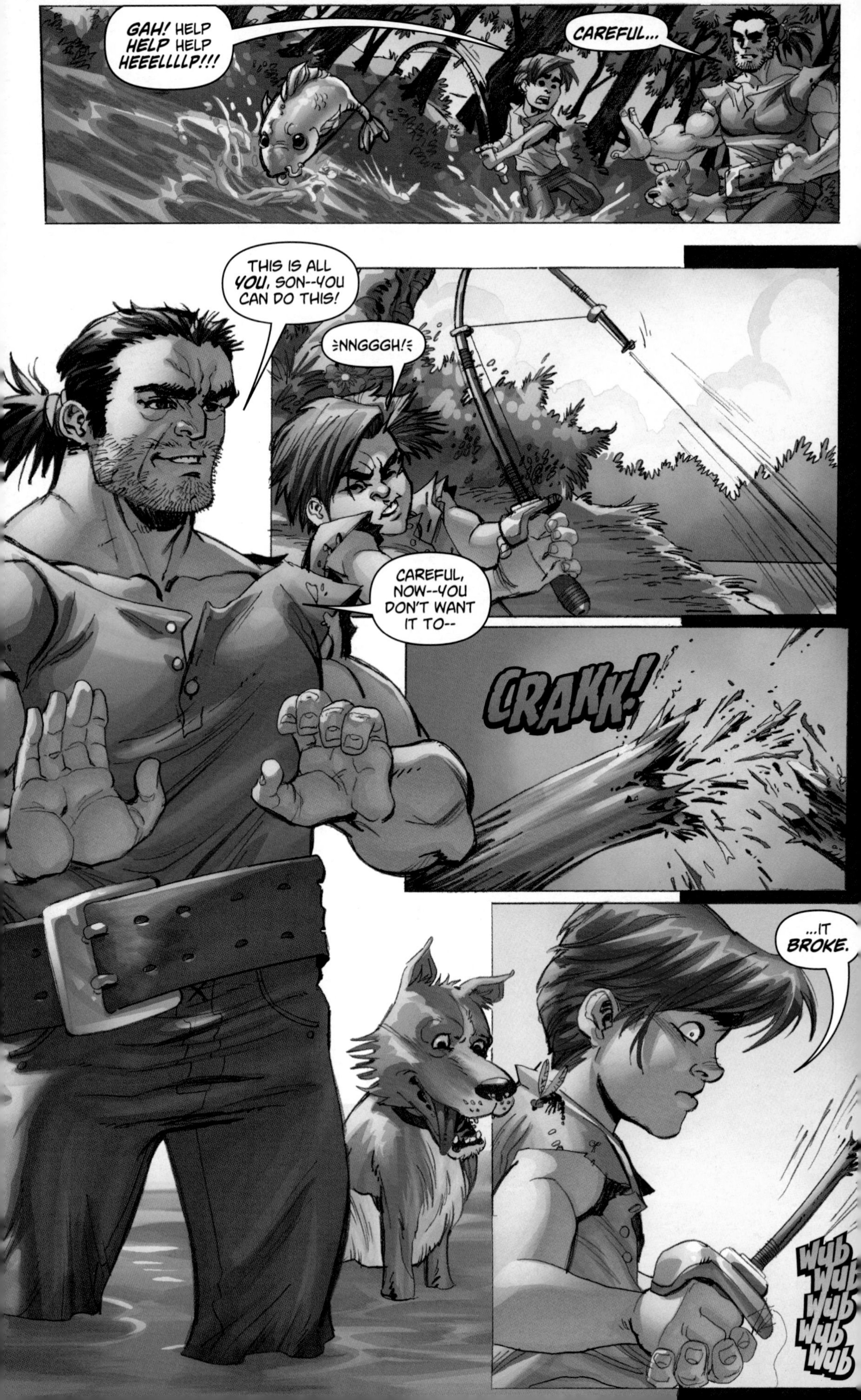
GAH! HELP HELP HELP HEEELLLLP!!!
CAREFUL...
THIS IS ALL YOU, SON--YOU CAN DO THIS!
NNGGGH!
CAREFUL, NOW--YOU DON'T WANT IT TO--
CRAKK!
...IT BROKE.
Wub Wub Wub Wub Wub

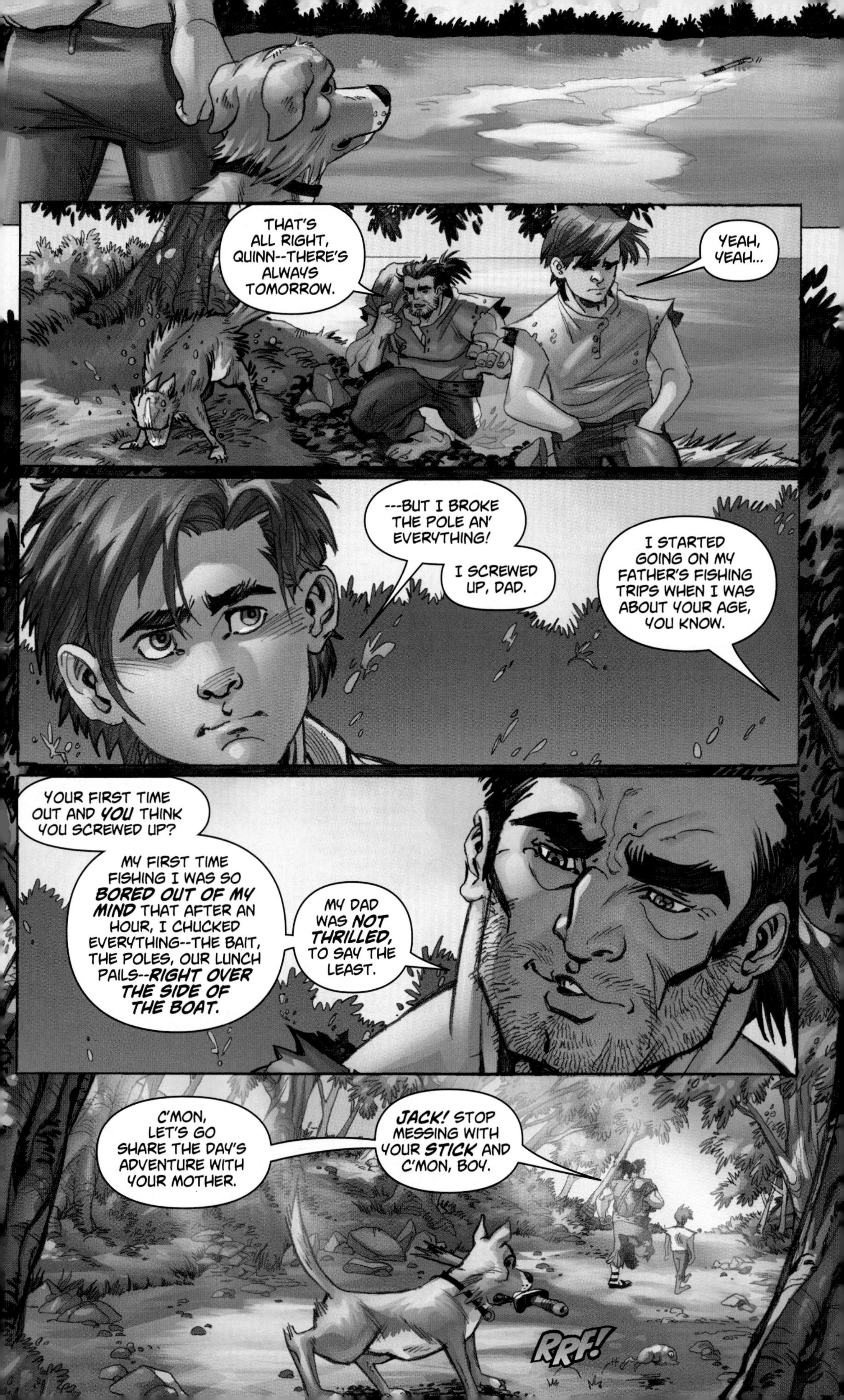

THAT'S ALL RIGHT, QUINN--THERE'S ALWAYS TOMORROW.
YEAH, YEAH...
---BUT I BROKE THE POLE AN' EVERYTHING!
I SCREWED UP, DAD.
I STARTED GOING ON MY FATHER'S FISHING TRIPS WHEN I WAS ABOUT YOUR AGE, YOU KNOW.
YOUR FIRST TIME OUT AND YOU THINK YOU SCREWED UP?
MY FIRST TIME FISHING I WAS SO BORED OUT OF MY MIND THAT AFTER AN HOUR, I CHUCKED EVERYTHING--THE BAIT, THE POLES, OUR LUNCH PAILS--RIGHT OVER THE SIDE OF THE BOAT.
MY DAD WAS NOT THRILLED, TO SAY THE LEAST.
C'MON, LET'S GO SHARE THE DAY'S ADVENTURE WITH YOUR MOTHER.
JACK! STOP MESSING WITH YOUR STICK AND C'MON, BOY.
RRF!

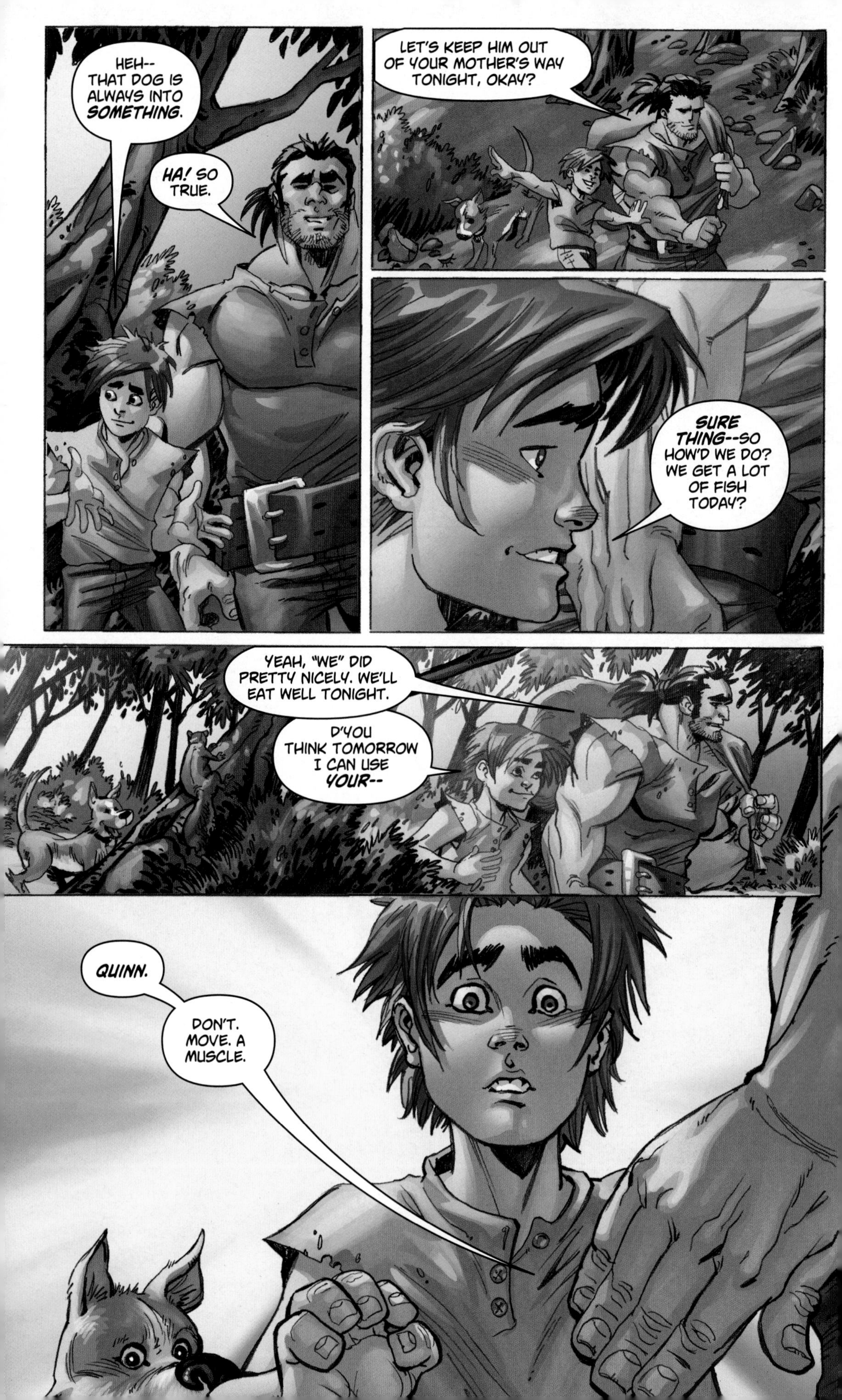
HEH--
THAT DOG IS
ALWAYS INTO
SOMETHING.
HA! SO
TRUE.
LET'S KEEP HIM OUT
OF YOUR MOTHER'S WAY
TONIGHT, OKAY?
SURE
THING--SO
HOW'D WE DO?
WE GET A LOT
OF FISH
TODAY?
YEAH, "WE" DID
PRETTY NICELY. WE'LL
EAT WELL TONIGHT.
D'YOU
THINK TOMORROW
I CAN USE
YOUR--
QUINN.
DON'T.
MOVE. A
MUSCLE.

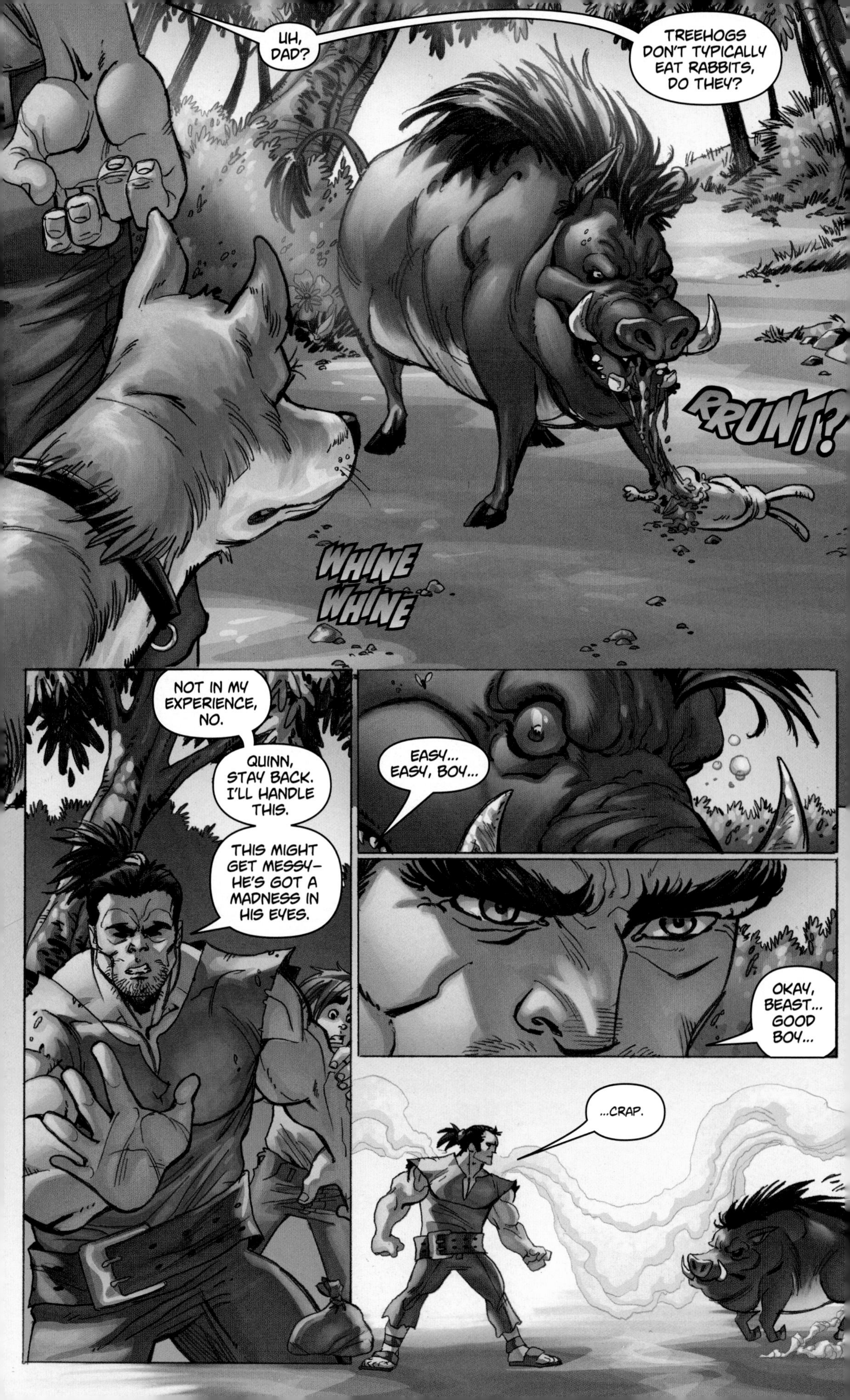
UH, DAD?
TREEHOGS DON'T TYPICALLY EAT RABBITS, DO THEY?
RRUNT?!
WHINE WHINE
NOT IN MY EXPERIENCE, NO.
QUINN, STAY BACK. I'LL HANDLE THIS.
THIS MIGHT GET MESSY— HE'S GOT A MADNESS IN HIS EYES.
EASY... EASY, BOY...
OKAY, BEAST... GOOD BOY...
...CRAP.

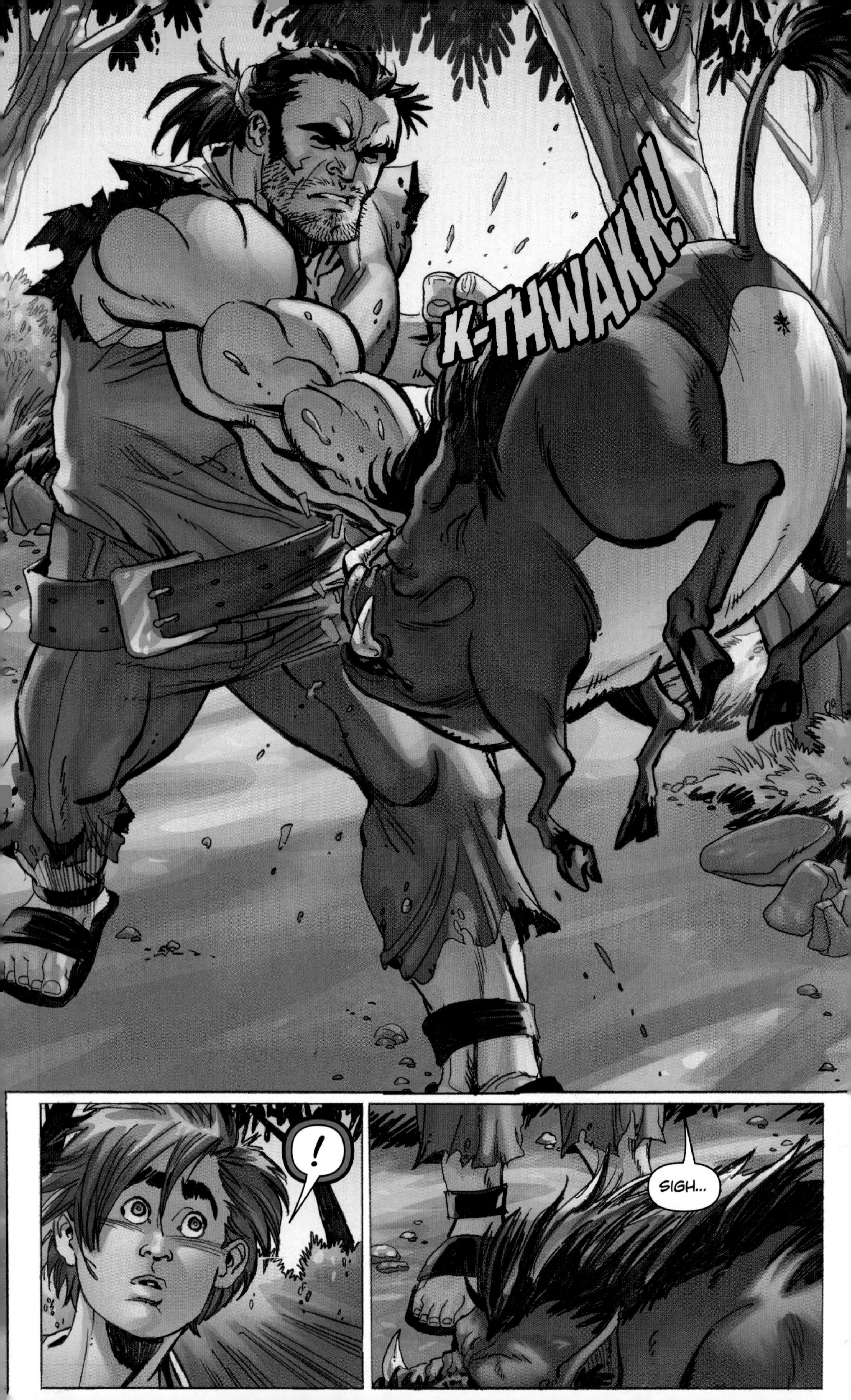
K-THWAKK!
!
SIGH...

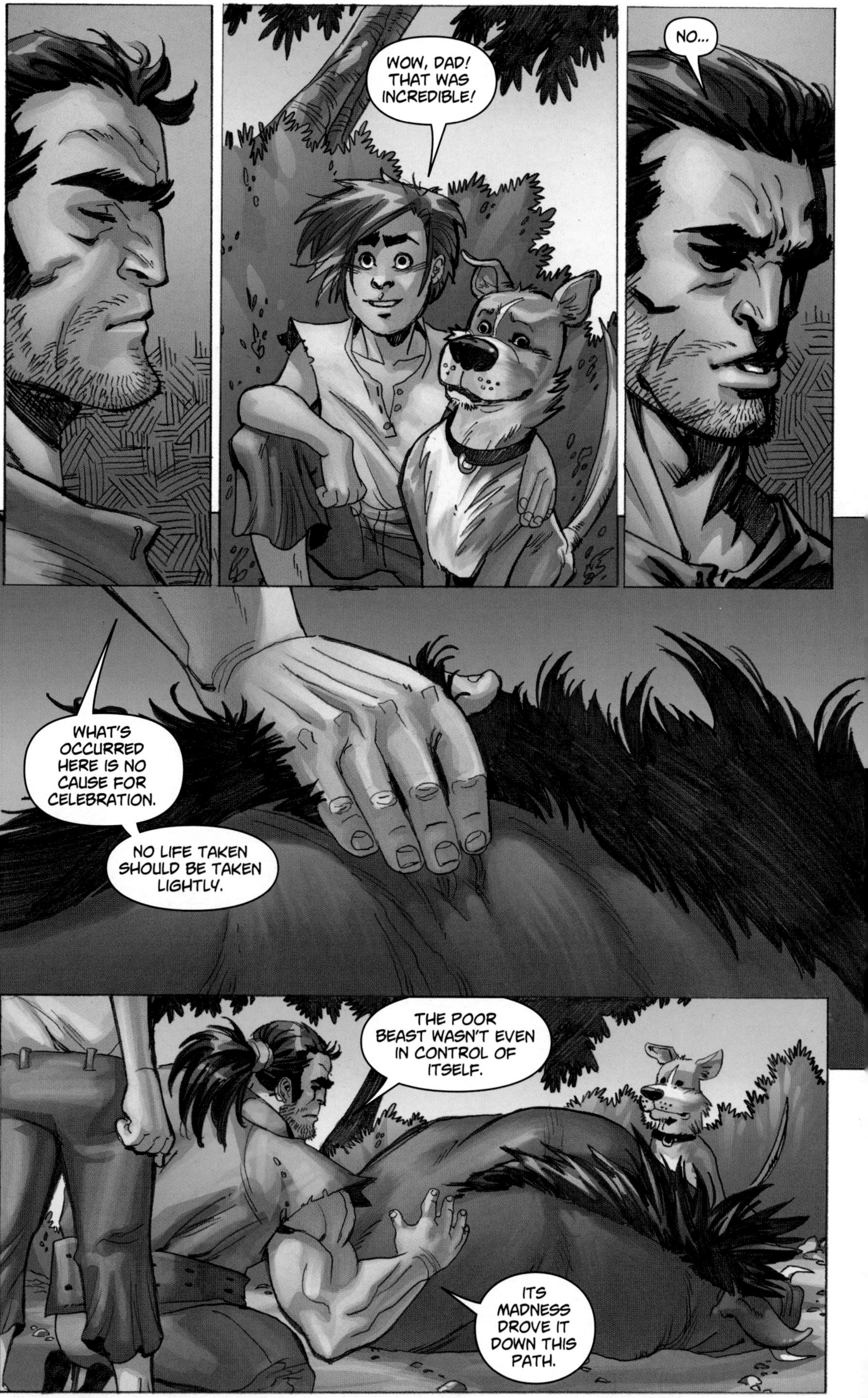

WOW, DAD! THAT WAS INCREDIBLE!
NO...
WHAT'S OCCURRED HERE IS NO CAUSE FOR CELEBRATION.
NO LIFE TAKEN SHOULD BE TAKEN LIGHTLY.
THE POOR BEAST WASN'T EVEN IN CONTROL OF ITSELF.
ITS MADNESS DROVE IT DOWN THIS PATH.

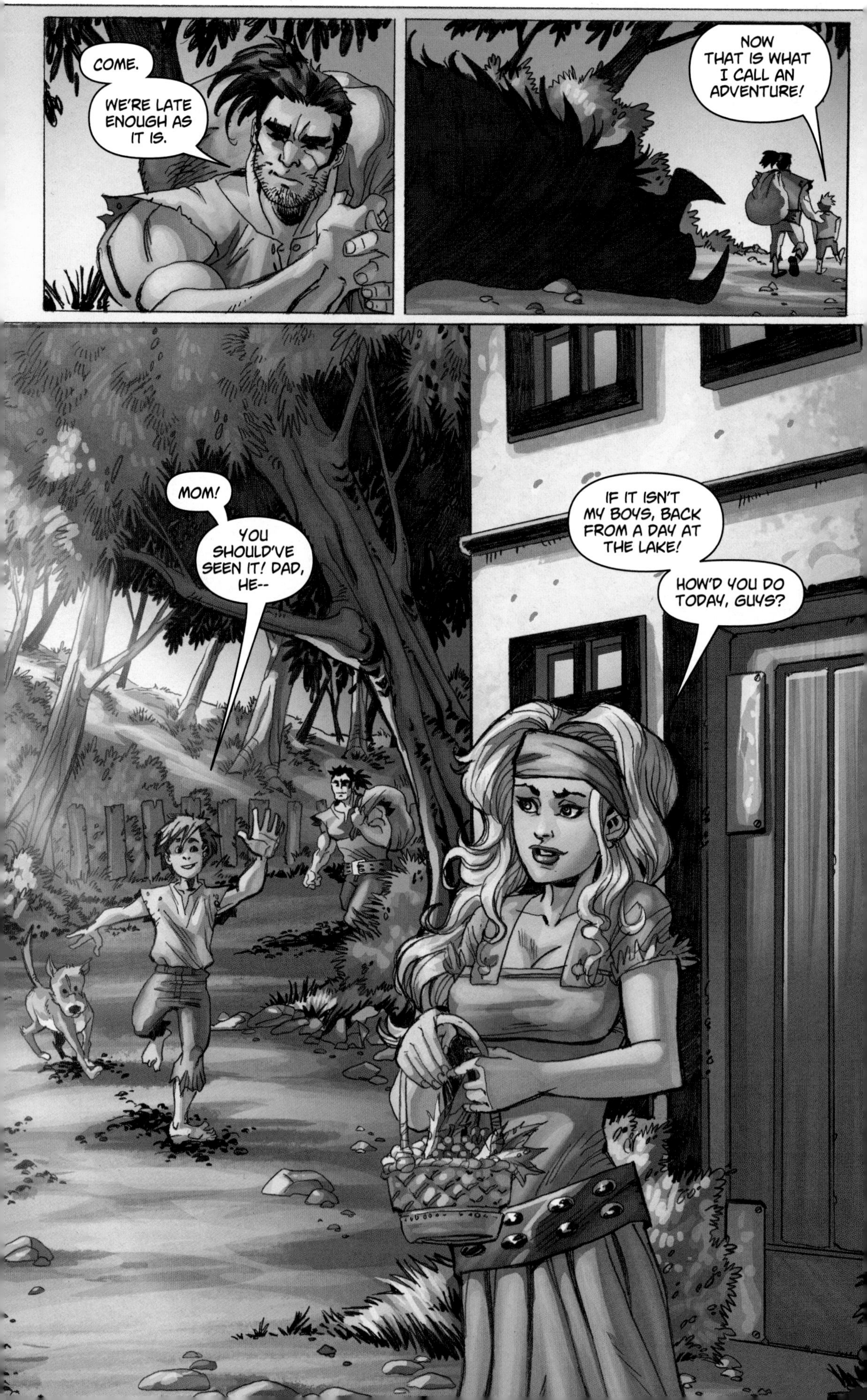
COME.
WE'RE LATE ENOUGH AS IT IS.
NOW THAT IS WHAT I CALL AN ADVENTURE!
MOM!
YOU SHOULD'VE SEEN IT! DAD, HE--
IF IT ISN'T MY BOYS, BACK FROM A DAY AT THE LAKE!
HOW'D YOU DO TODAY, GUYS?

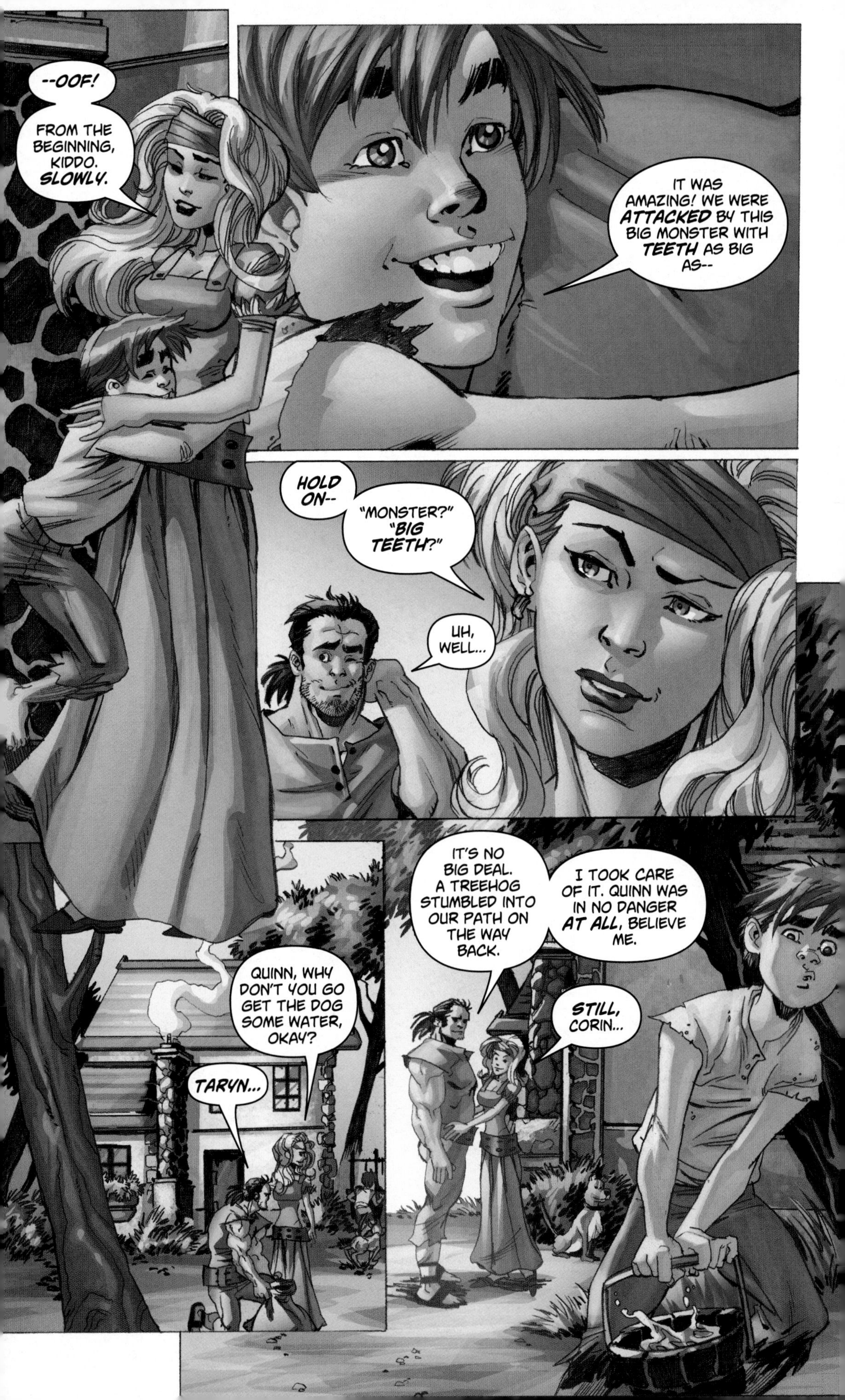
--OOF!
FROM THE BEGINNING, KIDDO. SLOWLY.
IT WAS AMAZING! WE WERE ATTACKED BY THIS BIG MONSTER WITH TEETH AS BIG AS--
HOLD ON--
"MONSTER?" "BIG TEETH?"
UH, WELL...
QUINN, WHY DON'T YOU GO GET THE DOG SOME WATER, OKAY?
TARYN...
IT'S NO BIG DEAL. A TREEHOG STUMBLED INTO OUR PATH ON THE WAY BACK.
I TOOK CARE OF IT. QUINN WAS IN NO DANGER AT ALL, BELIEVE ME.
STILL, CORIN...

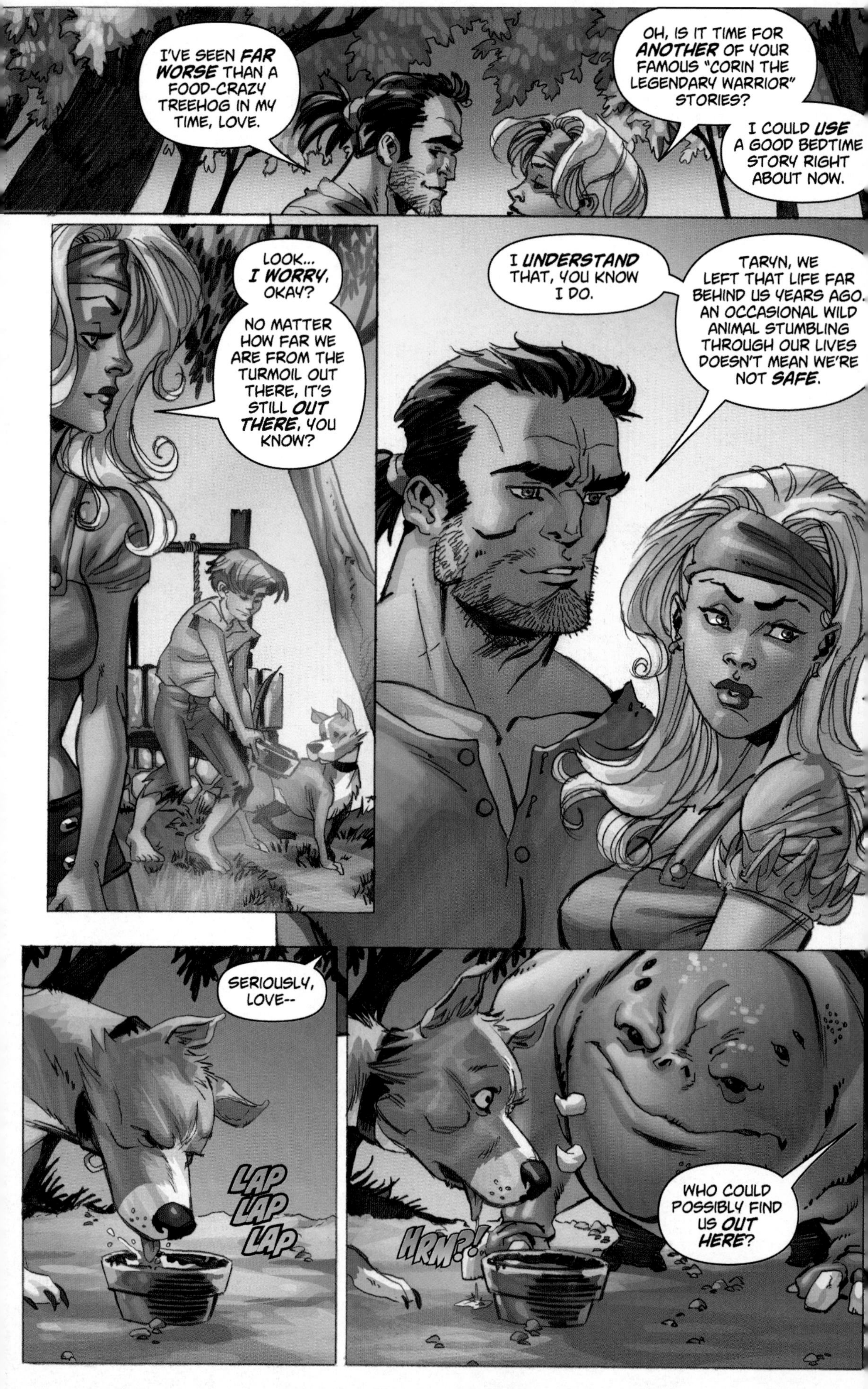
I'VE SEEN FAR WORSE THAN A FOOD-CRAZY TREEHOG IN MY TIME, LOVE.
OH, IS IT TIME FOR ANOTHER OF YOUR FAMOUS "CORIN THE LEGENDARY WARRIOR" STORIES?
I COULD USE A GOOD BEDTIME STORY RIGHT ABOUT NOW.
LOOK... I WORRY, OKAY?
NO MATTER HOW FAR WE ARE FROM THE TURMOIL OUT THERE, IT'S STILL OUT THERE, YOU KNOW?
I UNDERSTAND THAT, YOU KNOW I DO.
TARYN, WE LEFT THAT LIFE FAR BEHIND US YEARS AGO. AN OCCASIONAL WILD ANIMAL STUMBLING THROUGH OUR LIVES DOESN'T MEAN WE'RE NOT SAFE.
SERIOUSLY, LOVE--
LAP LAP LAP
HRM?!
WHO COULD POSSIBLY FIND US OUT HERE?

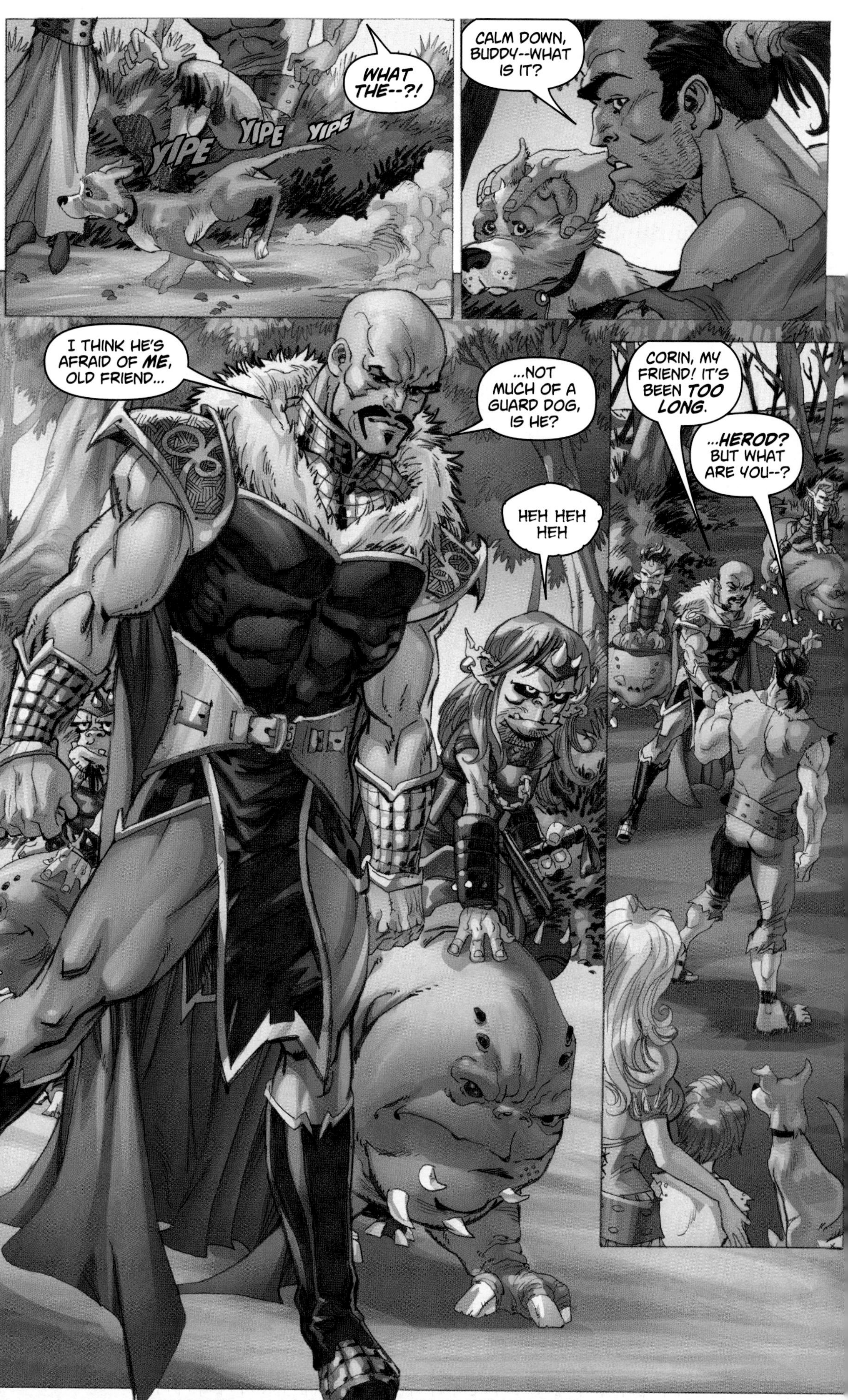
YIPE
YIPE
YIPE
WHAT THE--?!
CALM DOWN, BUDDY--WHAT IS IT?
I THINK HE'S AFRAID OF ME, OLD FRIEND...
...NOT MUCH OF A GUARD DOG, IS HE?
HEH HEH HEH
CORIN, MY FRIEND! IT'S BEEN TOO LONG.
...HEROD? BUT WHAT ARE YOU--?

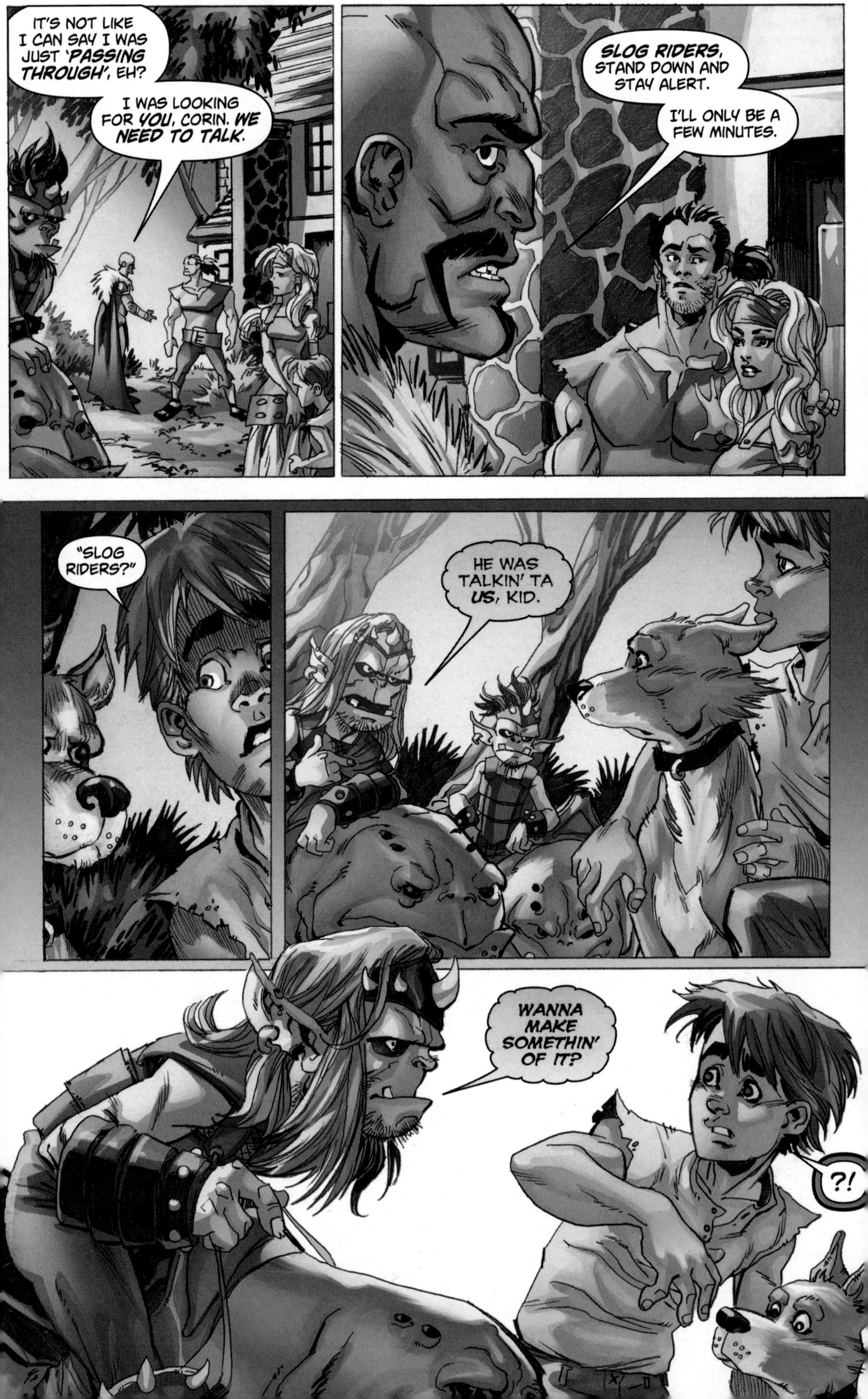
IT'S NOT LIKE I CAN SAY I WAS JUST 'PASSING THROUGH', EH?
I WAS LOOKING FOR YOU, CORIN. WE NEED TO TALK.
SLOG RIDERS, STAND DOWN AND STAY ALERT.
I'LL ONLY BE A FEW MINUTES.
"SLOG RIDERS?"
HE WAS TALKIN' TA US, KID.
WANNA MAKE SOMETHIN' OF IT?
?!

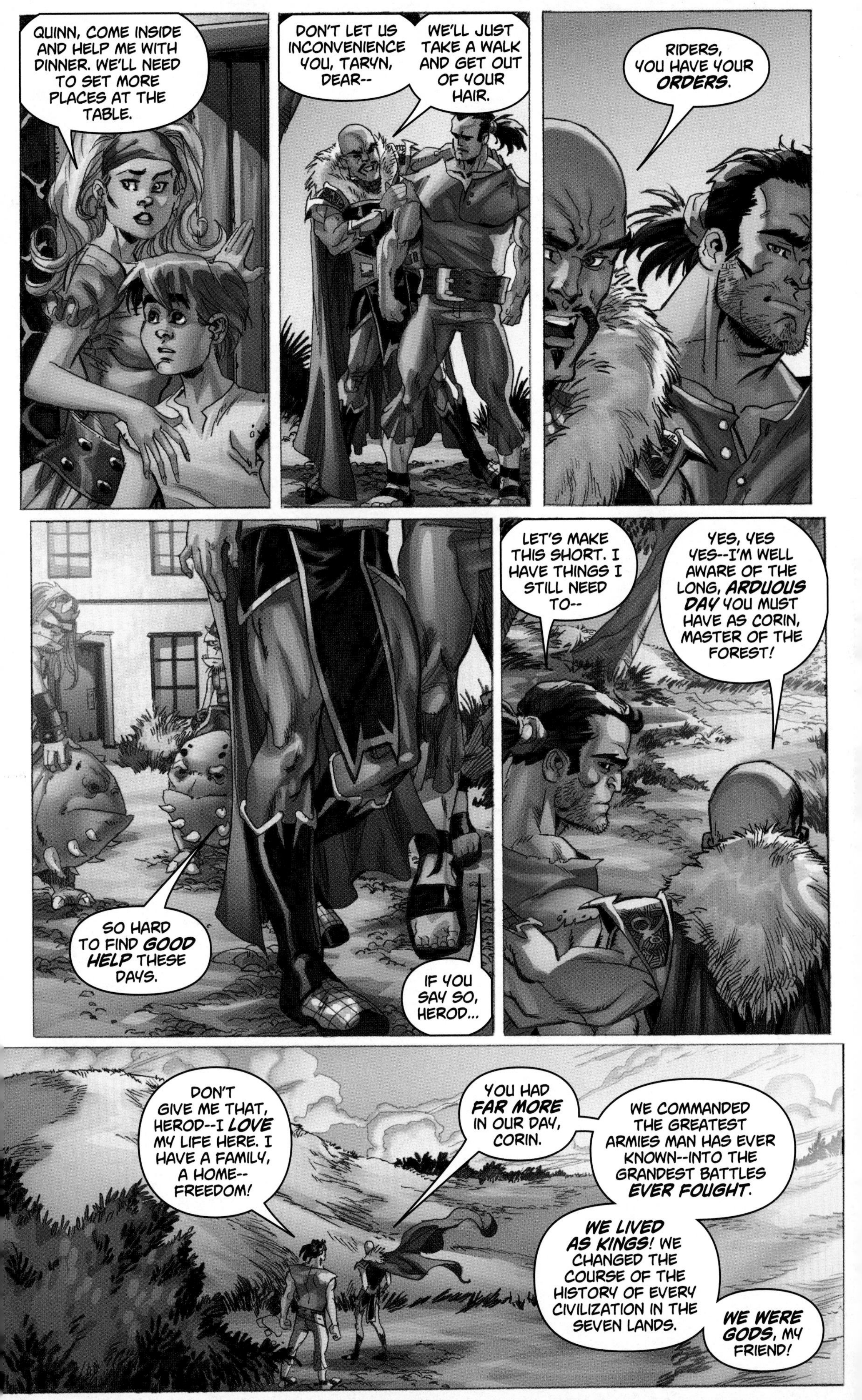
QUINN, COME INSIDE AND HELP ME WITH DINNER. WE'LL NEED TO SET MORE PLACES AT THE TABLE.
DON'T LET US INCONVENIENCE YOU, TARYN, DEAR--
WE'LL JUST TAKE A WALK AND GET OUT OF YOUR HAIR.
RIDERS, YOU HAVE YOUR ORDERS.
SO HARD TO FIND GOOD HELP THESE DAYS.
IF YOU SAY SO, HEROD...
LET'S MAKE THIS SHORT. I HAVE THINGS I STILL NEED TO--
YES, YES YES--I'M WELL AWARE OF THE LONG, ARDUOUS DAY YOU MUST HAVE AS CORIN, MASTER OF THE FOREST!
DON'T GIVE ME THAT, HEROD--I LOVE MY LIFE HERE. I HAVE A FAMILY, A HOME--FREEDOM!
YOU HAD FAR MORE IN OUR DAY, CORIN.
WE COMMANDED THE GREATEST ARMIES MAN HAS EVER KNOWN--INTO THE GRANDEST BATTLES EVER FOUGHT.
WE LIVED AS KINGS! WE CHANGED THE COURSE OF THE HISTORY OF EVERY CIVILIZATION IN THE SEVEN LANDS.
WE WERE GODS, MY FRIEND!

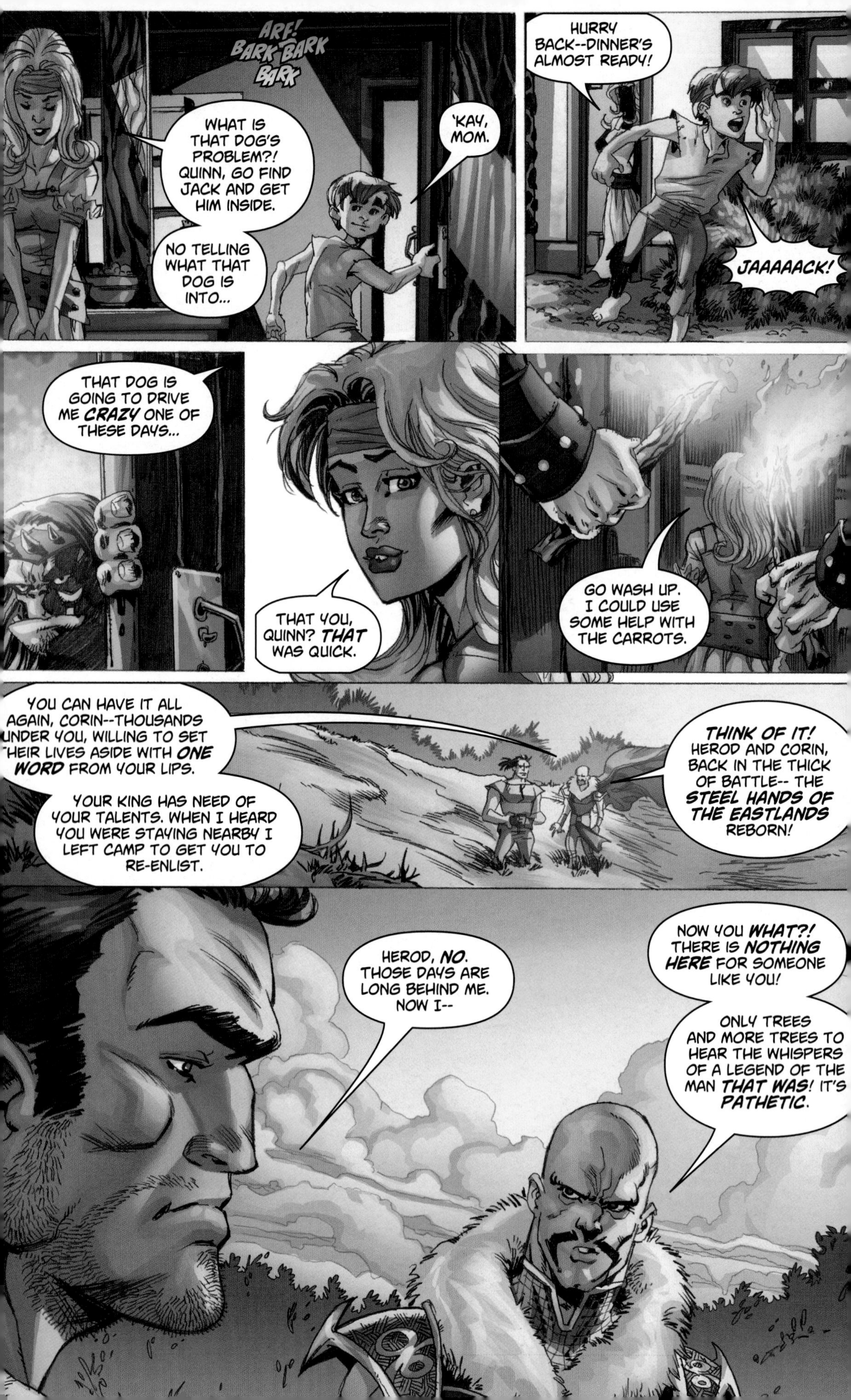
ARF! BARK BARK BARK
WHAT IS THAT DOG'S PROBLEM?! QUINN, GO FIND JACK AND GET HIM INSIDE.
NO TELLING WHAT THAT DOG IS INTO...
'KAY, MOM.
HURRY BACK--DINNER'S ALMOST READY!
JAAAAACK!
THAT DOG IS GOING TO DRIVE ME CRAZY ONE OF THESE DAYS...
THAT YOU, QUINN? THAT WAS QUICK.
GO WASH UP. I COULD USE SOME HELP WITH THE CARROTS.
YOU CAN HAVE IT ALL AGAIN, CORIN--THOUSANDS UNDER YOU, WILLING TO SET THEIR LIVES ASIDE WITH ONE WORD FROM YOUR LIPS.
YOUR KING HAS NEED OF YOUR TALENTS. WHEN I HEARD YOU WERE STAYING NEARBY I LEFT CAMP TO GET YOU TO RE-ENLIST.
THINK OF IT! HEROD AND CORIN, BACK IN THE THICK OF BATTLE-- THE STEEL HANDS OF THE EASTLANDS REBORN!
HEROD, NO. THOSE DAYS ARE LONG BEHIND ME. NOW I--
NOW YOU WHAT?! THERE IS NOTHING HERE FOR SOMEONE LIKE YOU!
ONLY TREES AND MORE TREES TO HEAR THE WHISPERS OF A LEGEND OF THE MAN THAT WAS! IT'S PATHETIC.

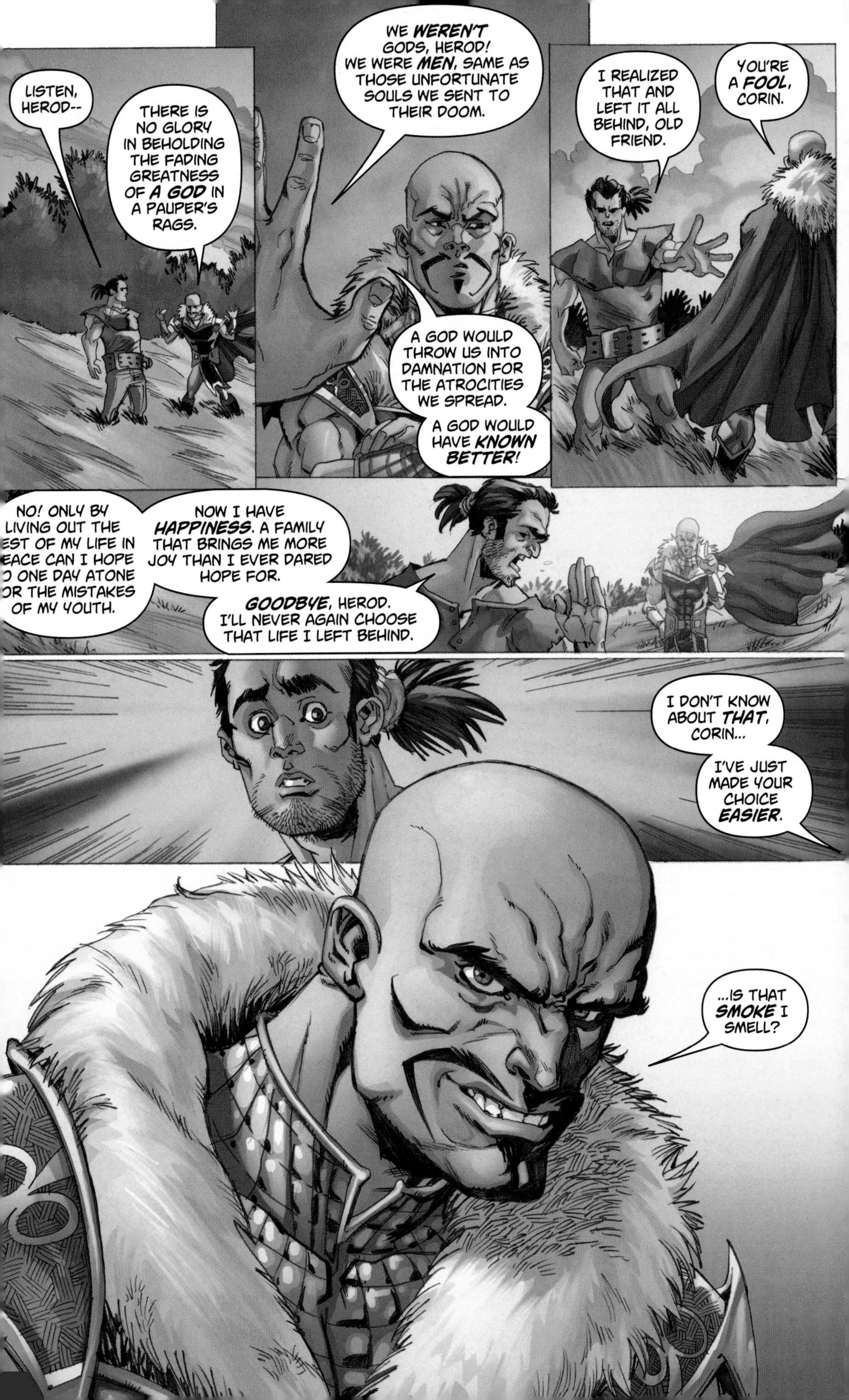
LISTEN, HEROD--
THERE IS NO GLORY IN BEHOLDING THE FADING GREATNESS OF A GOD IN A PAUPER'S RAGS.
WE WEREN'T GODS, HEROD! WE WERE MEN, SAME AS THOSE UNFORTUNATE SOULS WE SENT TO THEIR DOOM.
A GOD WOULD THROW US INTO DAMNATION FOR THE ATROCITIES WE SPREAD.
A GOD WOULD HAVE KNOWN BETTER!
I REALIZED THAT AND LEFT IT ALL BEHIND, OLD FRIEND.
YOU'RE A FOOL, CORIN.
NO! ONLY BY LIVING OUT THE EST OF MY LIFE IN EACE CAN I HOPE O ONE DAY ATONE OR THE MISTAKES OF MY YOUTH.
NOW I HAVE HAPPINESS. A FAMILY THAT BRINGS ME MORE JOY THAN I EVER DARED HOPE FOR.
GOODBYE, HEROD. I'LL NEVER AGAIN CHOOSE THAT LIFE I LEFT BEHIND.
I DON'T KNOW ABOUT THAT, CORIN...
I'VE JUST MADE YOUR CHOICE EASIER.
...IS THAT SMOKE I SMELL?

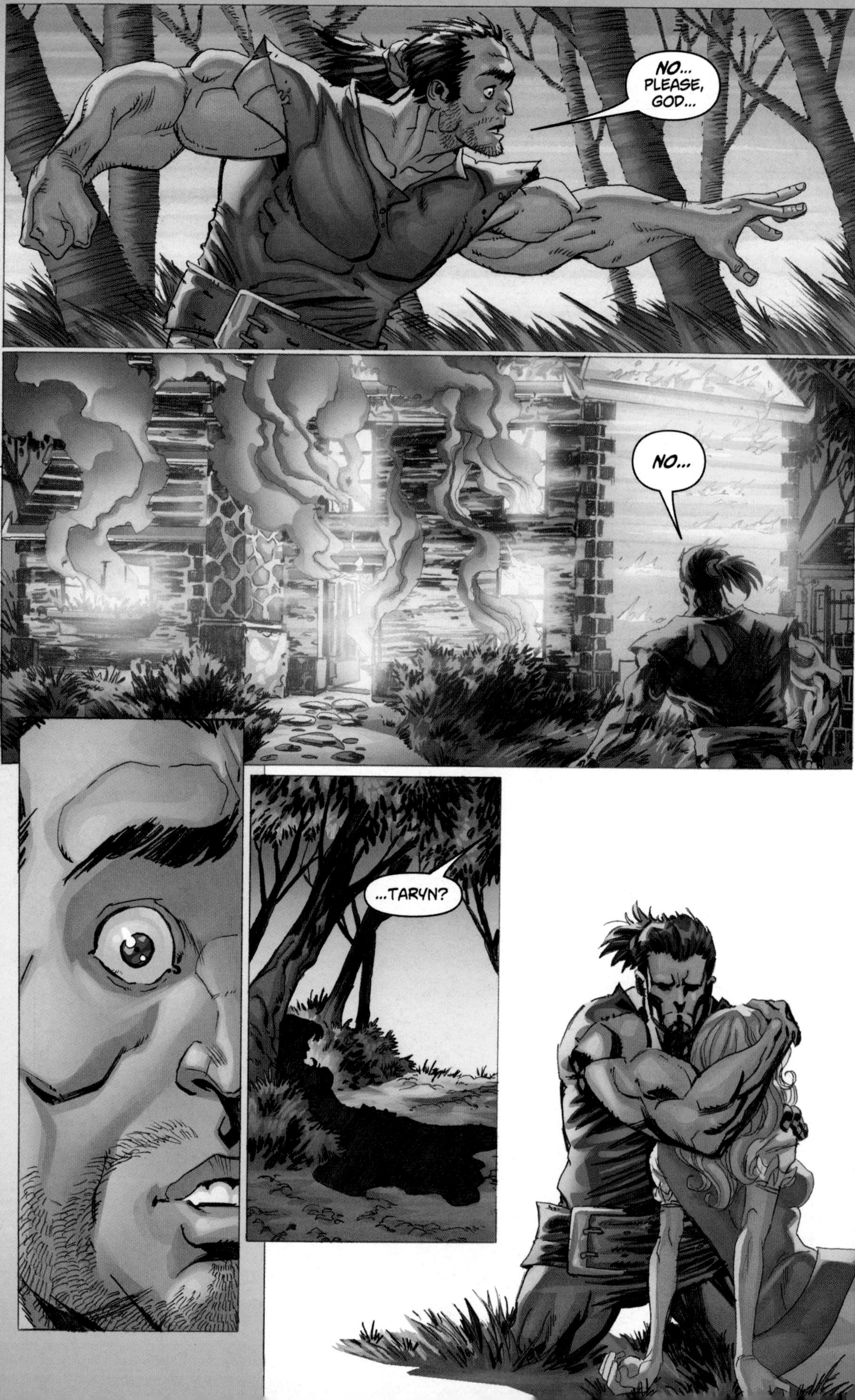
NO... PLEASE, GOD...
NO...
...TARYN?

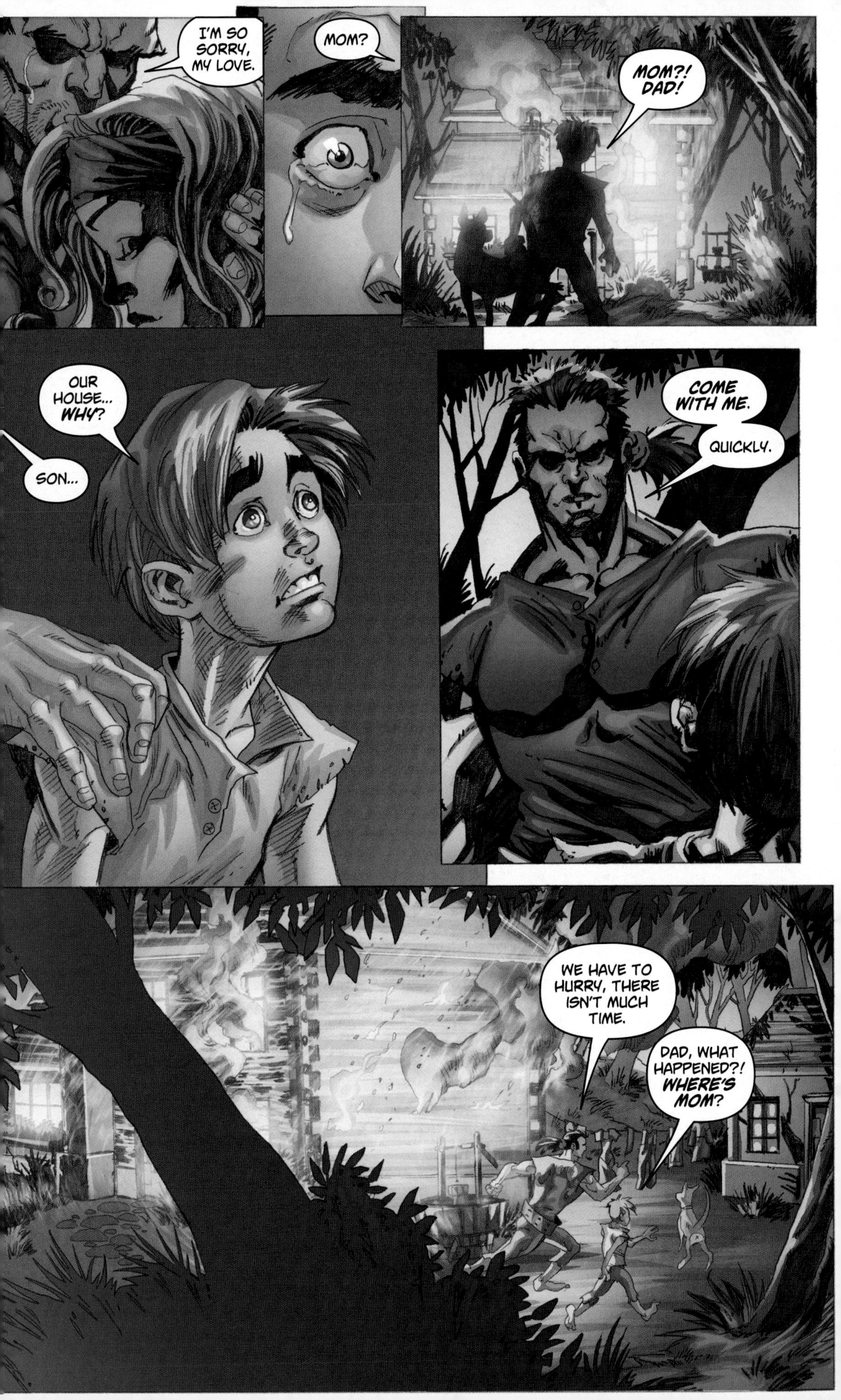

I'M SO SORRY, MY LOVE.
MOM?
MOM?! DAD!
OUR HOUSE... WHY?
SON...
COME WITH ME.
QUICKLY.
WE HAVE TO HURRY, THERE ISN'T MUCH TIME.
DAD, WHAT HAPPENED?! WHERE'S MOM?

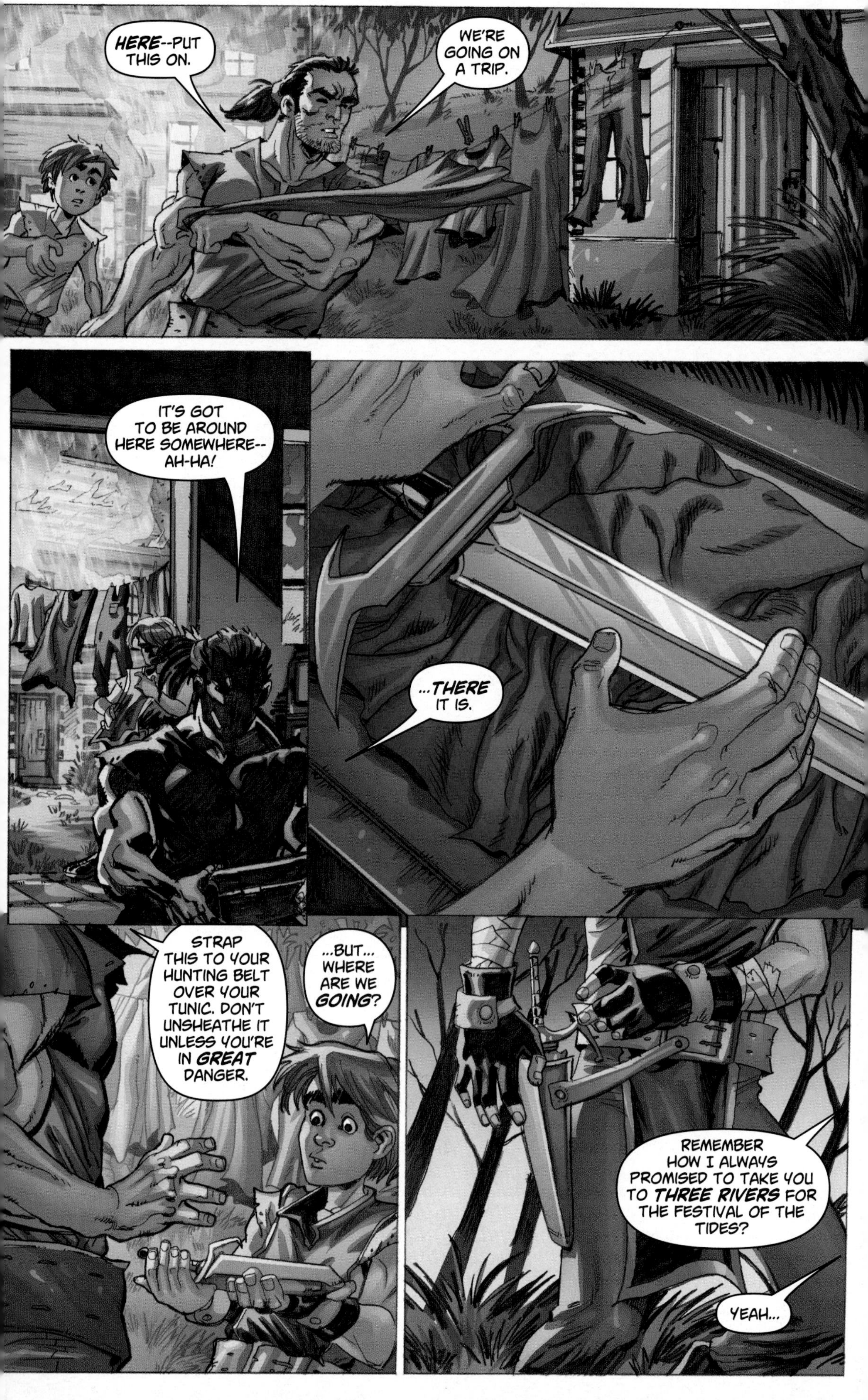

HERE--PUT THIS ON.
WE'RE GOING ON A TRIP.
IT'S GOT TO BE AROUND HERE SOMEWHERE-- AH-HA!
...THERE IT IS.
STRAP THIS TO YOUR HUNTING BELT OVER YOUR TUNIC. DON'T UNSHEATHE IT UNLESS YOU'RE IN GREAT DANGER.
...BUT... WHERE ARE WE GOING?
REMEMBER HOW I ALWAYS PROMISED TO TAKE YOU TO THREE RIVERS FOR THE FESTIVAL OF THE TIDES?
YEAH...

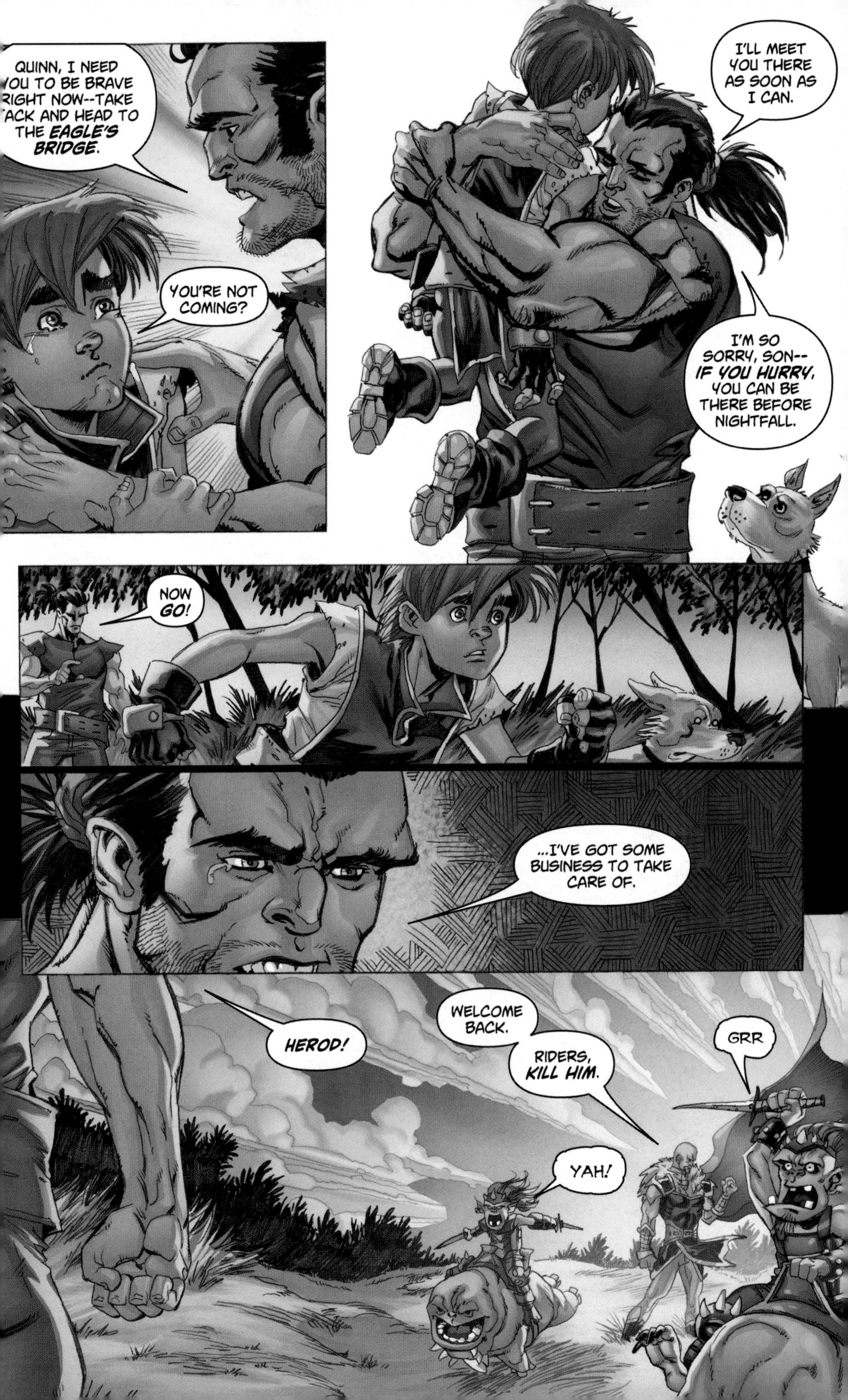

QUINN, I NEED OU TO BE BRAVE RIGHT NOW--TAKE ACK AND HEAD TO THE ***EAGLE'S BRIDGE***.
YOU'RE NOT COMING?
I'LL MEET YOU THERE AS SOON AS I CAN.
I'M SO SORRY, SON-- ***IF YOU HURRY***, YOU CAN BE THERE BEFORE NIGHTFALL.
NOW ***GO!***
...I'VE GOT SOME BUSINESS TO TAKE CARE OF.
HEROD!
WELCOME BACK.
RIDERS, ***KILL HIM***.
GRR
YAH!

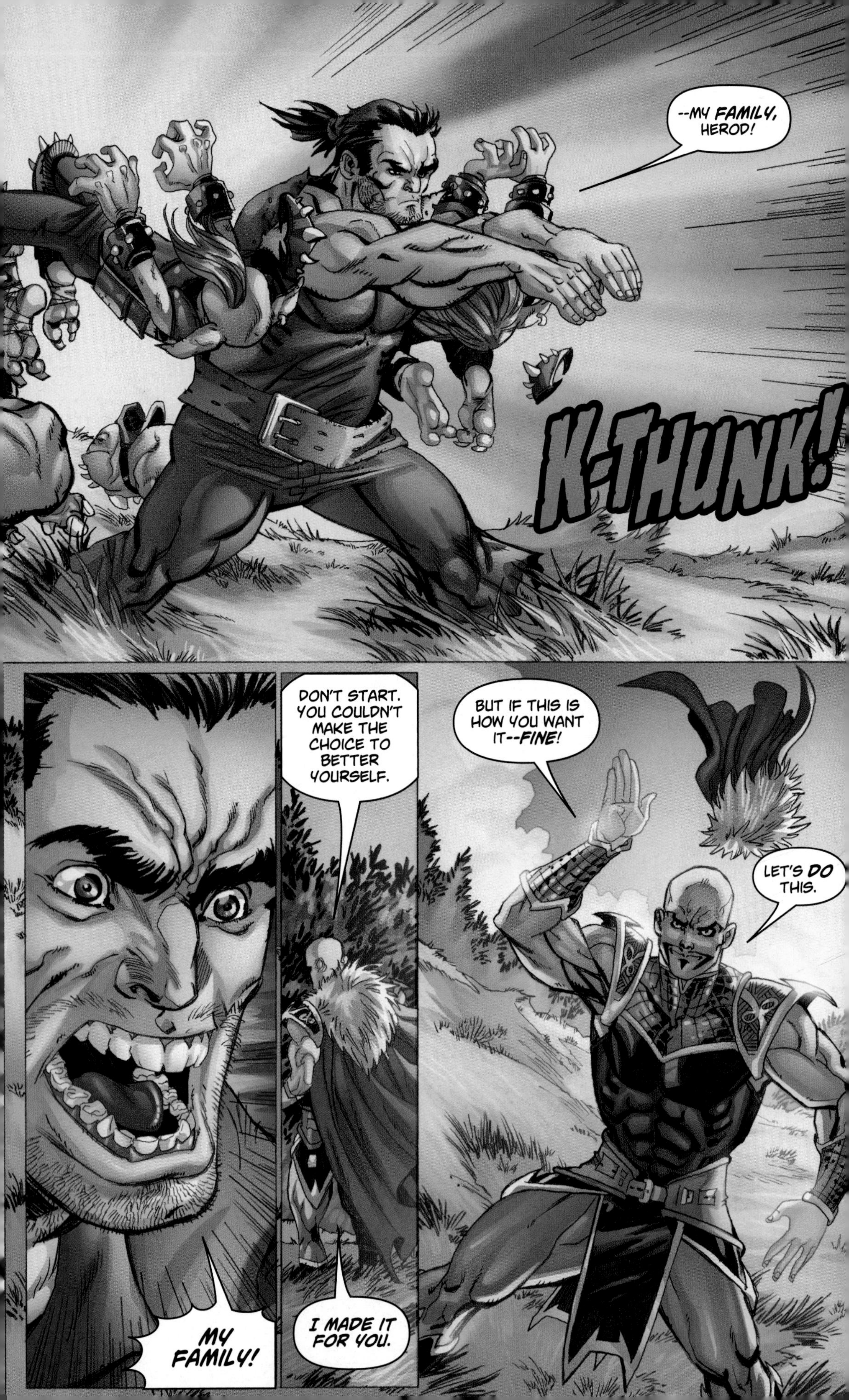
--MY FAMILY, HEROD!
K-THUNK!
MY FAMILY!
DON'T START. YOU COULDN'T MAKE THE CHOICE TO BETTER YOURSELF.
I MADE IT FOR YOU.
BUT IF THIS IS HOW YOU WANT IT--FINE!
LET'S DO THIS.

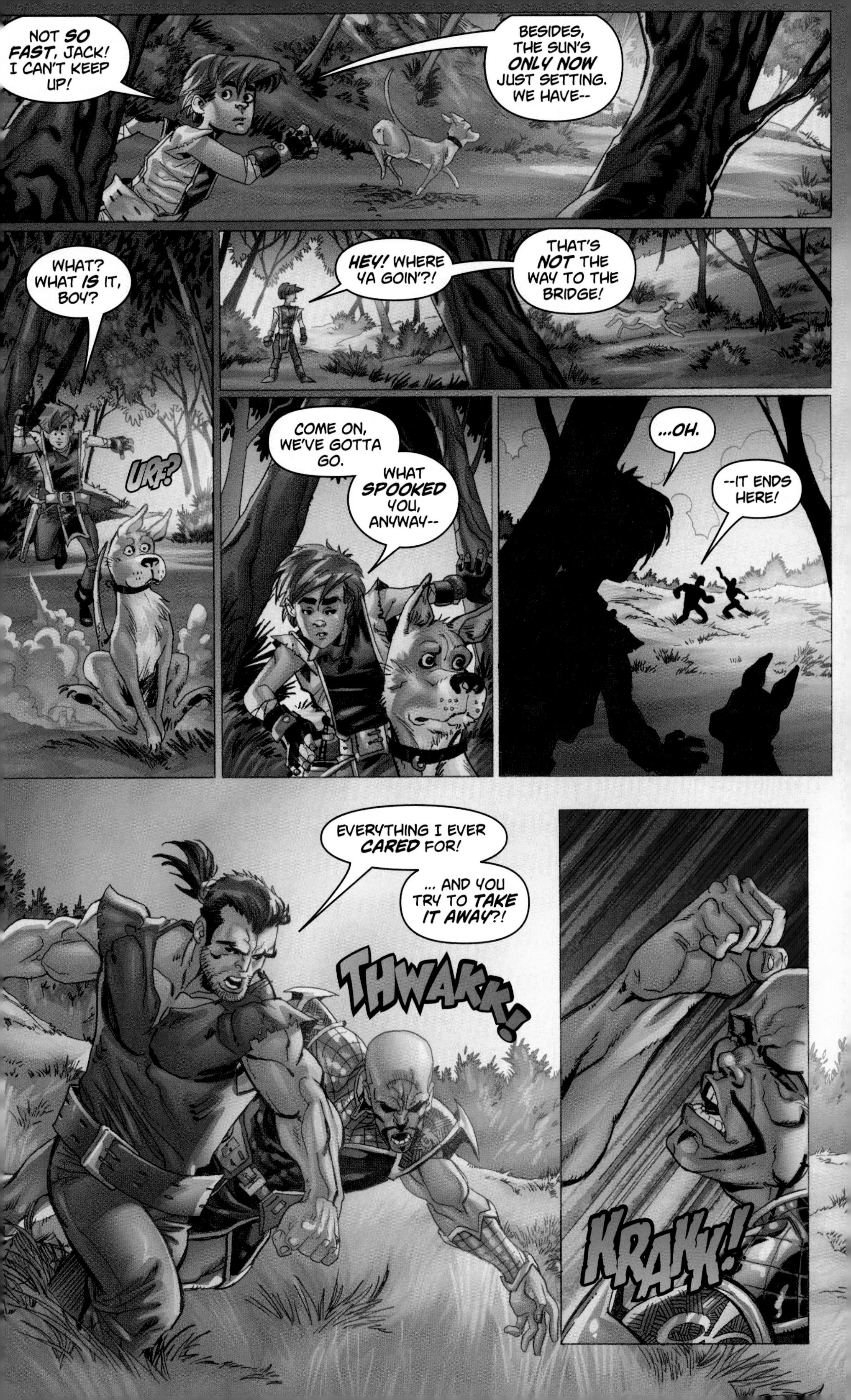
NOT SO FAST, JACK! I CAN'T KEEP UP!
BESIDES, THE SUN'S ONLY NOW JUST SETTING. WE HAVE--
WHAT? WHAT IS IT, BOY?
URF?
HEY! WHERE YA GOIN'?!
THAT'S NOT THE WAY TO THE BRIDGE!
COME ON, WE'VE GOTTA GO.
WHAT SPOOKED YOU, ANYWAY--
...OH.
--IT ENDS HERE!
EVERYTHING I EVER CARED FOR!
... AND YOU TRY TO TAKE IT AWAY?!
THWAKK!
KRAKK!

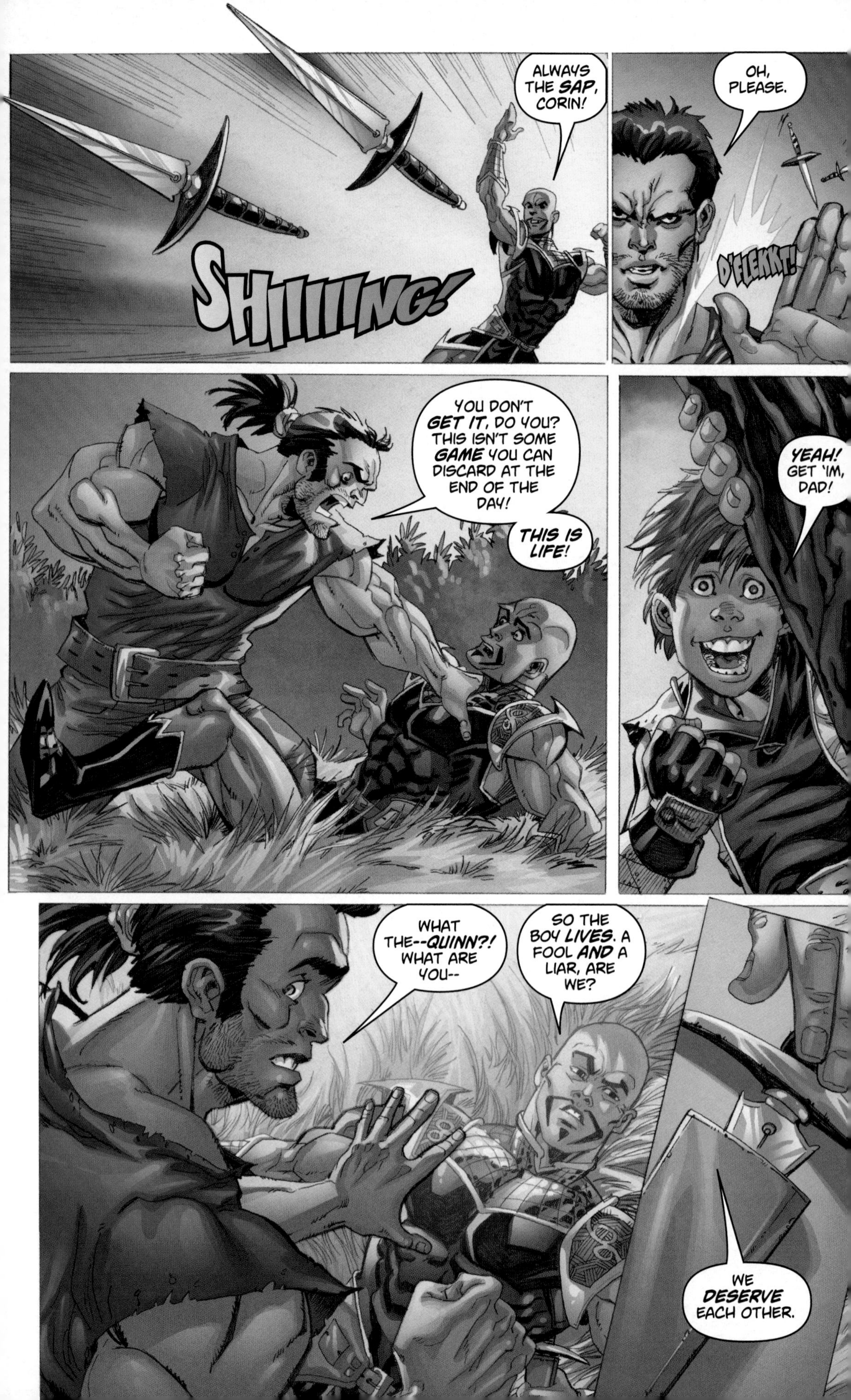
ALWAYS THE SAP, CORIN!
SHIIIIING!
OH, PLEASE.
D'ELEKKT!
YOU DON'T GET IT, DO YOU? THIS ISN'T SOME GAME YOU CAN DISCARD AT THE END OF THE DAY!
THIS IS LIFE!
YEAH! GET 'IM, DAD!
WHAT THE--QUINN?! WHAT ARE YOU--
SO THE BOY LIVES. A FOOL AND A LIAR, ARE WE?
WE DESERVE EACH OTHER.

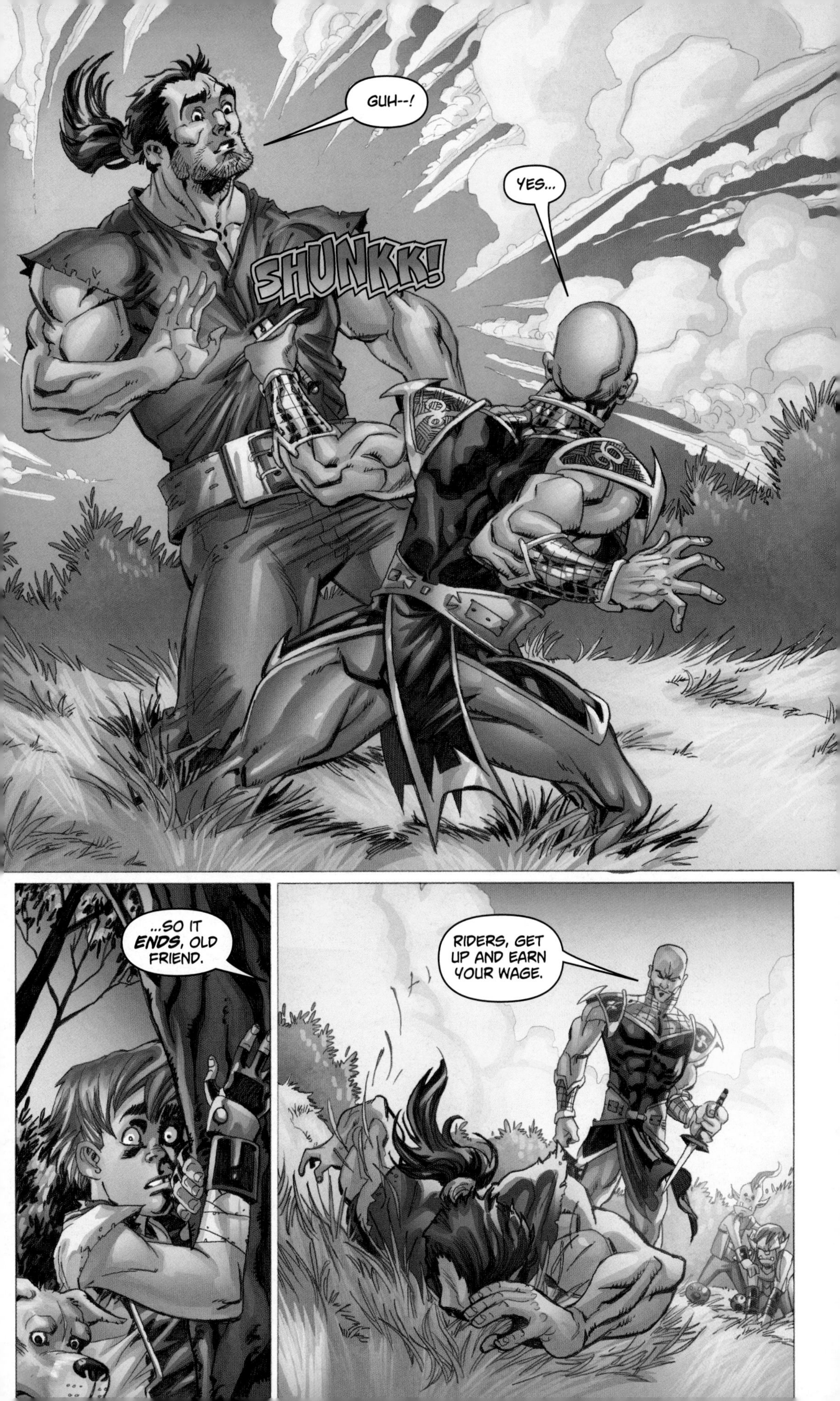
GUH--!
YES...
SHUNKK!
...SO IT ENDS, OLD FRIEND.
RIDERS, GET UP AND EARN YOUR WAGE.

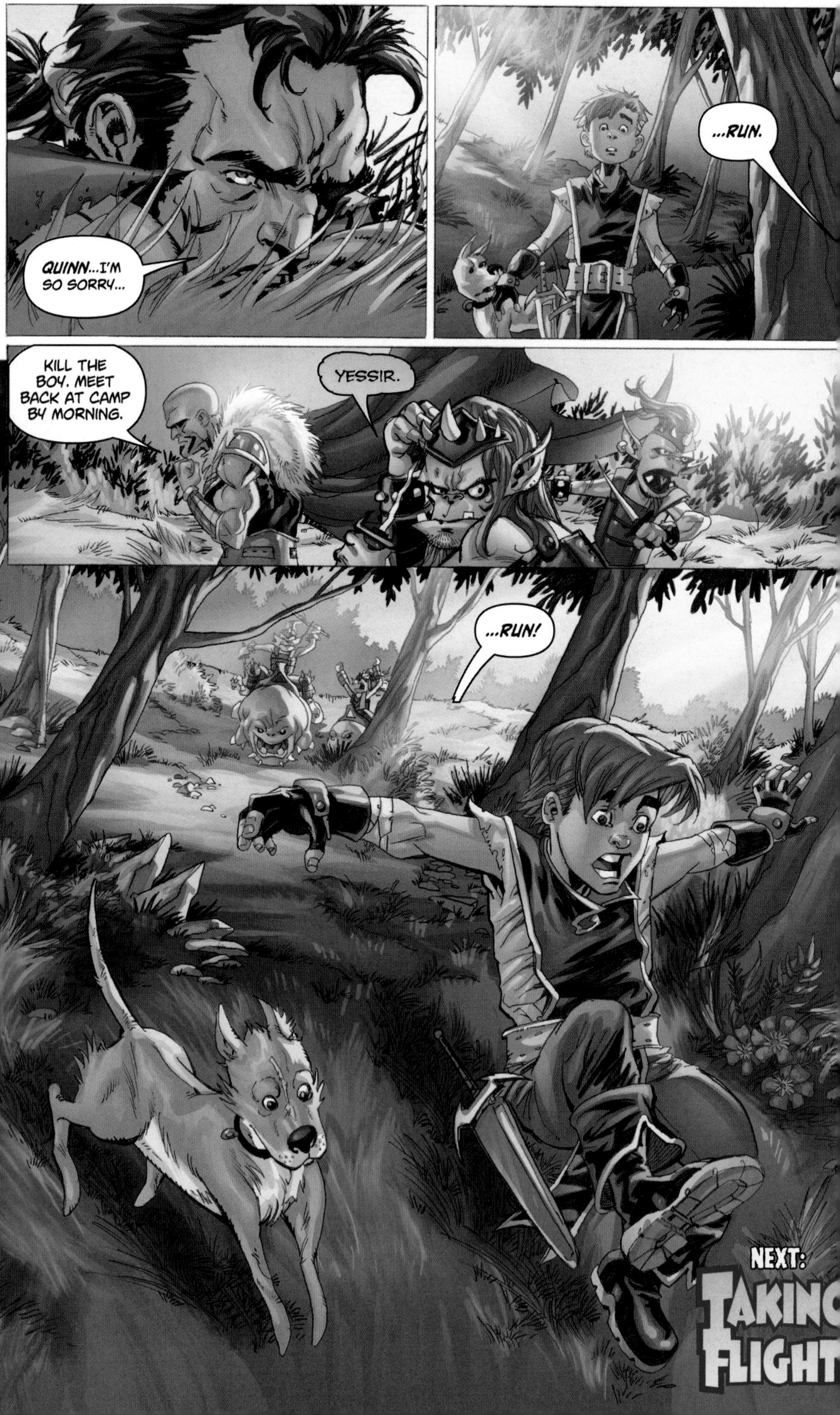
QUINN...I'M SO SORRY...
...RUN.
KILL THE BOY. MEET BACK AT CAMP BY MORNING.
YESSIR.
...RUN!
NEXT:
TAKING FLIGHT

SKYWORDS™

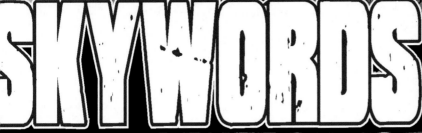

Got thoughts?
Fan art?
Ransom notes?

WRITE US @

skywardfans@gmail.com

It's here! *Finally-- we're thrilled to be here and hope you are, too. As I write this, I'm drawing issue six (yeah, I know) and having the time of my life. Thanks to all the fans and retailers that supported this book during its self-published days-- and welcome ACTION LAB as our new publisher! Give 'em a round of applause, folks! They deserve it. :)*

- jeremy

Hello,

I picked up all the issues at HeroesCon, except the Graphite Edition #1 I already had, and truly enjoyed them. You've really crafted a fun book here and that's something comics lack these days.

As far as the Graphite Editions go, please keep doing them. Your art is fantastic and they show it off well.

The story of this book is very intriguing. You've managed to diversify your characters and the world they live in early on. That makes me, and I'm sure everyone else, want to keep reading. It reminds me of the kind of world a Final Fantasy game might be set in and that's just awesome.

I'd also like to compliment you on the varying appearances of your characters. Not one single character in this series looks like any other character.

I think you have an awesome book here and I look forward to future issues.

-Adam Davis
jadster@ymail.com

Adam, it's been an honor counting you among my fans the past several years. It's always a pleasure seeing you at shows and your endless enthusiasm keeps guys like me going! Thanks-- we couldn't do it without ya. :)

Hi!
I didn't know which way to contact you would be the best, so I just went for this one. Anyway, I picked up the first volume of Skyward from your booth at SDCC this year, and I just wanted to say that the story and the artwork are amazing! I can't wait to see what happens next, and I'm already working on an Abigail costume (I hope that's ok...)!

Kudos and all the best,
- Hailey
hailey.mashburn@gmail.com

Listen up, Hailey-- you'd be the first SKYWARD cosplayer, so YES! Make it happen! That'd be so cool. Send photos when it's done and we'll run them in an upcoming issue!

I love you guys, seriously.

Hey Jeremy,
I picked up Skyward 0-3 at Heroes Con and read them that night. I think they're great! I was going to email sooner but work on my own book has kept me pretty busy. I like the style and the dialogue is easy to follow. The pacing is true to the form and the overall feeling you get when reading the story is that good, hard-to-explain, adventure/wonderment feeling. We need more all-ages adventures in the industry. Since I'm a big fan of Tellos, you need to make sure Todd Dezago sees these. I know he would love 'em if he hasn't seen them already!

Thanks and I'll definitely be picking up the entire series.

Christopher West
Westtwin Entertainment
www.westtwin.com

Oh, abolutely-- as a fan of the book as well, Todd and Mike's TELLOS proved we need more accessible action-fantasy comics in the industry. Todd has been incredibly helpful and supportive of me throughout my career, and I'm honored to call him a friend.

HEADS UP! Issue 2 is coming at ya in 30 days, so get excited! Also, don't forget to email me at the address at the top of this page with all your love, hate, general disdain, or tomfoolery-- Hey, this page is for YOU! We'll start running fan art next issue, too. Eyes on the sky!

- jeremy

2013 CONVENTION SCHEDULE

3/1 - 3/3
Emerald City Comicon
(Seattle, WA)

3/9
Captain's Comics Expo
(Charleston, SC)

3/15 - 3/17
Megacon
(Orlando, FL)

3/22 - 3/24
FablesCon
(Rochester, MN)

4/26 - 4/28
C2E2
(Chicago, IL)

5/4
Free Comic Book Day @ Acme Comics
(Greensboro, NC)

6/7 - 6/9
HeroesCon
(Charlotte, NC)

7/17 - 7/21
SDCC (Comic-Con)
(San Diego, CA)

8/30 - 9/2
Dragon*Con
(Atlanta, GA)

9/7 - 9/8
Baltimore Comic-Con
(Baltimore, MD)

10/10 - 10/13
New York Comic Con
(New York, NY)

10/26 - 10/27
Comic Book City Con
(Greensboro, NC)

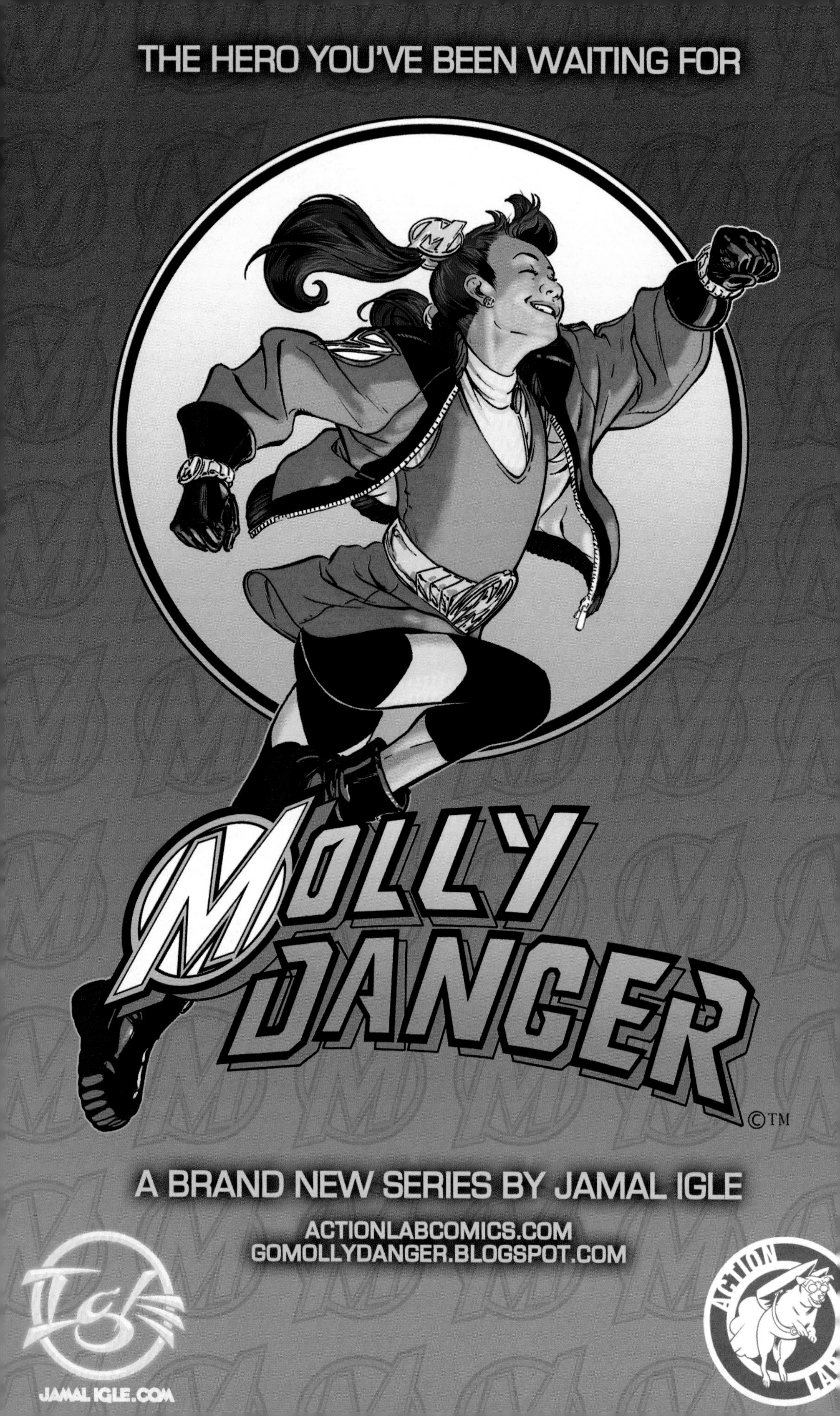
THE HERO YOU'VE BEEN WAITING FOR
MOLLY DANGER
©TM
A BRAND NEW SERIES BY JAMAL IGLE
ACTIONLABCOMICS.COM
GOMOLLYDANGER.BLOGSPOT.COM
JAMAL IGLE.COM
ACTION LAB

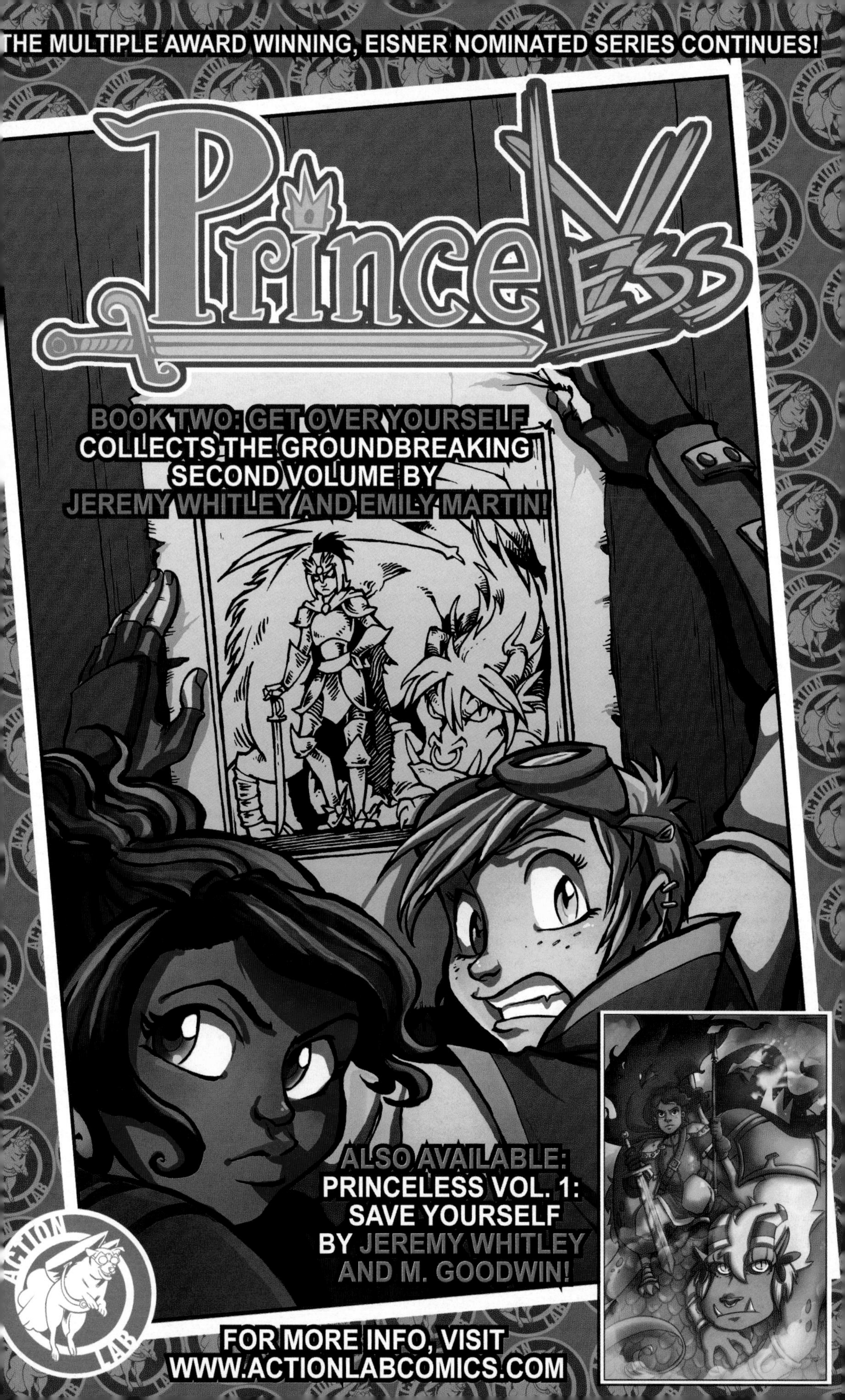
THE MULTIPLE AWARD WINNING, EISNER NOMINATED SERIES CONTINUES!
Princeless
BOOK TWO: GET OVER YOURSELF
COLLECTS THE GROUNDBREAKING
SECOND VOLUME BY
JEREMY WHITLEY AND EMILY MARTIN!
ALSO AVAILABLE:
PRINCELESS VOL. 1:
SAVE YOURSELF
BY JEREMY WHITLEY
AND M. GOODWIN!
ACTION LAB
FOR MORE INFO, VISIT
WWW.ACTIONLABCOMICS.COM

READ MORE NOW

ACTIONLABCOMICS.COM

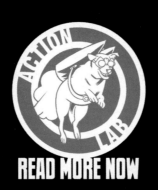

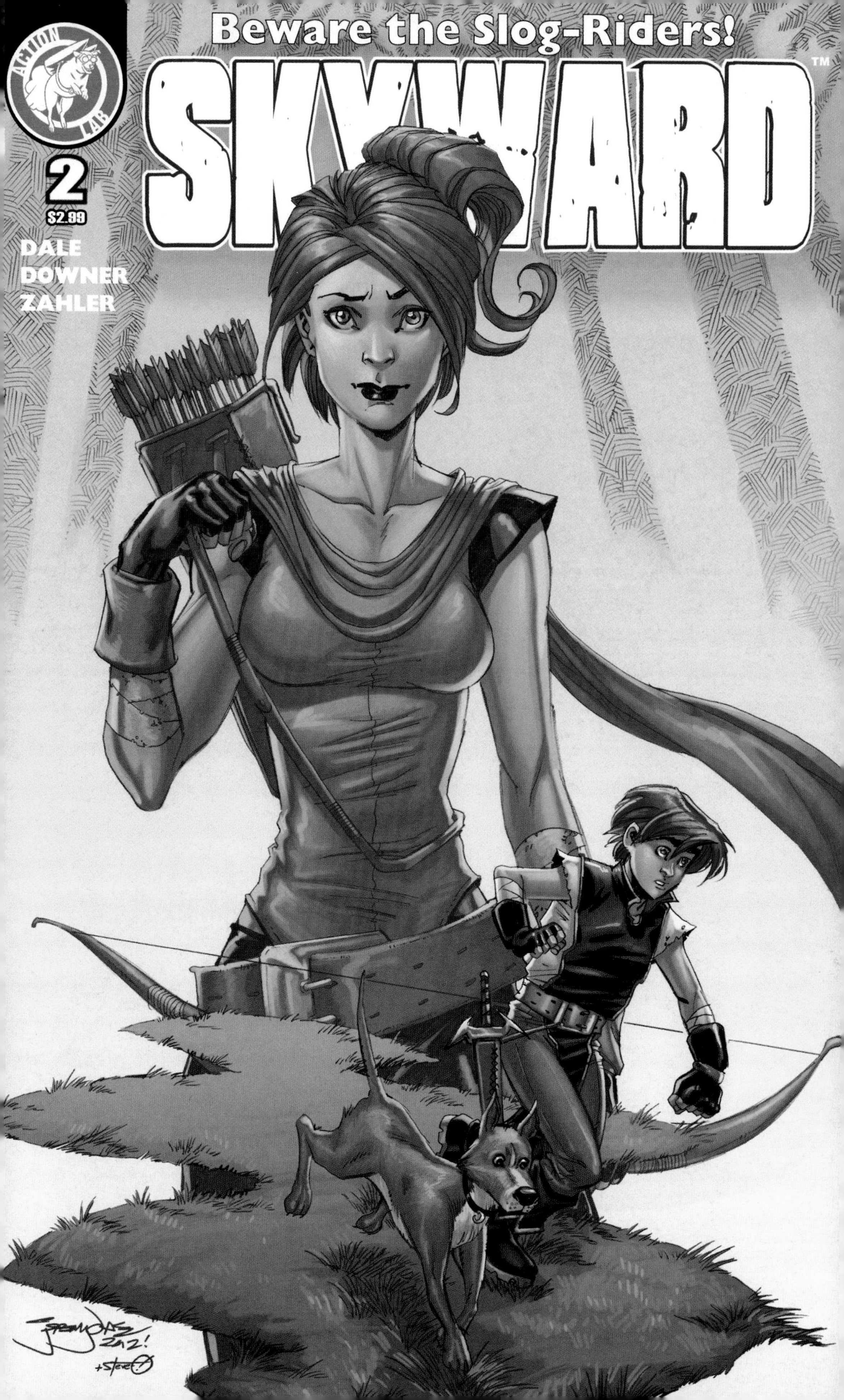
Beware the Slog-Riders!
ACTION LAB
SKYWARD™
2
$2.99
DALE
DOWNER
ZAHLER

SKYWARD

2

Jeremy Dale
Creator, Writer, Artist
@jeremydale

Steve Downer
Colors
@downersteve

Thom Zahler
Letters
@loveandcapes

**Cover by Jeremy Dale
and Steve Downer**

Kelly Dale
Editor
@kellyedale

PREVIOUSLY: Having watched his parents lose their lives, young Quinn takes off into the woods, chased by Herod's sinister Slog-Riders. Meanwhile...

KEVIN FREEMAN- PRESIDENT
SHAWN PRYOR- VP DIGITAL MEDIA
DAVE DWONCH- CREATIVE DIRECTOR
SHAWN GABBORIN- EDITOR IN CHIEF
JASON MARTIN- EDITOR
JEREMY WHITLEY- DIRECTOR OF MARKETING
CHAD CICCONI- LOOKING FOR PEACE IN A SAVAGE LAND
COLLEEN BOYD- ASSOCIATE EDITOR

Jeremy Dale
the talent

Kelly Dale
editor

Kirby
Canine Relations

SKYWARD #2. August 2013. Published by Action Lab Entertainment. Copyright 2010-2013 Jeremy Dale. All rights reserved. SKYWARD (including all prominent characters featured herein), its logo and all character logos are trademarks of Jeremy Dale, unless otherwise noted. Action Lab and its logos are trademarks and copyrights of Action Lab. All rights reserved. No part of this publication may be reproduced or transmitted in any form or by any means (except for short excerpts for review purposes) without the express permission of Action Lab Entertainment or Jeremy Dale. All names, characters, events and locales in this publication are entirely fictional. Any resemblance to actual persons (living and/or dead), events of places, without satiric intent, is coincidental. For more information visit

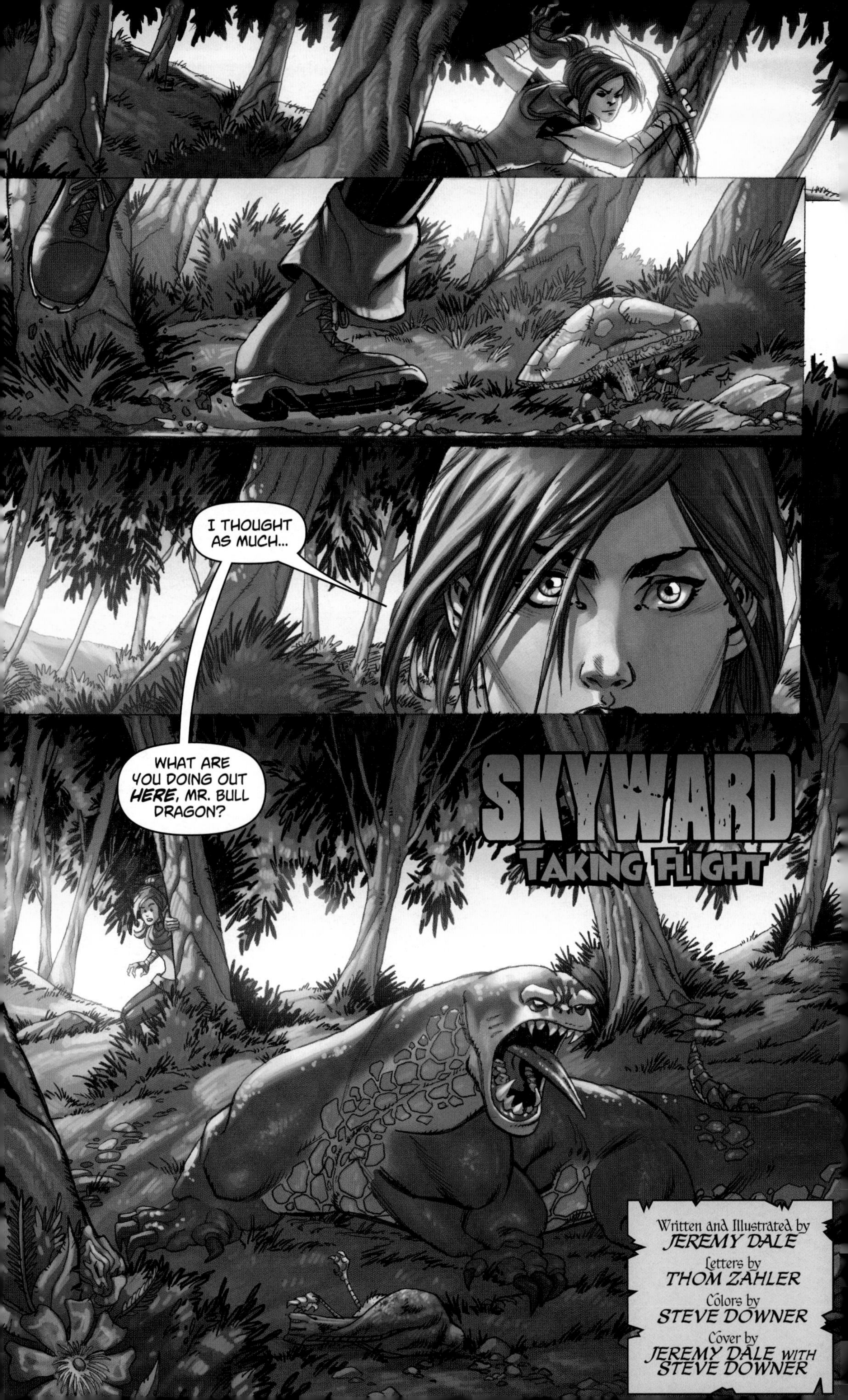

I THOUGHT AS MUCH...
WHAT ARE YOU DOING OUT HERE, MR. BULL DRAGON?
SKYWARD
TAKING FLIGHT
Written and Illustrated by JEREMY DALE
Letters by THOM ZAHLER
Colors by STEVE DOWNER
Cover by JEREMY DALE WITH STEVE DOWNER

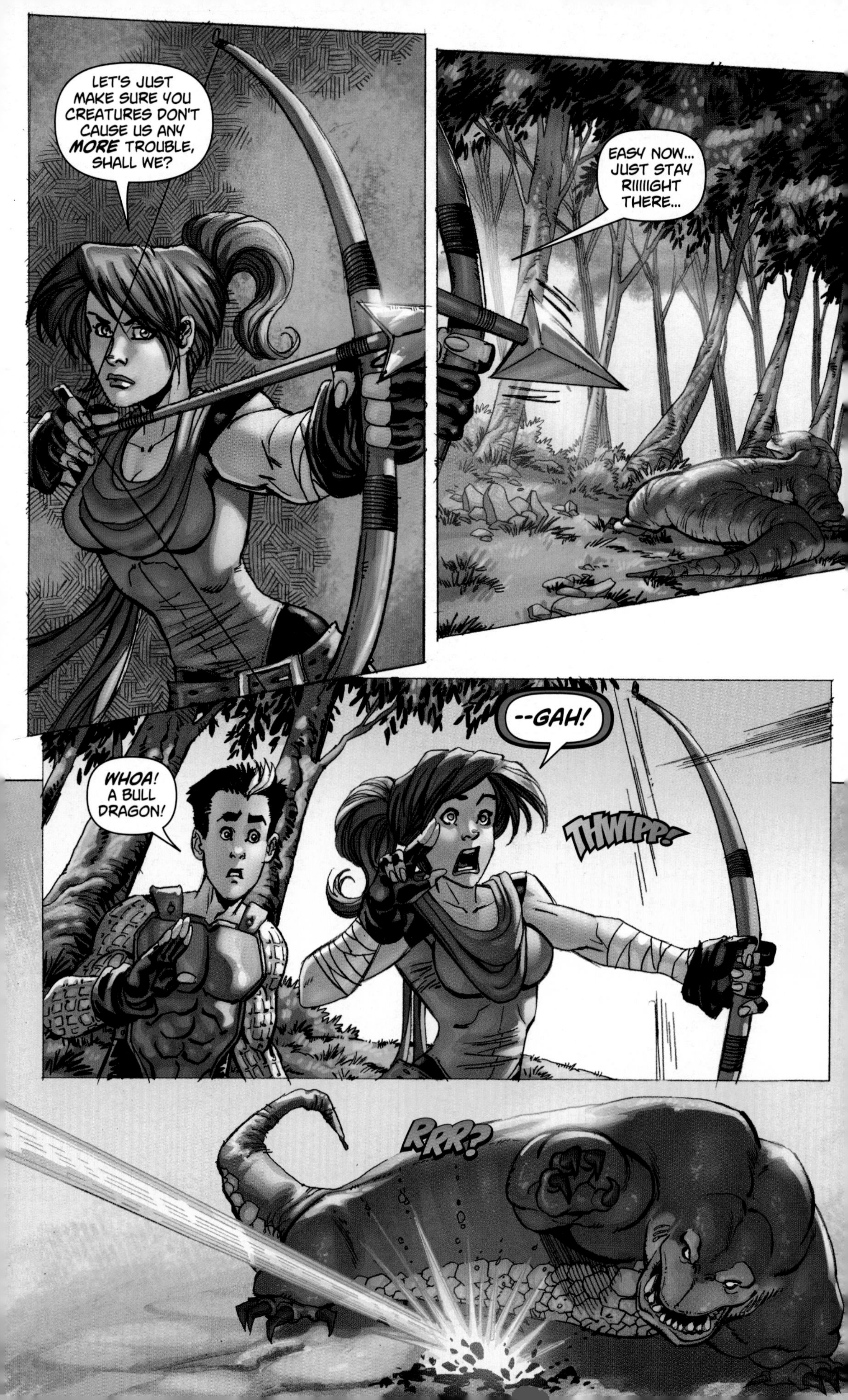
LET'S JUST MAKE SURE YOU CREATURES DON'T CAUSE US ANY *MORE* TROUBLE, SHALL WE?
EASY NOW... JUST STAY RIIIIIGHT THERE...
WHOA! A BULL DRAGON!
--GAH!
THWIPP!
RRR?

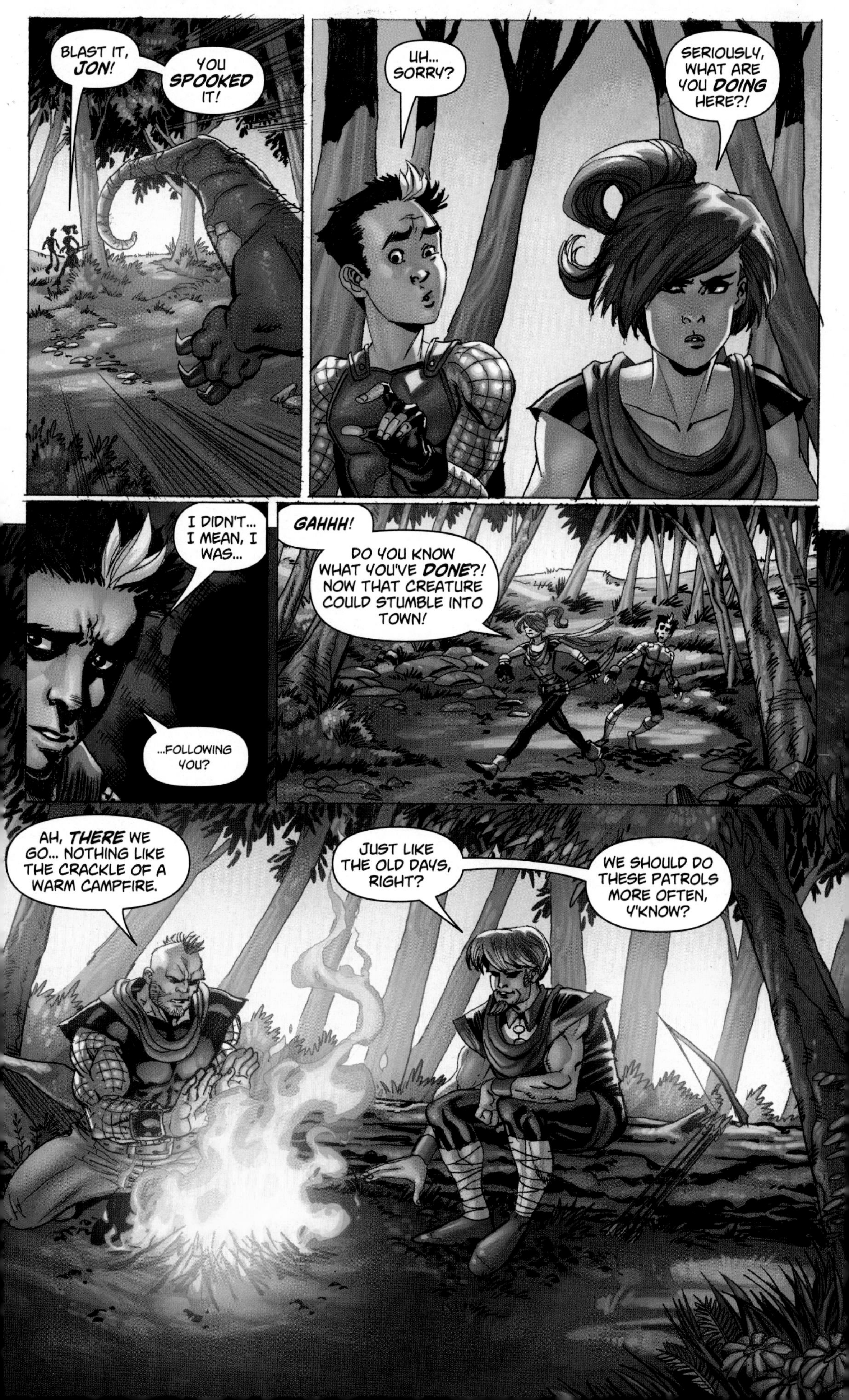
BLAST IT, JON!
YOU SPOOKED IT!
UH... SORRY?
SERIOUSLY, WHAT ARE YOU DOING HERE?!
I DIDN'T... I MEAN, I WAS...
...FOLLOWING YOU?
GAHHH!
DO YOU KNOW WHAT YOU'VE DONE?! NOW THAT CREATURE COULD STUMBLE INTO TOWN!
AH, THERE WE GO... NOTHING LIKE THE CRACKLE OF A WARM CAMPFIRE.
JUST LIKE THE OLD DAYS, RIGHT?
WE SHOULD DO THESE PATROLS MORE OFTEN, Y'KNOW?

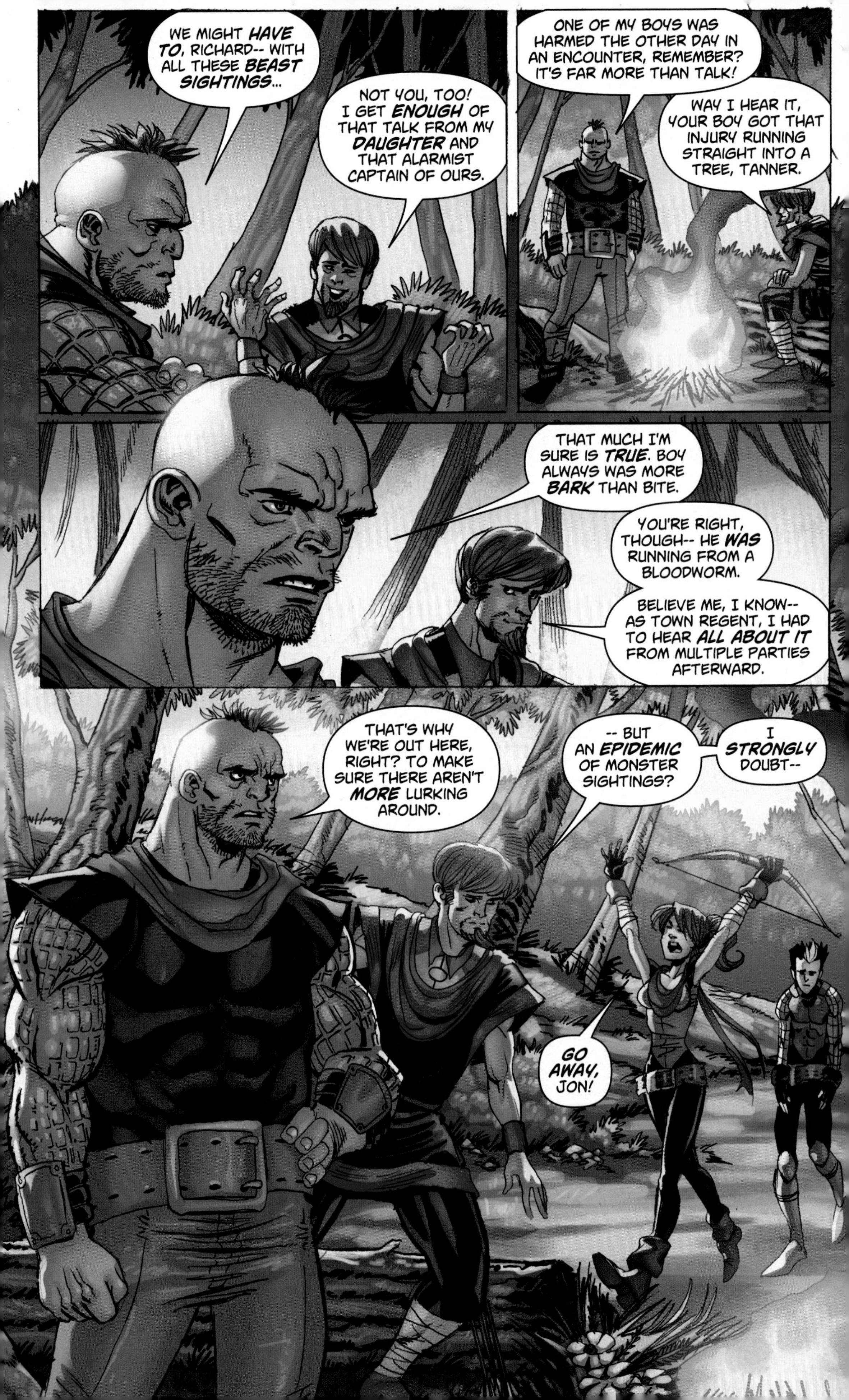
WE MIGHT HAVE TO, RICHARD-- WITH ALL THESE BEAST SIGHTINGS...
NOT YOU, TOO! I GET ENOUGH OF THAT TALK FROM MY DAUGHTER AND THAT ALARMIST CAPTAIN OF OURS.
ONE OF MY BOYS WAS HARMED THE OTHER DAY IN AN ENCOUNTER, REMEMBER? IT'S FAR MORE THAN TALK!
WAY I HEAR IT, YOUR BOY GOT THAT INJURY RUNNING STRAIGHT INTO A TREE, TANNER.
THAT MUCH I'M SURE IS TRUE. BOY ALWAYS WAS MORE BARK THAN BITE.
YOU'RE RIGHT, THOUGH-- HE WAS RUNNING FROM A BLOODWORM.
BELIEVE ME, I KNOW-- AS TOWN REGENT, I HAD TO HEAR ALL ABOUT IT FROM MULTIPLE PARTIES AFTERWARD.
THAT'S WHY WE'RE OUT HERE, RIGHT? TO MAKE SURE THERE AREN'T MORE LURKING AROUND.
I STRONGLY DOUBT--
-- BUT AN EPIDEMIC OF MONSTER SIGHTINGS?
GO AWAY, JON!

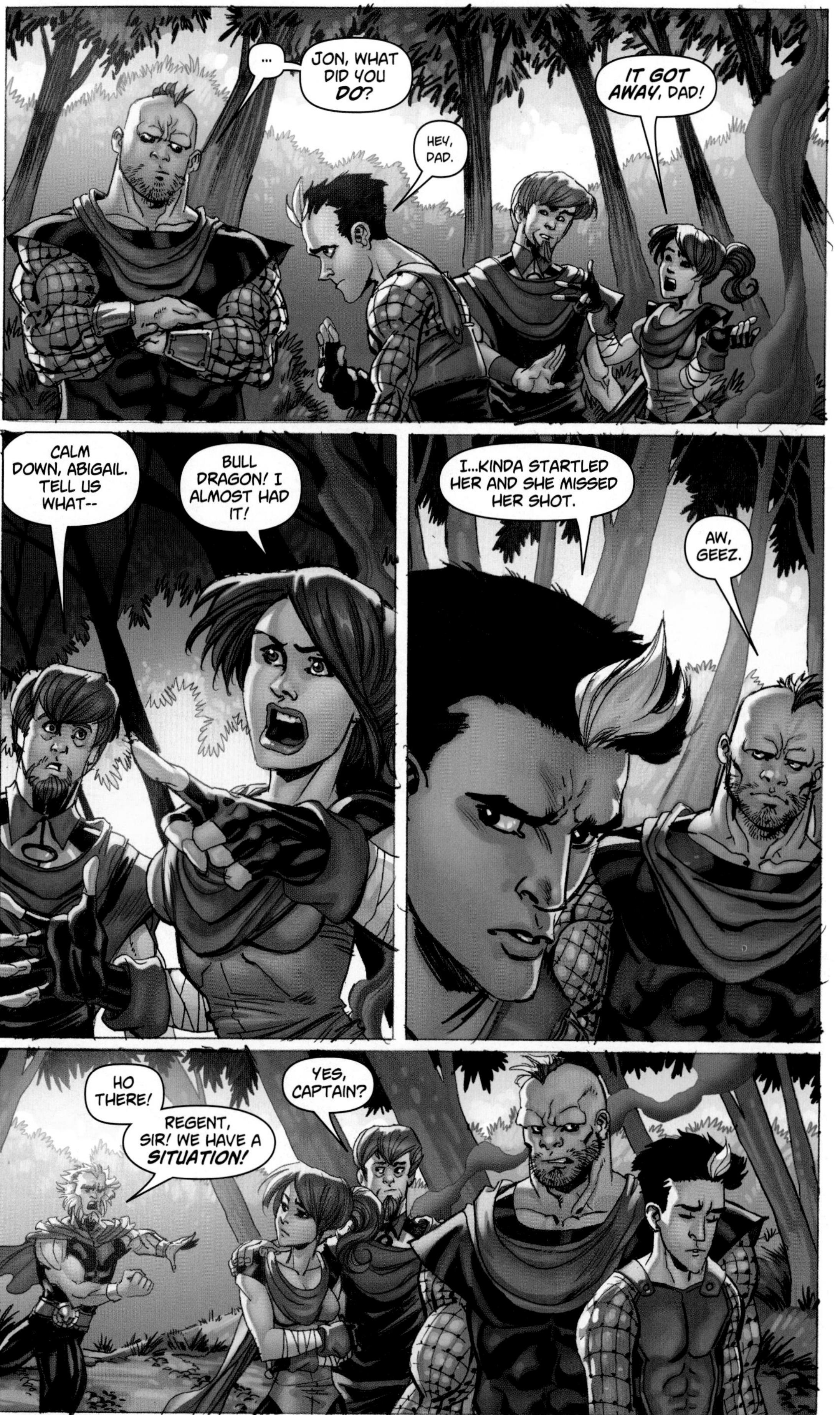
...
JON, WHAT DID YOU DO?
HEY, DAD.
IT GOT AWAY, DAD!
CALM DOWN, ABIGAIL. TELL US WHAT--
BULL DRAGON! I ALMOST HAD IT!
I...KINDA STARTLED HER AND SHE MISSED HER SHOT.
AW, GEEZ.
HO THERE!
REGENT, SIR! WE HAVE A SITUATION!
YES, CAPTAIN?

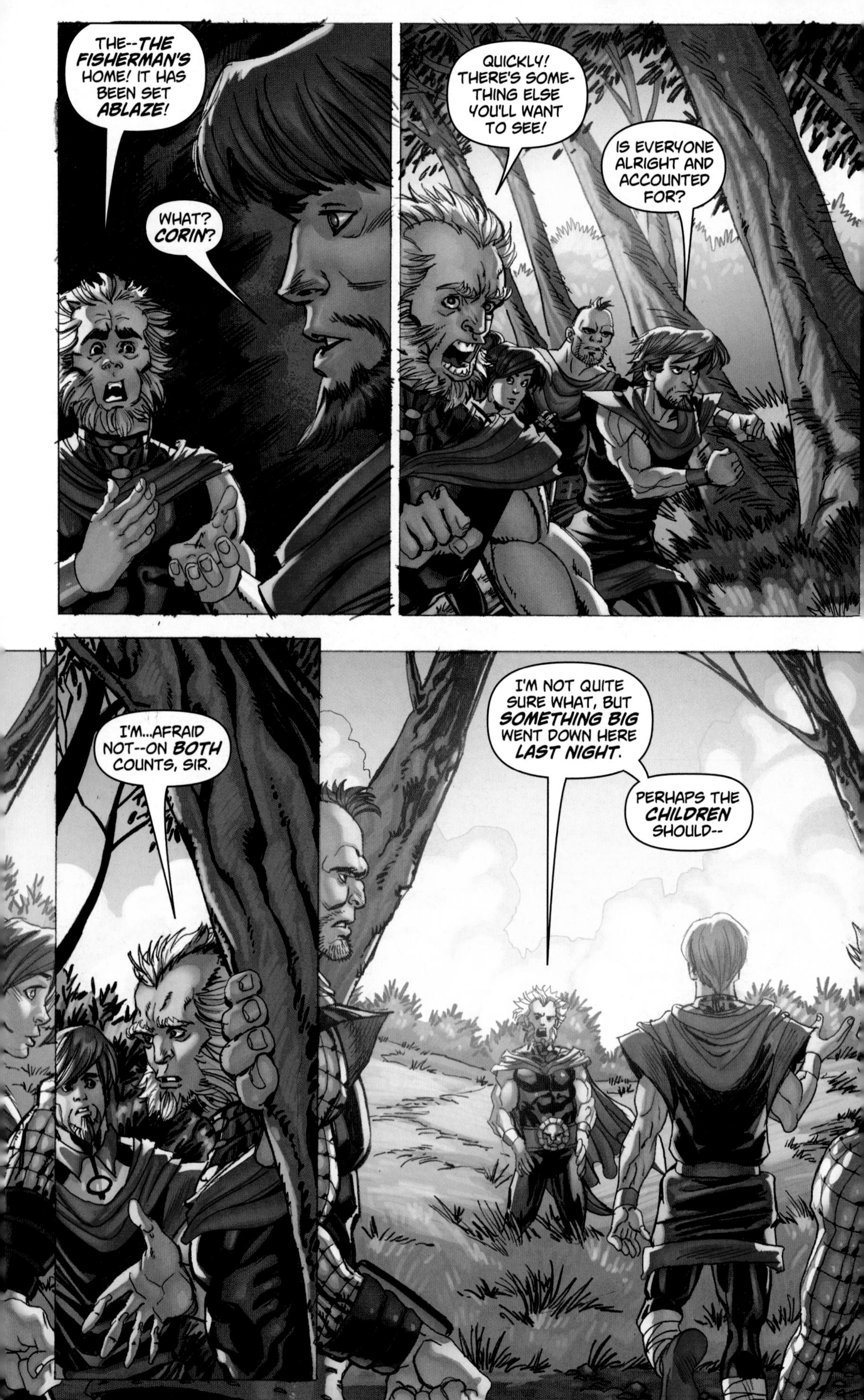
THE--THE FISHERMAN'S HOME! IT HAS BEEN SET ABLAZE!
WHAT? CORIN?
QUICKLY! THERE'S SOME-THING ELSE YOU'LL WANT TO SEE!
IS EVERYONE ALRIGHT AND ACCOUNTED FOR?
I'M...AFRAID NOT--ON BOTH COUNTS, SIR.
I'M NOT QUITE SURE WHAT, BUT SOMETHING BIG WENT DOWN HERE LAST NIGHT.
PERHAPS THE CHILDREN SHOULD--

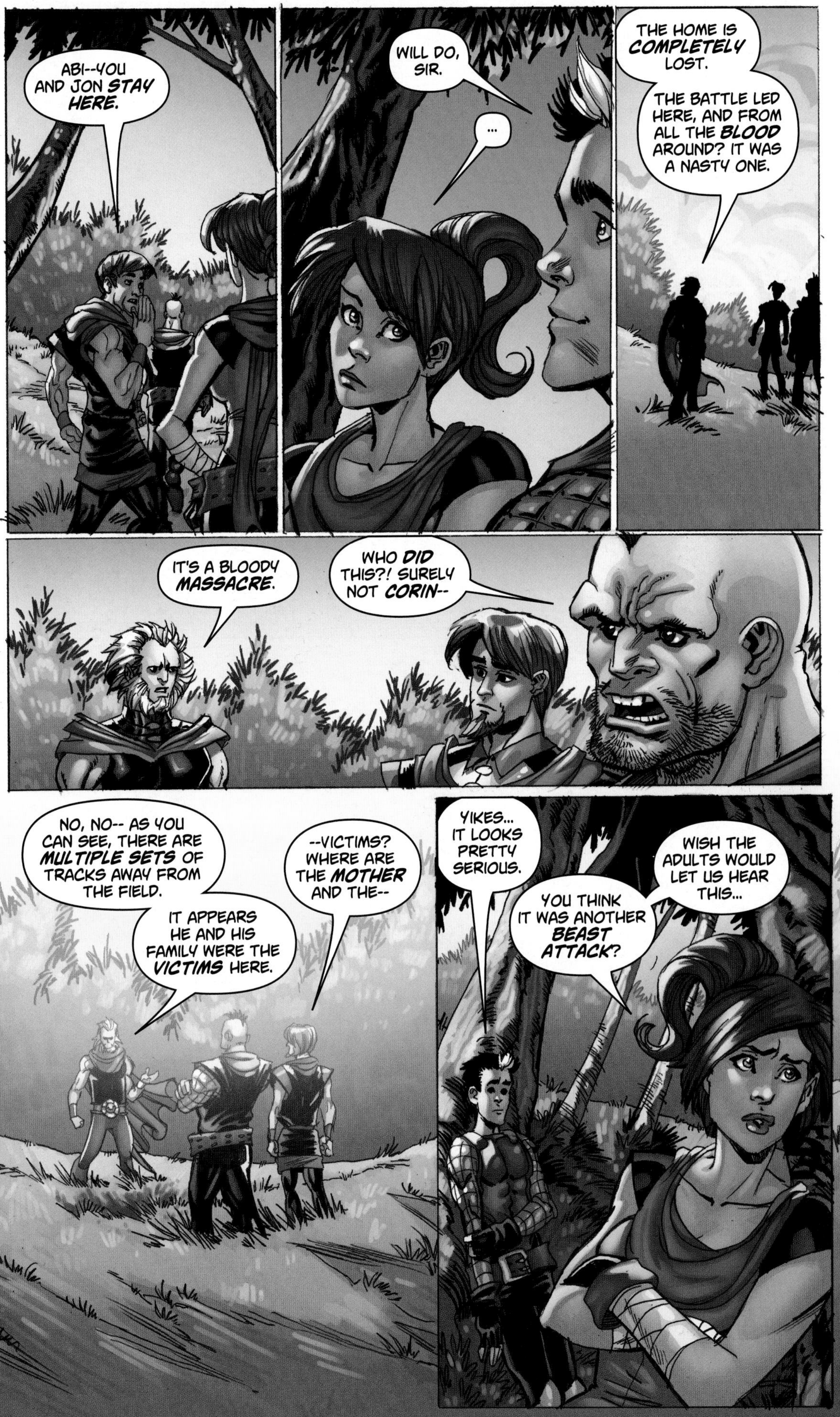

ABI--YOU AND JON STAY HERE.
WILL DO, SIR.
...
THE HOME IS COMPLETELY LOST.
THE BATTLE LED HERE, AND FROM ALL THE BLOOD AROUND? IT WAS A NASTY ONE.
IT'S A BLOODY MASSACRE.
WHO DID THIS?! SURELY NOT CORIN--
NO, NO-- AS YOU CAN SEE, THERE ARE MULTIPLE SETS OF TRACKS AWAY FROM THE FIELD.
IT APPEARS HE AND HIS FAMILY WERE THE VICTIMS HERE.
--VICTIMS? WHERE ARE THE MOTHER AND THE--
YIKES... IT LOOKS PRETTY SERIOUS.
YOU THINK IT WAS ANOTHER BEAST ATTACK?
WISH THE ADULTS WOULD LET US HEAR THIS...

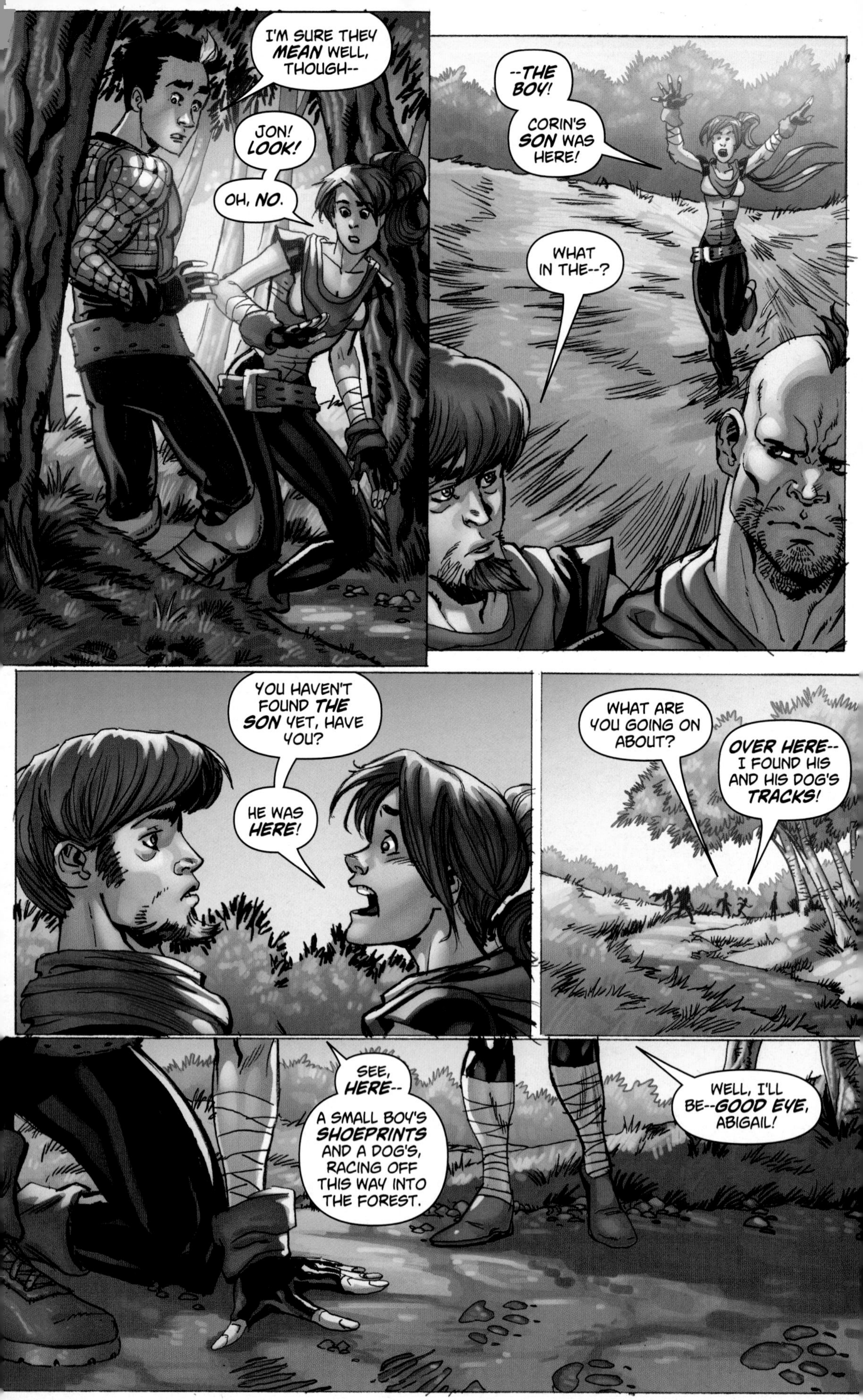
I'M SURE THEY MEAN WELL, THOUGH--
JON! LOOK!
OH, NO.
--THE BOY!
CORIN'S SON WAS HERE!
WHAT IN THE--?
YOU HAVEN'T FOUND THE SON YET, HAVE YOU?
HE WAS HERE!
WHAT ARE YOU GOING ON ABOUT?
OVER HERE-- I FOUND HIS AND HIS DOG'S TRACKS!
SEE, HERE--
A SMALL BOY'S SHOEPRINTS AND A DOG'S, RACING OFF THIS WAY INTO THE FOREST.
WELL, I'LL BE--GOOD EYE, ABIGAIL!

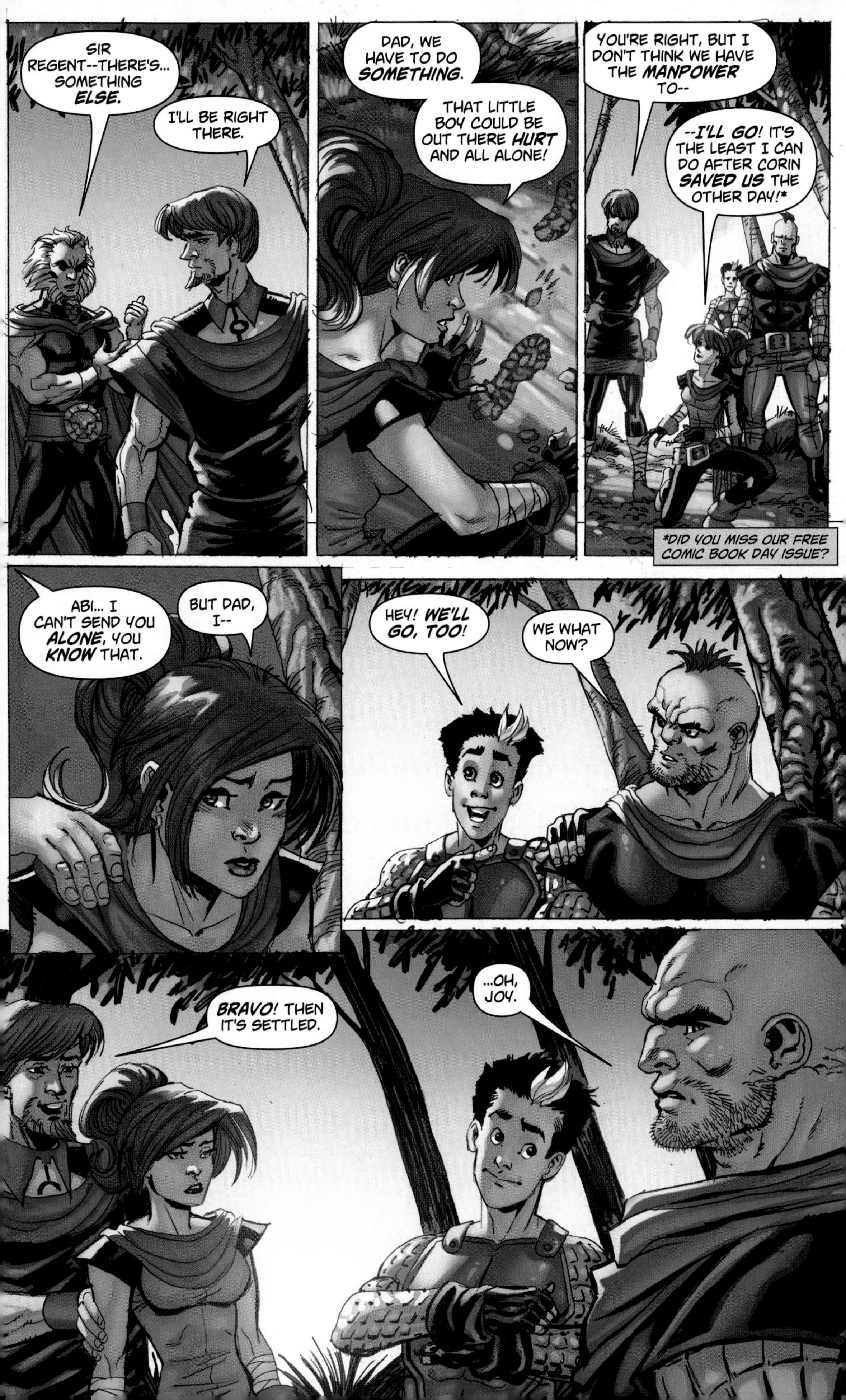
SIR REGENT--THERE'S... SOMETHING ELSE.
I'LL BE RIGHT THERE.
DAD, WE HAVE TO DO SOMETHING.
THAT LITTLE BOY COULD BE OUT THERE HURT AND ALL ALONE!
YOU'RE RIGHT, BUT I DON'T THINK WE HAVE THE MANPOWER TO--
--I'LL GO! IT'S THE LEAST I CAN DO AFTER CORIN SAVED US THE OTHER DAY!*
*DID YOU MISS OUR FREE COMIC BOOK DAY ISSUE?
ABI... I CAN'T SEND YOU ALONE, YOU KNOW THAT.
BUT DAD, I--
HEY! WE'LL GO, TOO!
WE WHAT NOW?
BRAVO! THEN IT'S SETTLED.
...OH, JOY.

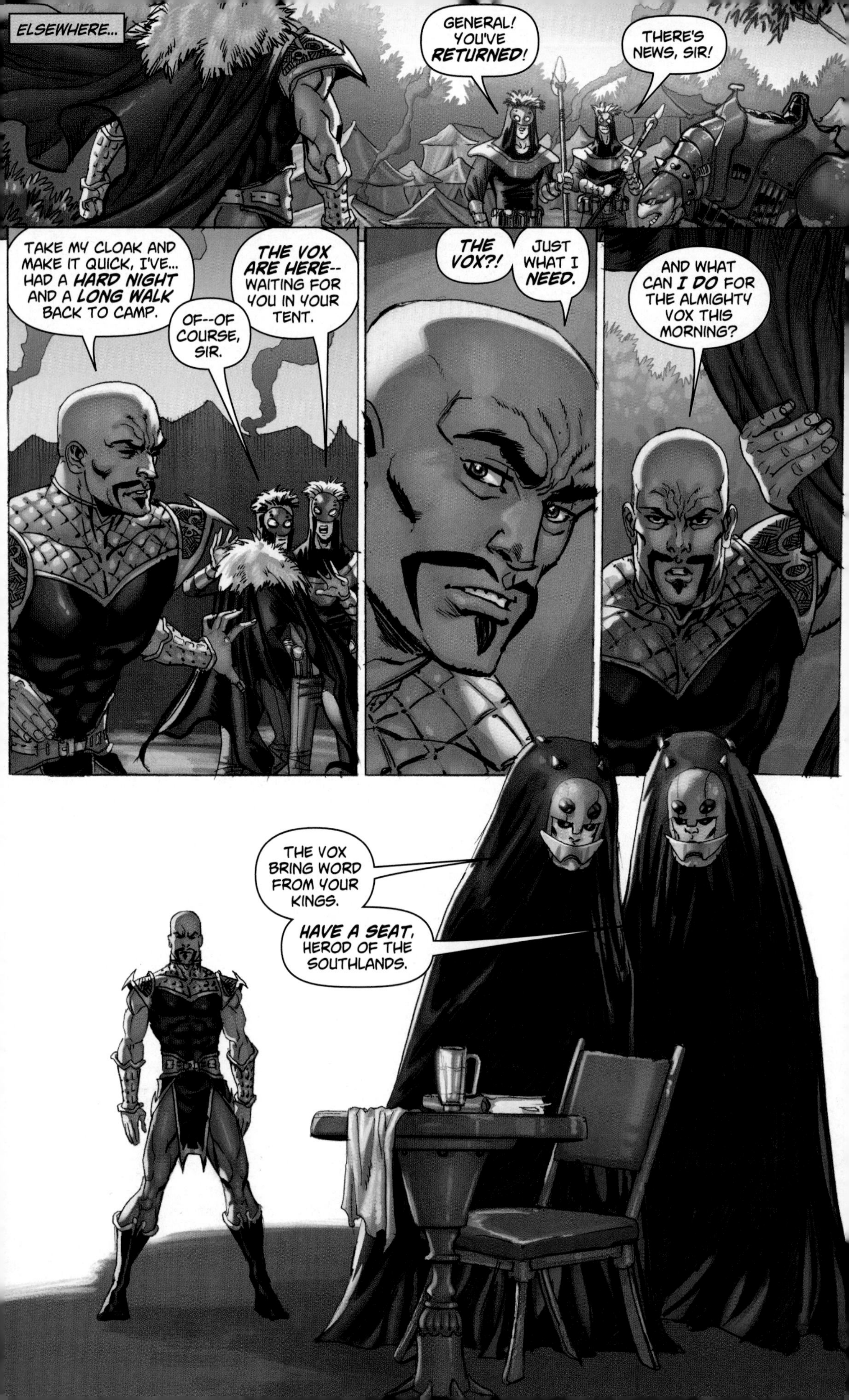
ELSEWHERE...
GENERAL! YOU'VE RETURNED!
THERE'S NEWS, SIR!
TAKE MY CLOAK AND MAKE IT QUICK, I'VE... HAD A HARD NIGHT AND A LONG WALK BACK TO CAMP.
OF--OF COURSE, SIR.
THE VOX ARE HERE-- WAITING FOR YOU IN YOUR TENT.
THE VOX?!
JUST WHAT I NEED.
AND WHAT CAN I DO FOR THE ALMIGHTY VOX THIS MORNING?
THE VOX BRING WORD FROM YOUR KINGS.
HAVE A SEAT, HEROD OF THE SOUTHLANDS.

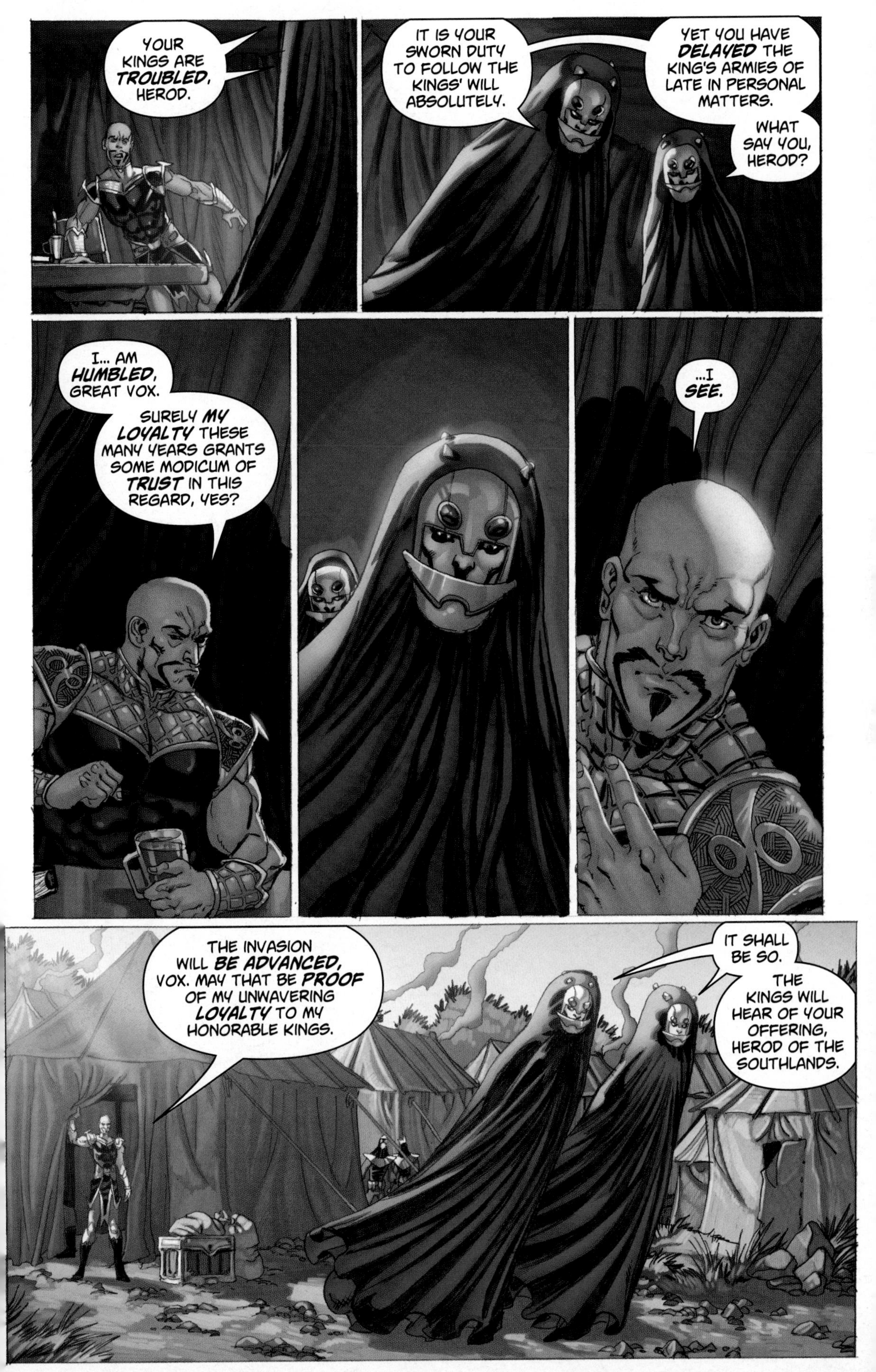
YOUR KINGS ARE TROUBLED, HEROD.
IT IS YOUR SWORN DUTY TO FOLLOW THE KINGS' WILL ABSOLUTELY.
YET YOU HAVE DELAYED THE KING'S ARMIES OF LATE IN PERSONAL MATTERS.
WHAT SAY YOU, HEROD?
I... AM HUMBLED, GREAT VOX.
SURELY MY LOYALTY THESE MANY YEARS GRANTS SOME MODICUM OF TRUST IN THIS REGARD, YES?
...I SEE.
THE INVASION WILL BE ADVANCED, VOX. MAY THAT BE PROOF OF MY UNWAVERING LOYALTY TO MY HONORABLE KINGS.
IT SHALL BE SO.
THE KINGS WILL HEAR OF YOUR OFFERING, HEROD OF THE SOUTHLANDS.

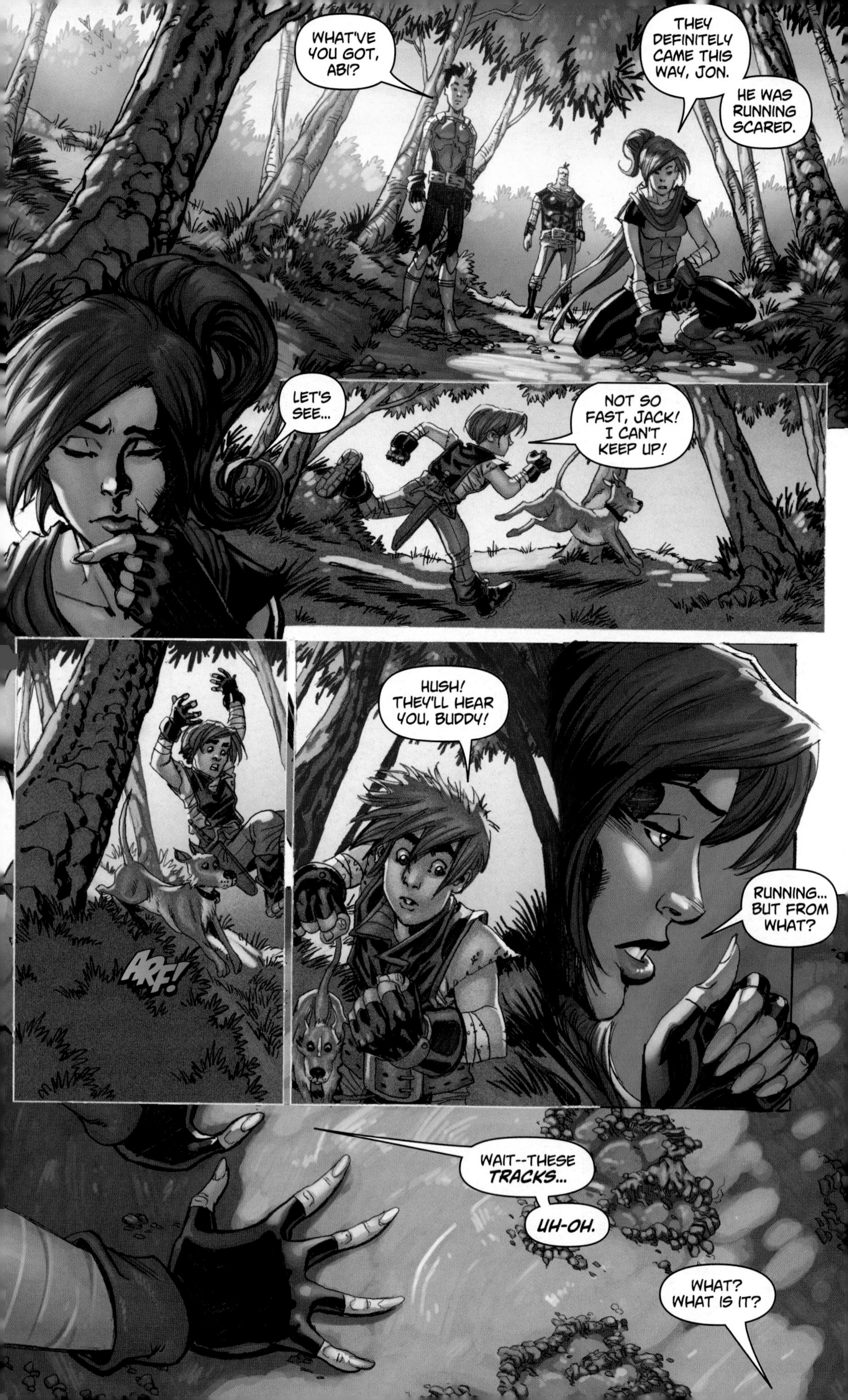
WHAT'VE YOU GOT, ABI?
THEY DEFINITELY CAME THIS WAY, JON.
HE WAS RUNNING SCARED.
LET'S SEE...
NOT SO FAST, JACK! I CAN'T KEEP UP!
ARF!
HUSH! THEY'LL HEAR YOU, BUDDY!
RUNNING... BUT FROM WHAT?
WAIT--THESE *TRACKS*...
UH-OH.
WHAT? WHAT IS IT?

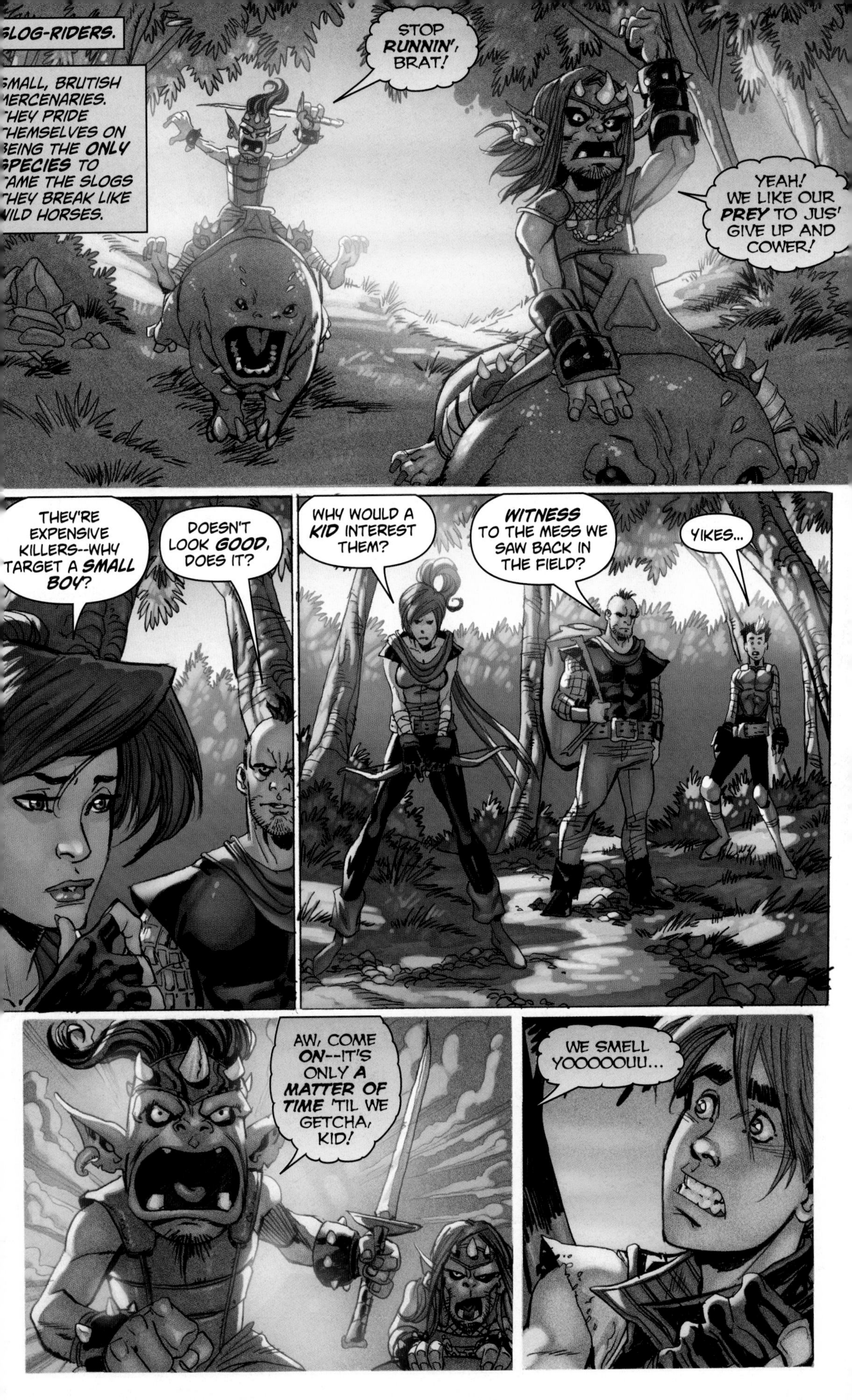

SLOG-RIDERS.
SMALL, BRUTISH MERCENARIES. THEY PRIDE THEMSELVES ON BEING THE ONLY SPECIES TO TAME THE SLOGS THEY BREAK LIKE WILD HORSES.
STOP RUNNIN', BRAT!
YEAH! WE LIKE OUR PREY TO JUS' GIVE UP AND COWER!
THEY'RE EXPENSIVE KILLERS--WHY TARGET A SMALL BOY?
DOESN'T LOOK GOOD, DOES IT?
WHY WOULD A KID INTEREST THEM?
WITNESS TO THE MESS WE SAW BACK IN THE FIELD?
YIKES...
AW, COME ON--IT'S ONLY A MATTER OF TIME 'TIL WE GETCHA, KID!
WE SMELL YOOOOOUU...

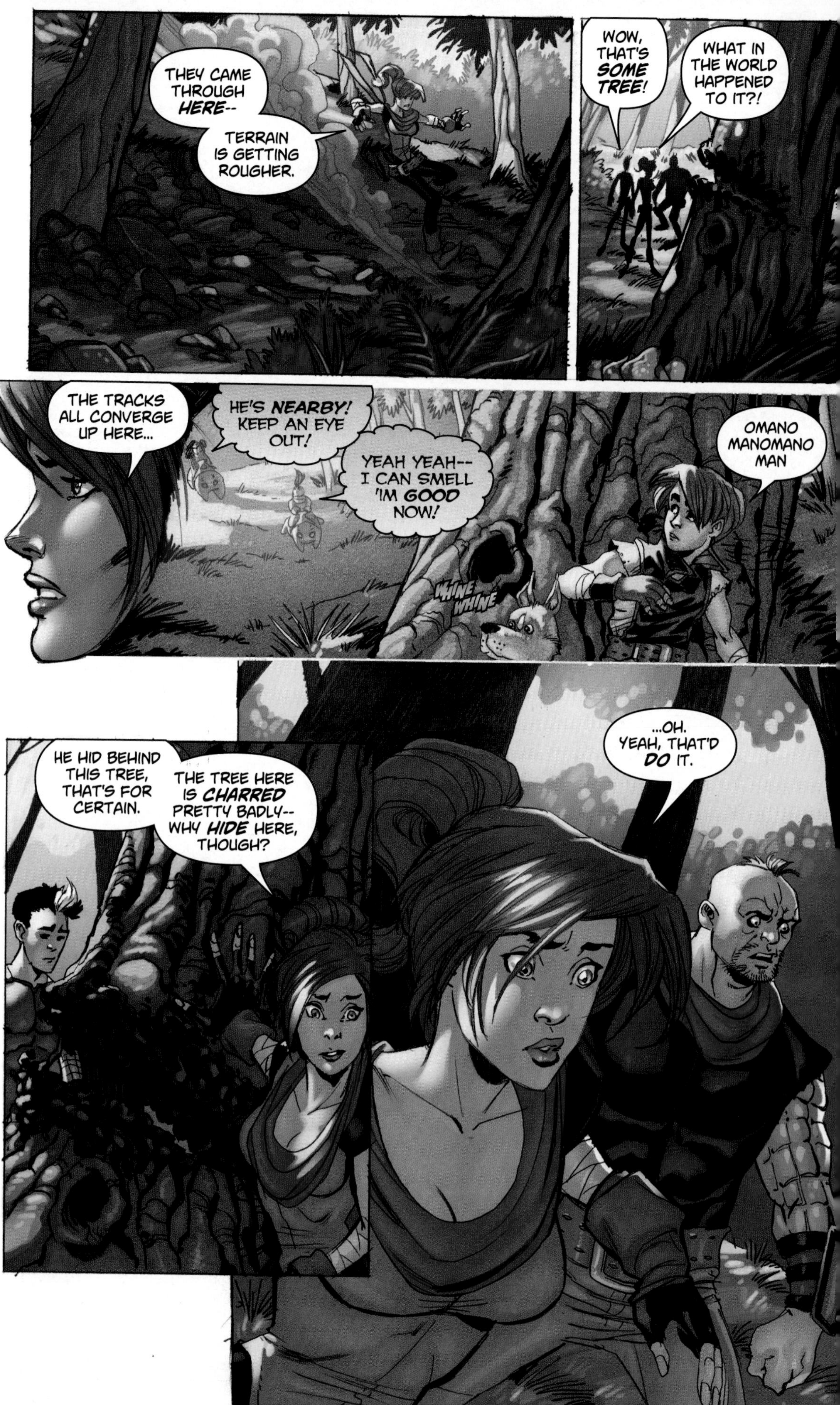

THEY CAME THROUGH **HERE**--
TERRAIN IS GETTING ROUGHER.
WOW, THAT'S **SOME TREE**!
WHAT IN THE WORLD HAPPENED TO IT?!
THE TRACKS ALL CONVERGE UP HERE...
HE'S **NEARBY**! KEEP AN EYE OUT!
YEAH YEAH-- I CAN SMELL 'IM **GOOD** NOW!
OMANO MANOMANO MAN
WHINE WHINE
HE HID BEHIND THIS TREE, THAT'S FOR CERTAIN.
THE TREE HERE IS **CHARRED** PRETTY BADLY-- WHY **HIDE** HERE, THOUGH?
...OH. YEAH, THAT'D **DO** IT.

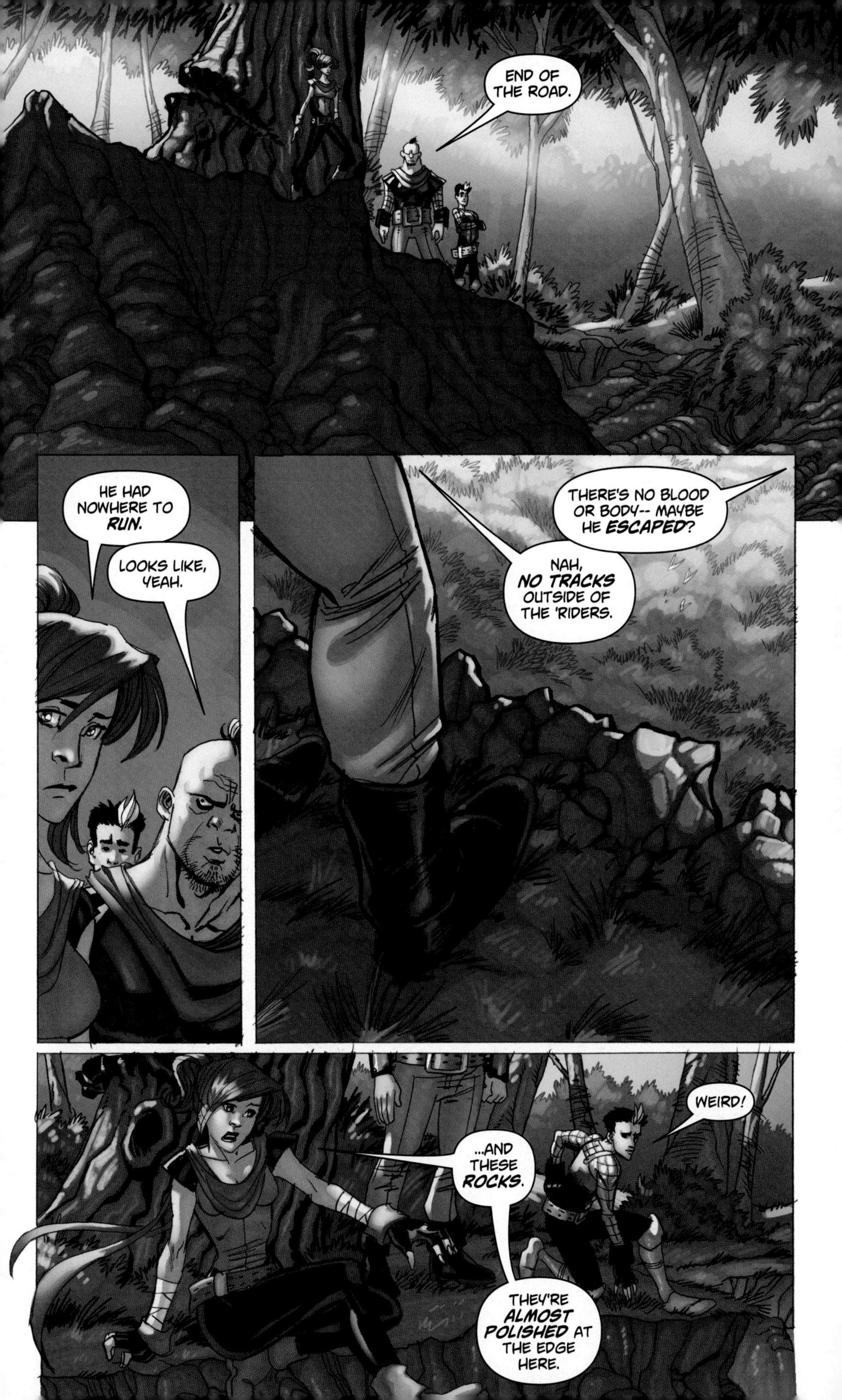

END OF THE ROAD.
HE HAD NOWHERE TO RUN.
LOOKS LIKE, YEAH.
THERE'S NO BLOOD OR BODY-- MAYBE HE ESCAPED?
NAH, NO TRACKS OUTSIDE OF THE 'RIDERS.
WEIRD!
...AND THESE ROCKS.
THEY'RE ALMOST POLISHED AT THE EDGE HERE.

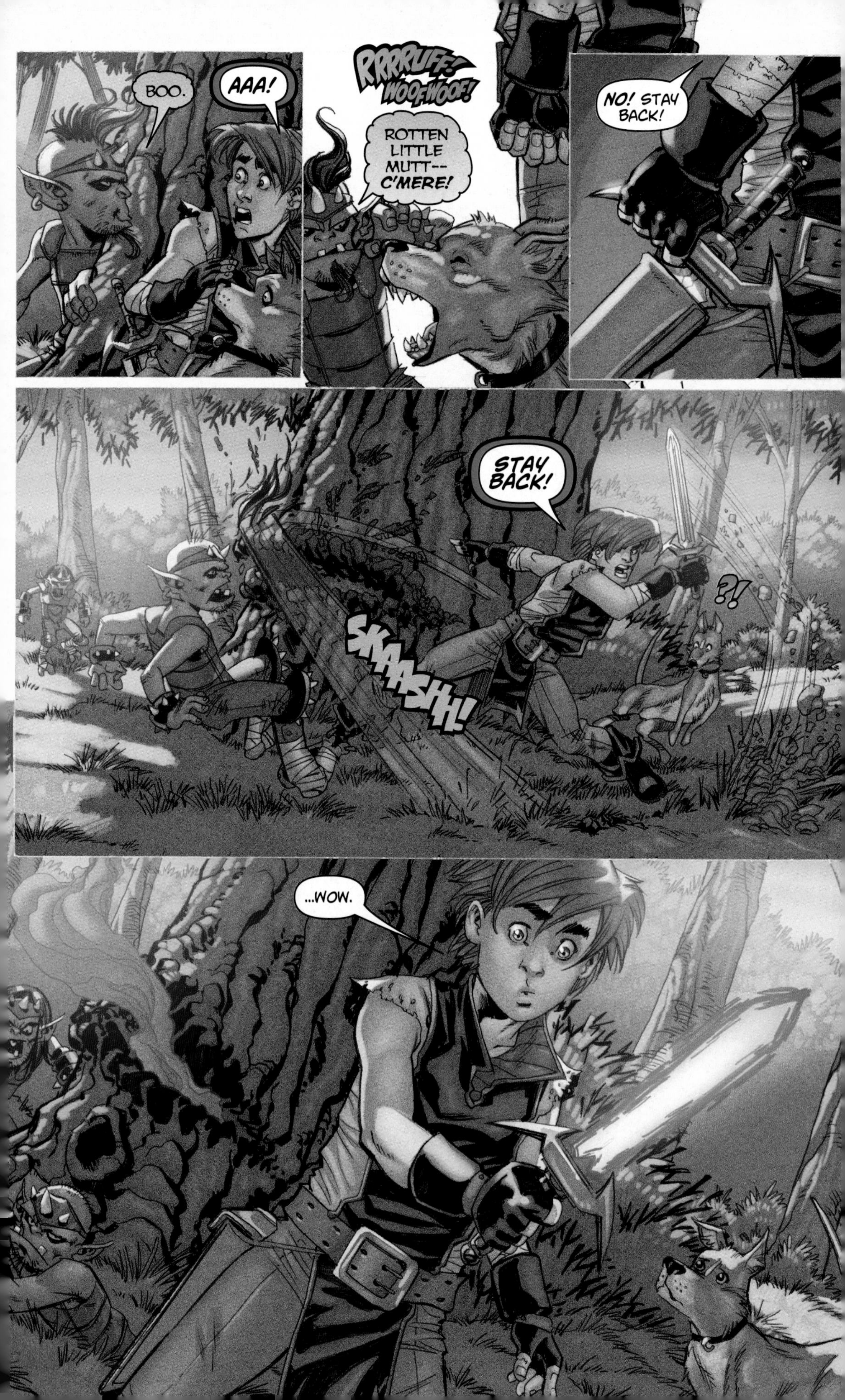
BOO.
AAA!
RRRRUFF! WOOFWOOF!
ROTTEN LITTLE MUTT-- C'MERE!
NO! STAY BACK!
STAY BACK!
SKAASHH!
?!
...WOW.

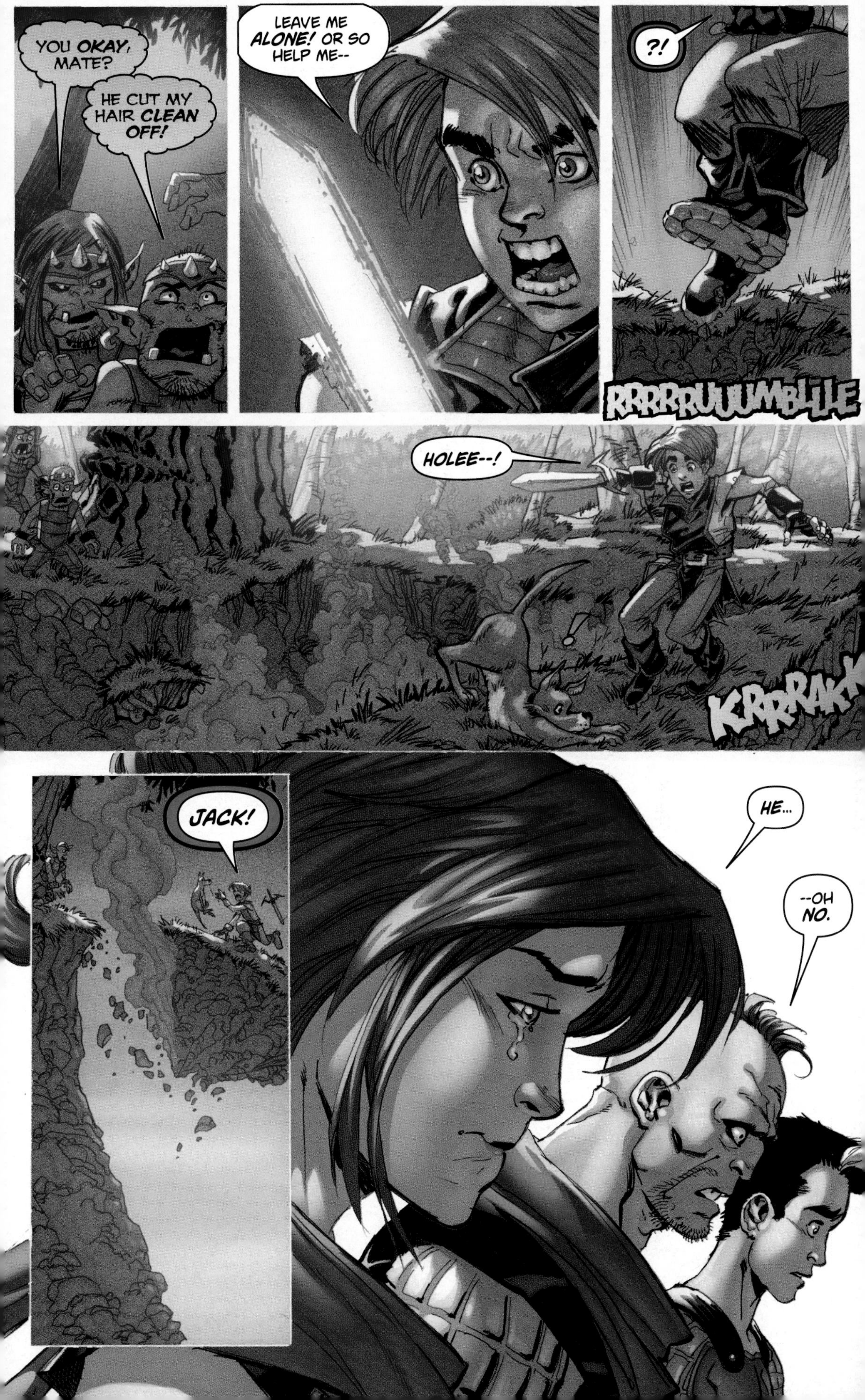

YOU OKAY, MATE?
HE CUT MY HAIR CLEAN OFF!
LEAVE ME ALONE! OR SO HELP ME--
?!
RRRRRUUUMBLLLE
HOLEE--!
KRRRAKK
JACK!
HE...
--OH NO.

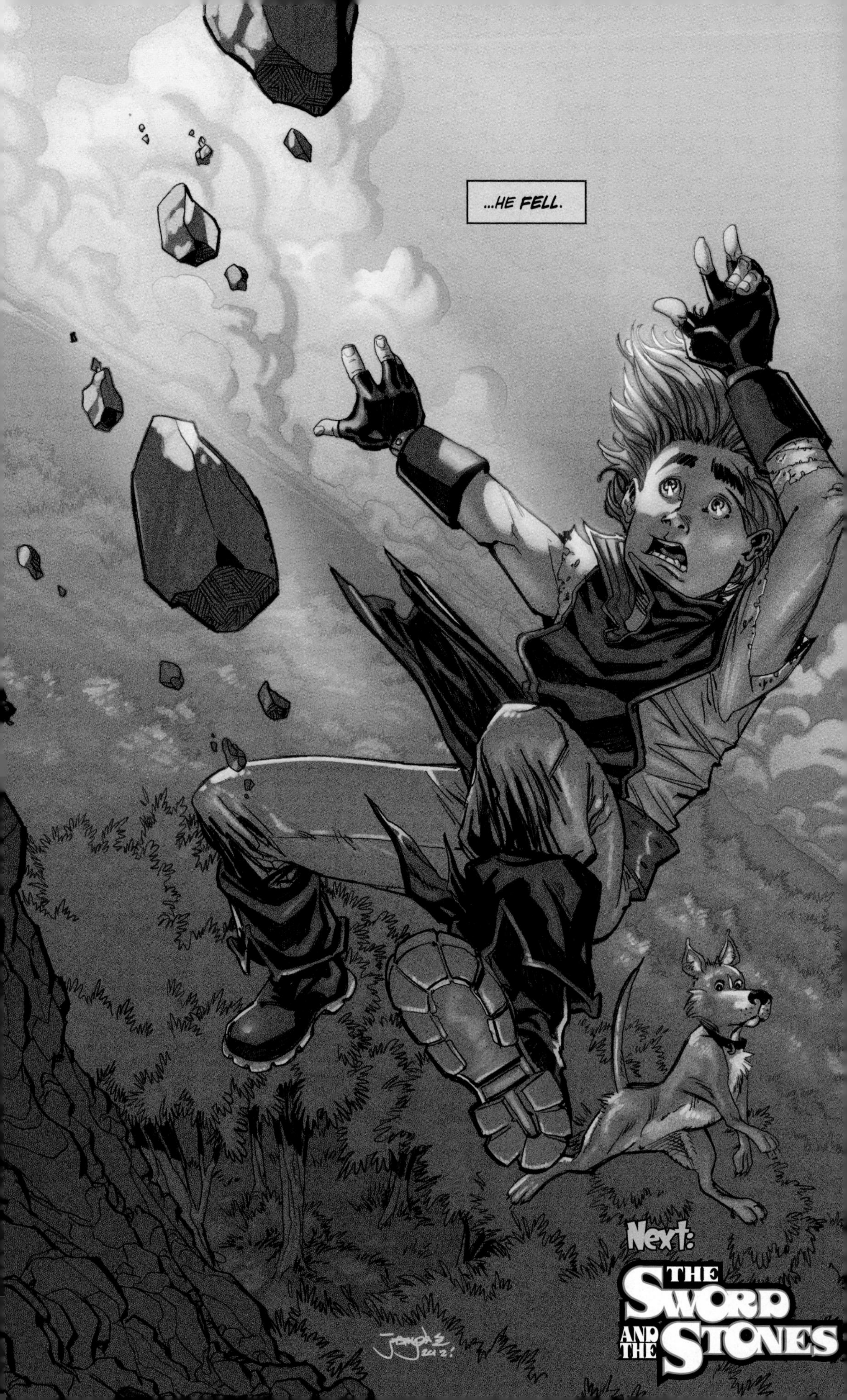
...HE FELL.
Next:
THE SWORD AND THE STONES

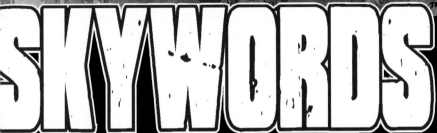

SKYWORDS™

Got thoughts?
Fan art?
Ransom notes?

WRITE US @

skywardfans@gmail.com

Wow! *Issue two is here and so are your letters! Wow, what a response. Mind you, I'm still sorting through your emails pre-Action Lab still, but from what I'm seeing? We're here to stay a while, folks! Thanks for the enthusiasm!*

Eyes on the sky!
- jeremy

Jeremy,

I received issues 0-3 of Skyward in the mail yesterday and read them all in one sitting tonight. I seem to have a kindred spirit for stories that involve a boy and his dog and this is no exception. Although I don't know much about Quinn or Jack yet, the story captivated my interest. I enjoyed the artwork and the characters seem to have come to life and make me want to know more. I liked the introduction of Garrick and his interesting bird friend. Plus the cliffhanger with the rabbit warriors makes one ready to read the next issue.

Not sure when issue 4 will be out or how it will be distributed but hopefully I will find out. I came across your book thru Facebook from a post from someone else. Can't recall who so you won't be able to thank them but this led me to your book. I noticed you do a lot of conventions but none that close to me. I live in Iowa, and will be going to Fallcon (Oct 6th) and yes we do have one in Iowa called the I-con (Nov 10th) It would be cool to get a sketch from you sometime. Looking forward to hearing when issue 4 might come out and that you find a publisher for this book. Its truly a adventurous read!

Craig
batmanboy@hotmail.com

Craig, thanks so much! As hopefully you know now, we're now in the capable hands of the lads at Action Lab, and couldn't be more thrilled-- it's not often one gets a chance to be at the ground level of a monster in the making.

- jeremy

Hey, Jeremy,

We've run into each other several times over the years. I first met you at HeroesCon (2007, maybe?) and fell in love with your art. It's the perfect mix of dynamic and animated, reminiscent of Mike Wieringo's style.

I got the first issue of "Skyward" at HeroesCon last year (I believe) and thought it was really good. This year, I was really busy at my table, so I had my wife & kids run over to get issues 2 and 3 (I know one of my sons got you to sketch Captain America for him). I read those two issues after getting home, and wow…they are amazing!

I love this story for so many reasons. It's a great mix of action and fantasy, which reminds me of comics and cartoons I love like this, such as "Tellos", "Bone", and "Pirates of Darkwater". I'm definitely interested to see where the story goes!

On a side note, I bought "After School Agent" at HeroesCon last year, and again, great job on your issue!

Hope to hear back from you. Keep up the great work, man!

Matthew D. Smith
mdsmithcomics@gmail.com

Thanks, Matt! My issue of After School Agent is out now at finer comic shops worldwide, for those interested! Also, pick up my issue of Matthew D. Smith's SIMON SAYS out now! I did art for the latest issue. :)

Hello,

My name is Scott Fine and we met at Fabletown and Beyond last weekend. I just wanted to touch base with you and thank you for being at an awesome show!

I know you said Skyward will be in Diamond sometime this summer. I'm looking forward to carrying the title and was wondering if you would have any promotional material for it. It's never too early to start building hype! The book looks great!

Looking forward to stocking your book!

-Scott Fine
Level Up Entertainment
levelup.llc@gmail.com

Folks, if you weren't at FABLESCON in March, you really missed out! A haven for all things mythic fiction in comics, everyone that attended had one of the best shows they've ever had, from comic creators to fans and back again. Scott, expect to hear more from me about making SKYWARD a mainstay at your establishment! Thanks for the kind words!

NEXT! *Quinn takes a fall, the chase continues, and strange creatures lurk deep in woods-- but are they friend or foe? It's all in SKYWARD #3, in your face in 30 days! GET EXCITED!*

- jeremy

2013 CONVENTION SCHEDULE

7/17 - 7/21
SDCC (Comic-Con)
(San Diego, CA)

8/30 - 9/2
Dragon*Con
(Atlanta, GA)

9/7 - 9/8
Baltimore Comic-Con
(Baltimore, MD)

10/10 - 10/13
New York Comic Con
(New York, NY)

10/26 - 10/27
Comic Book City Con
(Greensboro, NC)

SKYWARD EXTRAS

Fan Art!

Send your fanart to:
skywardfans@gmail.com

So cool! Thanks to all the fans that are sending in SKYWARD fan art! Keep sending 'em and we'll keep running them in these pages!

- jeremy

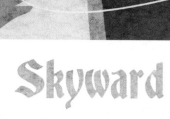

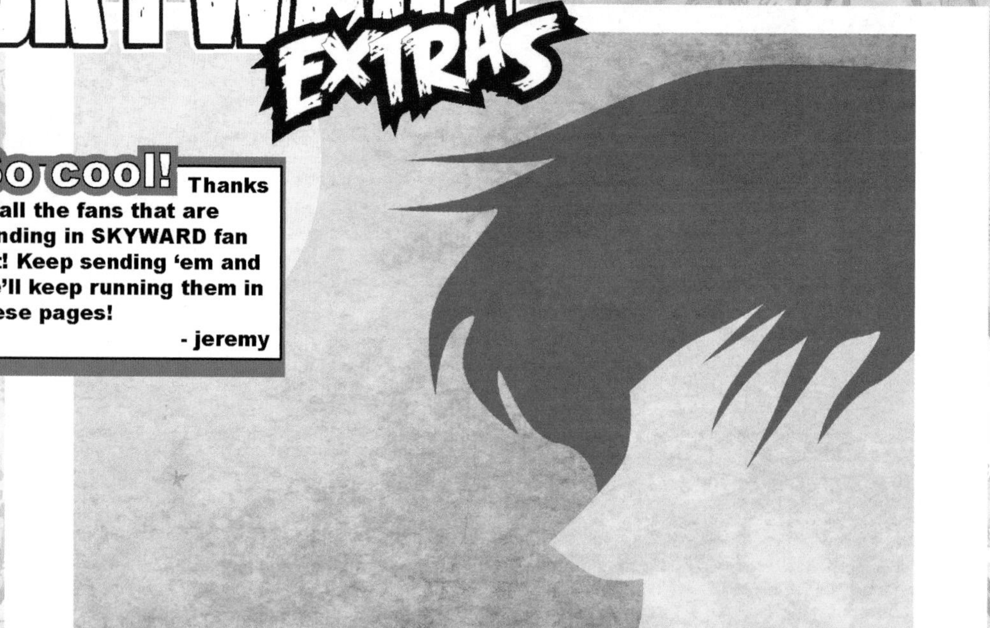

Skyward

FanArt

Art by CiLc
cilc.deviantart.com

FanArt

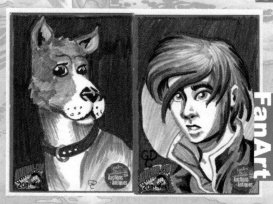

Art by GC Dale
hoosiermouse.deviantart.com

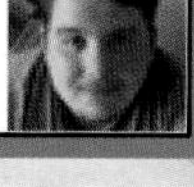

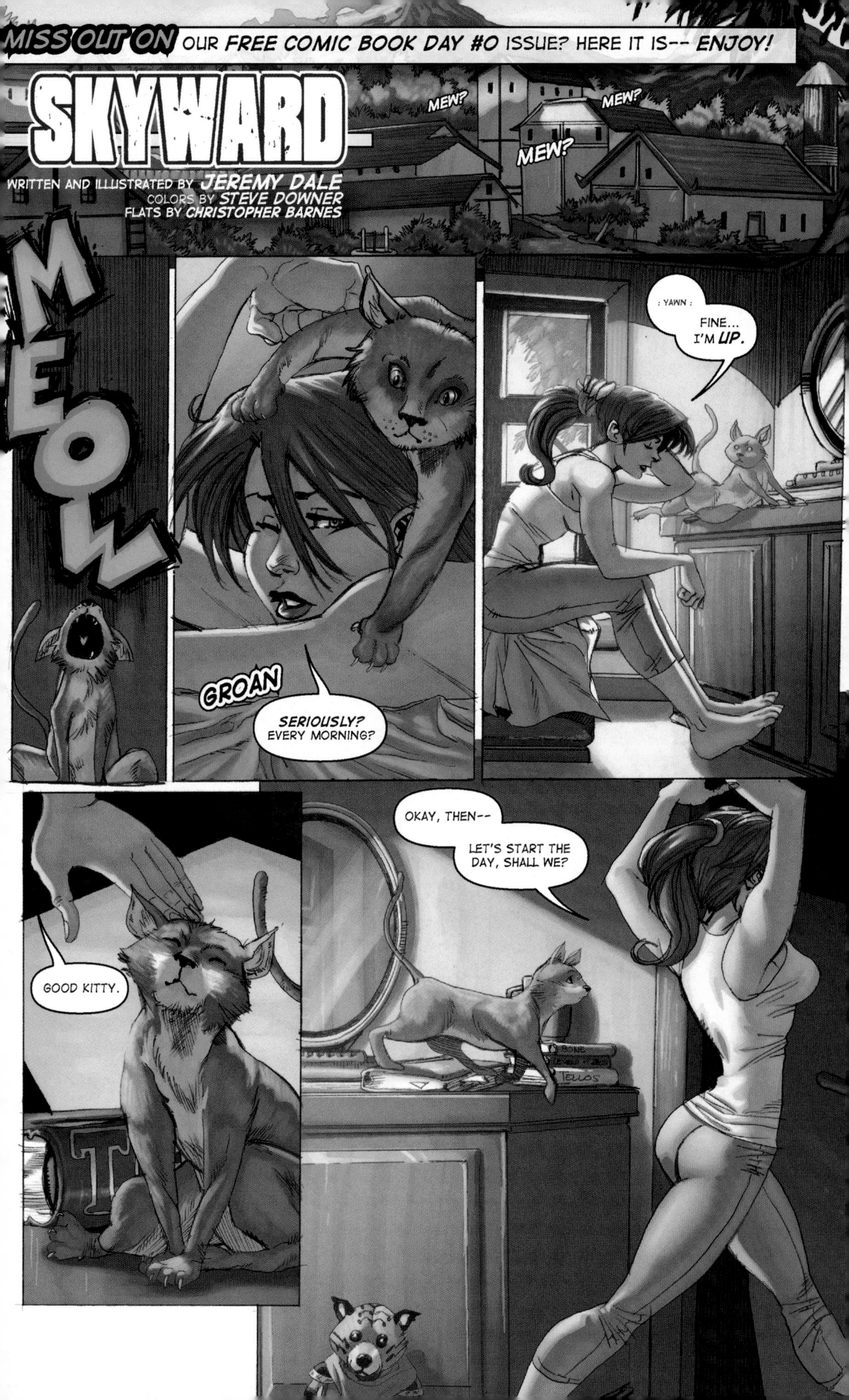

MISS OUT ON OUR FREE COMIC BOOK DAY #0 ISSUE? HERE IT IS-- ENJOY!
SKYWARD
WRITTEN AND ILLUSTRATED BY JEREMY DALE
COLORS BY STEVE DOWNER
FLATS BY CHRISTOPHER BARNES
MEW?
MEW?
MEW?
MEOW
GROAN
SERIOUSLY? EVERY MORNING?
: YAWN :
FINE... I'M UP.
GOOD KITTY.
OKAY, THEN--
LET'S START THE DAY, SHALL WE?

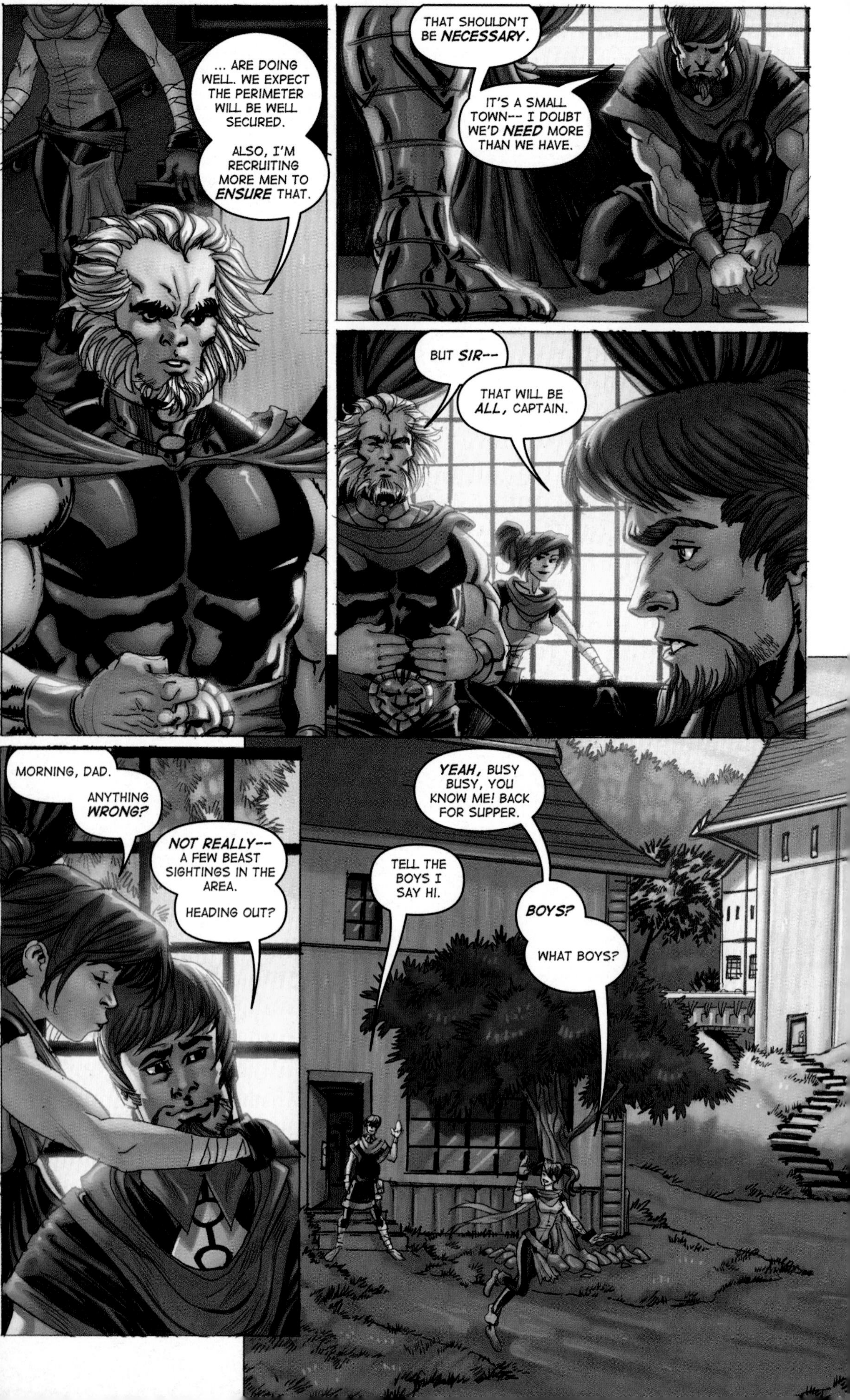
... ARE DOING WELL. WE EXPECT THE PERIMETER WILL BE WELL SECURED.
ALSO, I'M RECRUITING MORE MEN TO ENSURE THAT.
THAT SHOULDN'T BE NECESSARY.
IT'S A SMALL TOWN-- I DOUBT WE'D NEED MORE THAN WE HAVE.
BUT SIR--
THAT WILL BE ALL, CAPTAIN.
MORNING, DAD.
ANYTHING WRONG?
NOT REALLY-- A FEW BEAST SIGHTINGS IN THE AREA.
HEADING OUT?
YEAH, BUSY BUSY, YOU KNOW ME! BACK FOR SUPPER.
TELL THE BOYS I SAY HI.
BOYS?
WHAT BOYS?

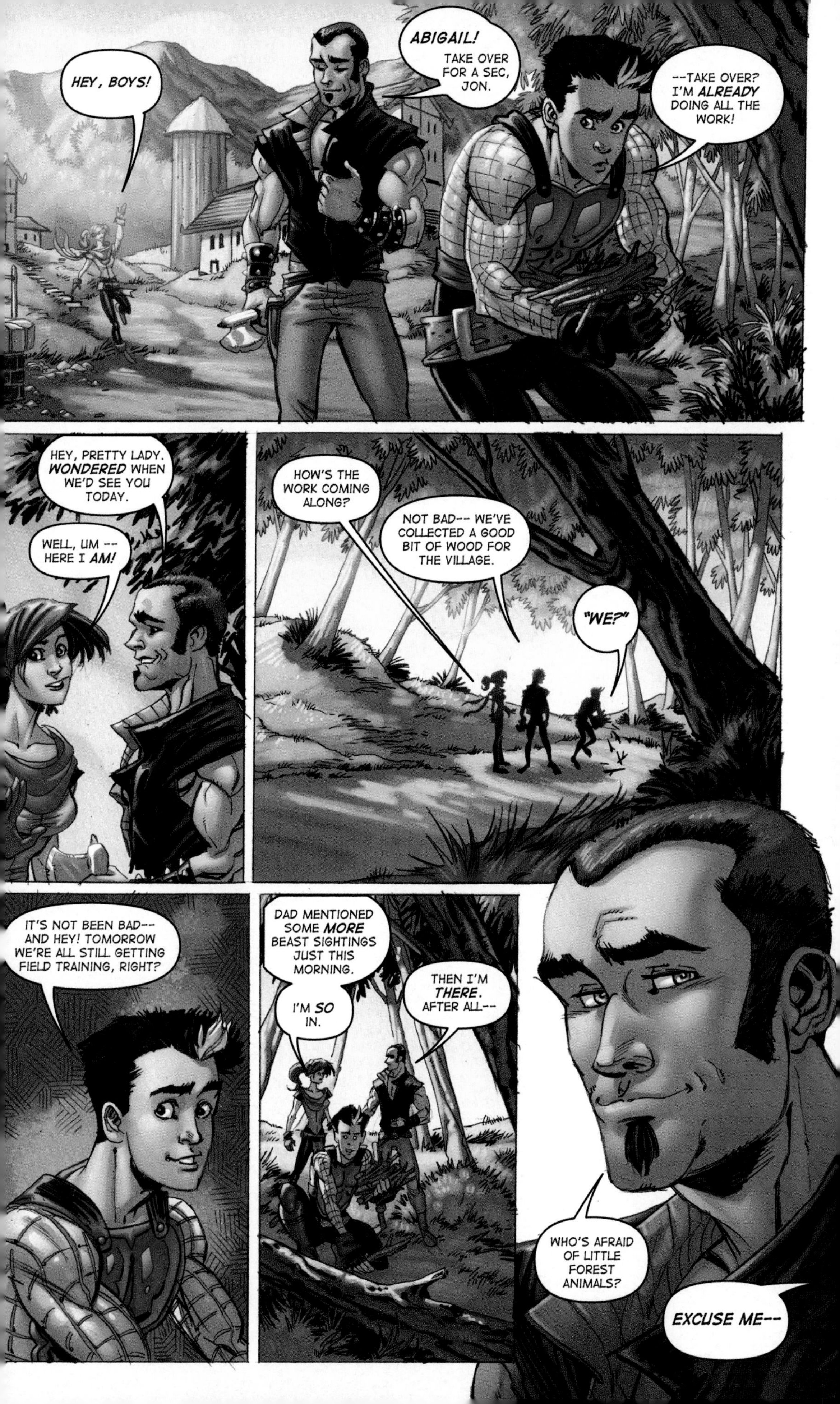
HEY, BOYS!
ABIGAIL!
TAKE OVER FOR A SEC, JON.
--TAKE OVER? I'M ALREADY DOING ALL THE WORK!
HEY, PRETTY LADY. WONDERED WHEN WE'D SEE YOU TODAY.
WELL, UM -- HERE I AM!
HOW'S THE WORK COMING ALONG?
NOT BAD-- WE'VE COLLECTED A GOOD BIT OF WOOD FOR THE VILLAGE.
"WE?"
IT'S NOT BEEN BAD-- AND HEY! TOMORROW WE'RE ALL STILL GETTING FIELD TRAINING, RIGHT?
DAD MENTIONED SOME MORE BEAST SIGHTINGS JUST THIS MORNING.
I'M SO IN.
THEN I'M THERE. AFTER ALL--
WHO'S AFRAID OF LITTLE FOREST ANIMALS?
EXCUSE ME--

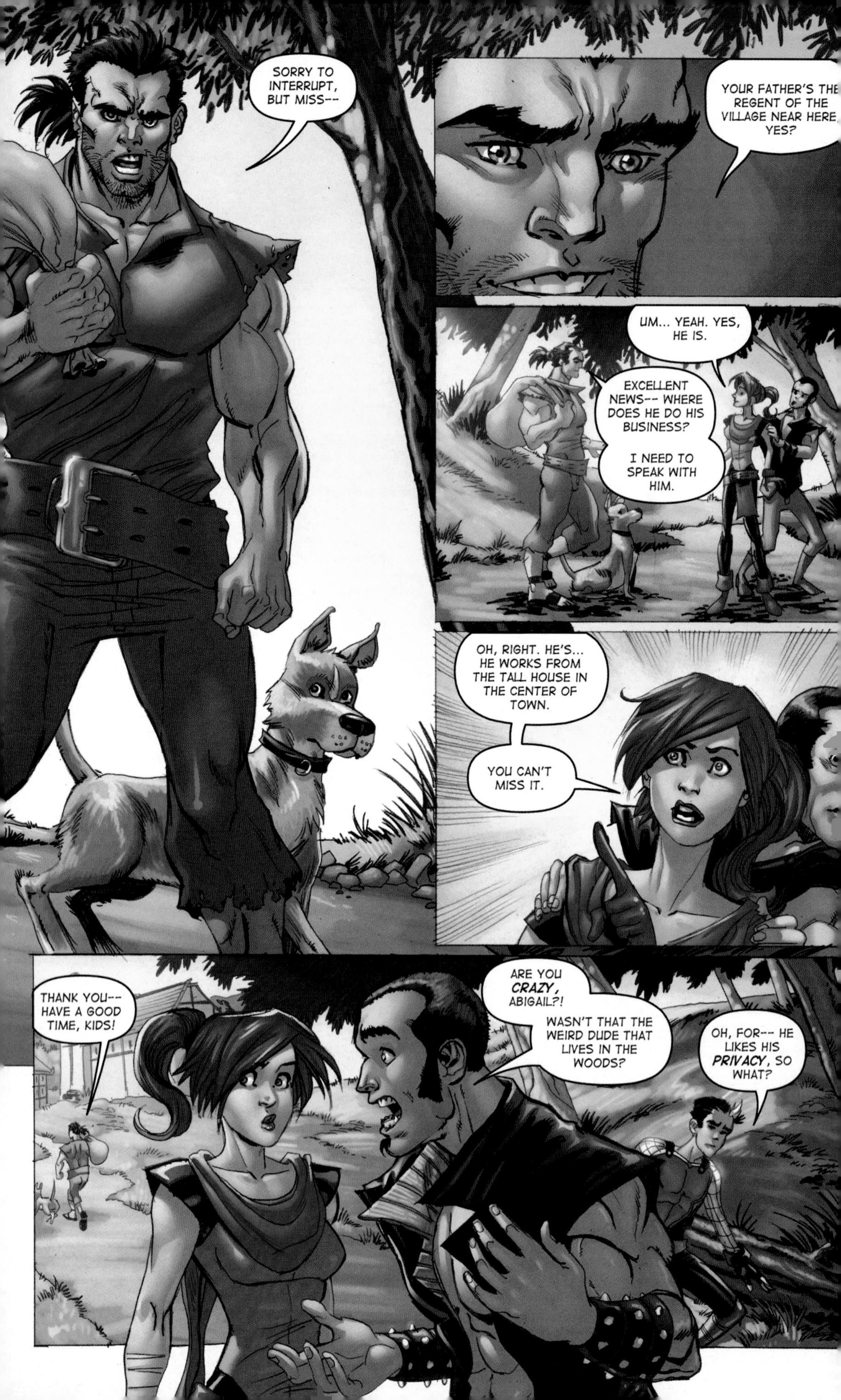
SORRY TO INTERRUPT, BUT MISS--
YOUR FATHER'S THE REGENT OF THE VILLAGE NEAR HERE, YES?
UM... YEAH. YES, HE IS.
EXCELLENT NEWS-- WHERE DOES HE DO HIS BUSINESS?
I NEED TO SPEAK WITH HIM.
OH, RIGHT. HE'S... HE WORKS FROM THE TALL HOUSE IN THE CENTER OF TOWN.
YOU CAN'T MISS IT.
THANK YOU-- HAVE A GOOD TIME, KIDS!
ARE YOU *CRAZY*, ABIGAIL?!
WASN'T THAT THE WEIRD DUDE THAT LIVES IN THE WOODS?
OH, FOR-- HE LIKES HIS *PRIVACY*, SO WHAT?

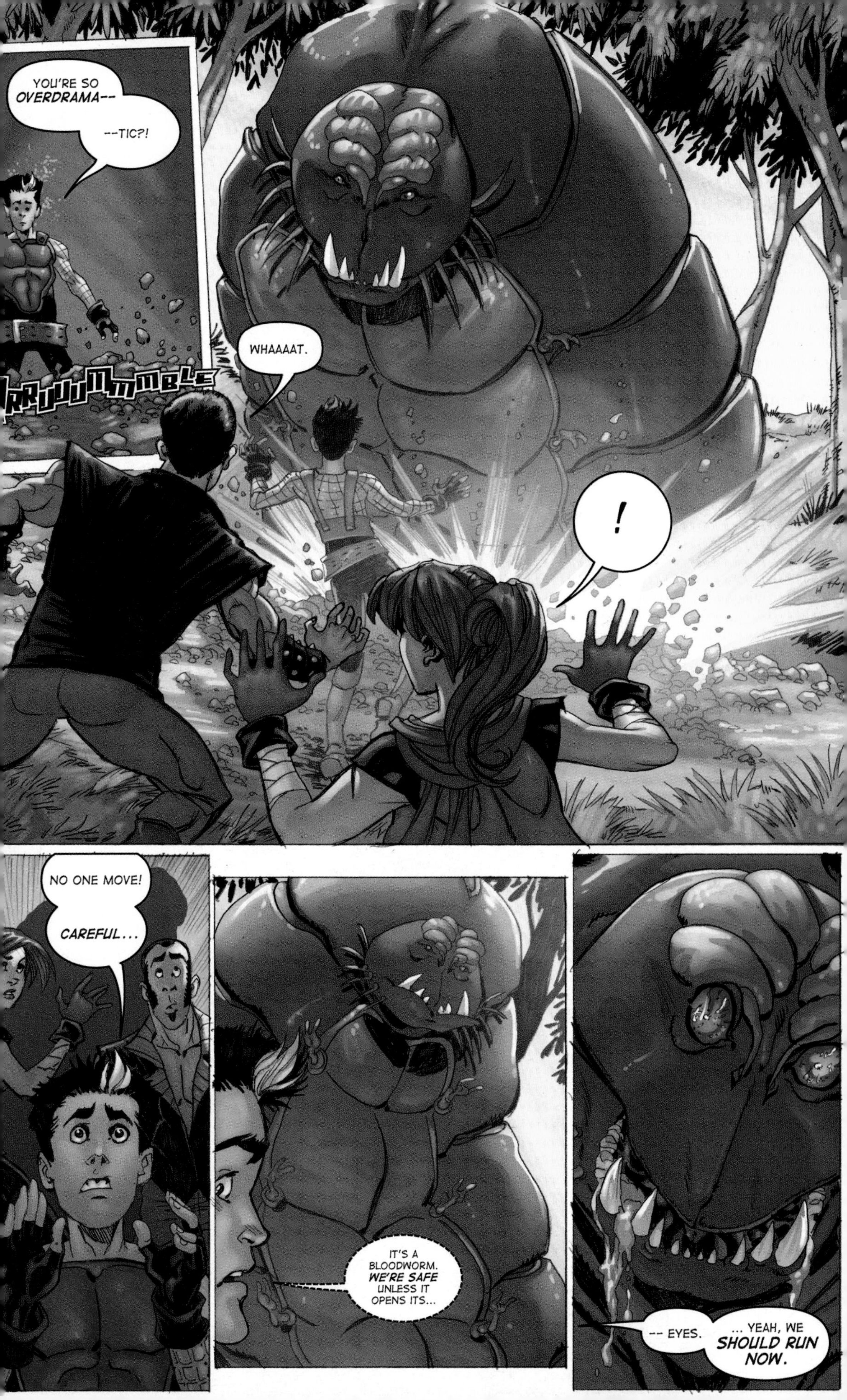

YOU'RE SO OVERDRAMA--
--TIC?!
RRUUUMMMBLE
WHAAAAT.
!
NO ONE MOVE!
CAREFUL...
IT'S A BLOODWORM. WE'RE SAFE UNLESS IT OPENS ITS...
-- EYES.
... YEAH, WE SHOULD RUN NOW.

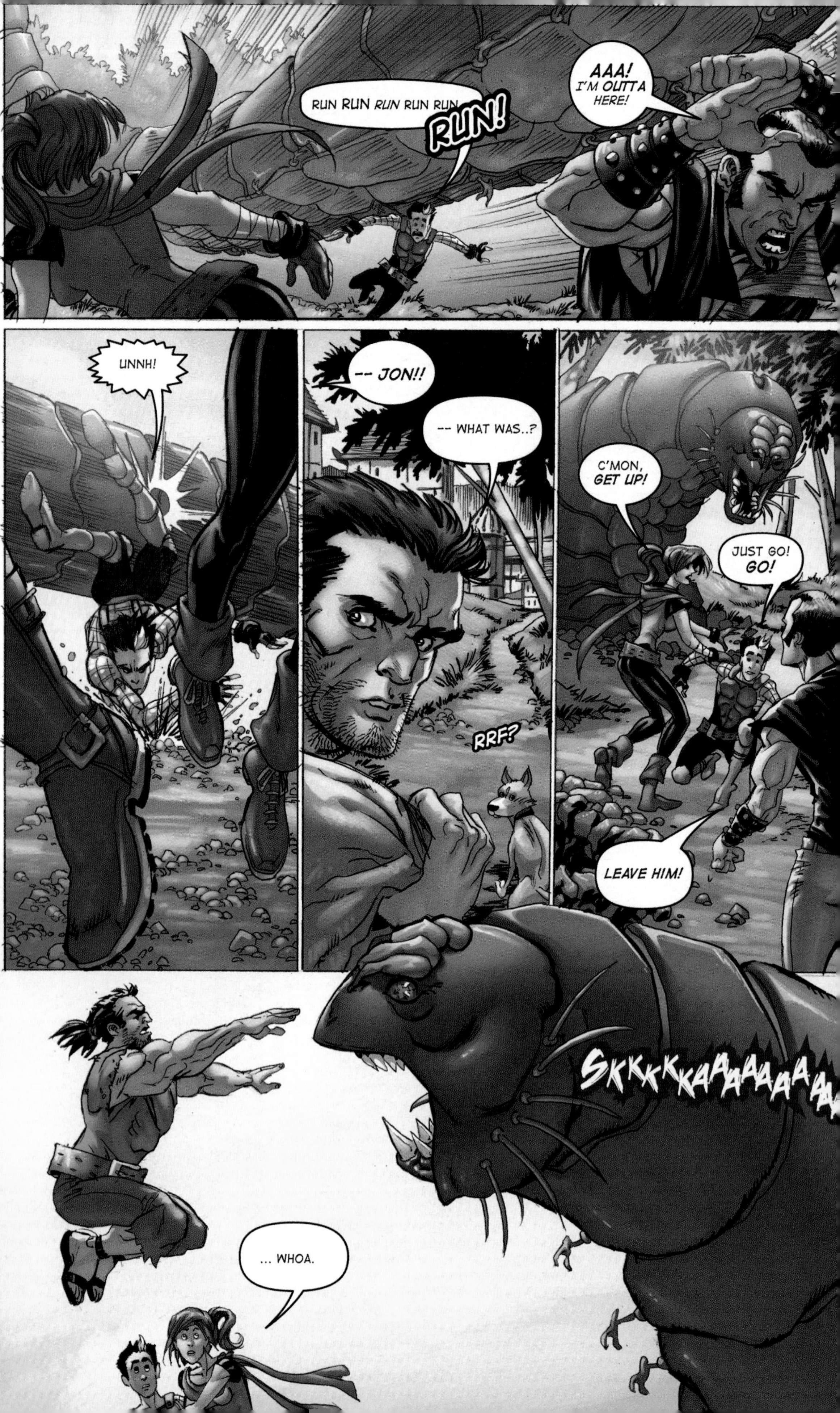
RUN RUN RUN RUN RUN
RUN!
AAA! I'M OUTTA HERE!
UNNH!
-- JON!!
-- WHAT WAS..?
RRF?
C'MON, GET UP!
JUST GO! GO!
LEAVE HIM!
SKKKKAAAAAAAA
... WHOA.

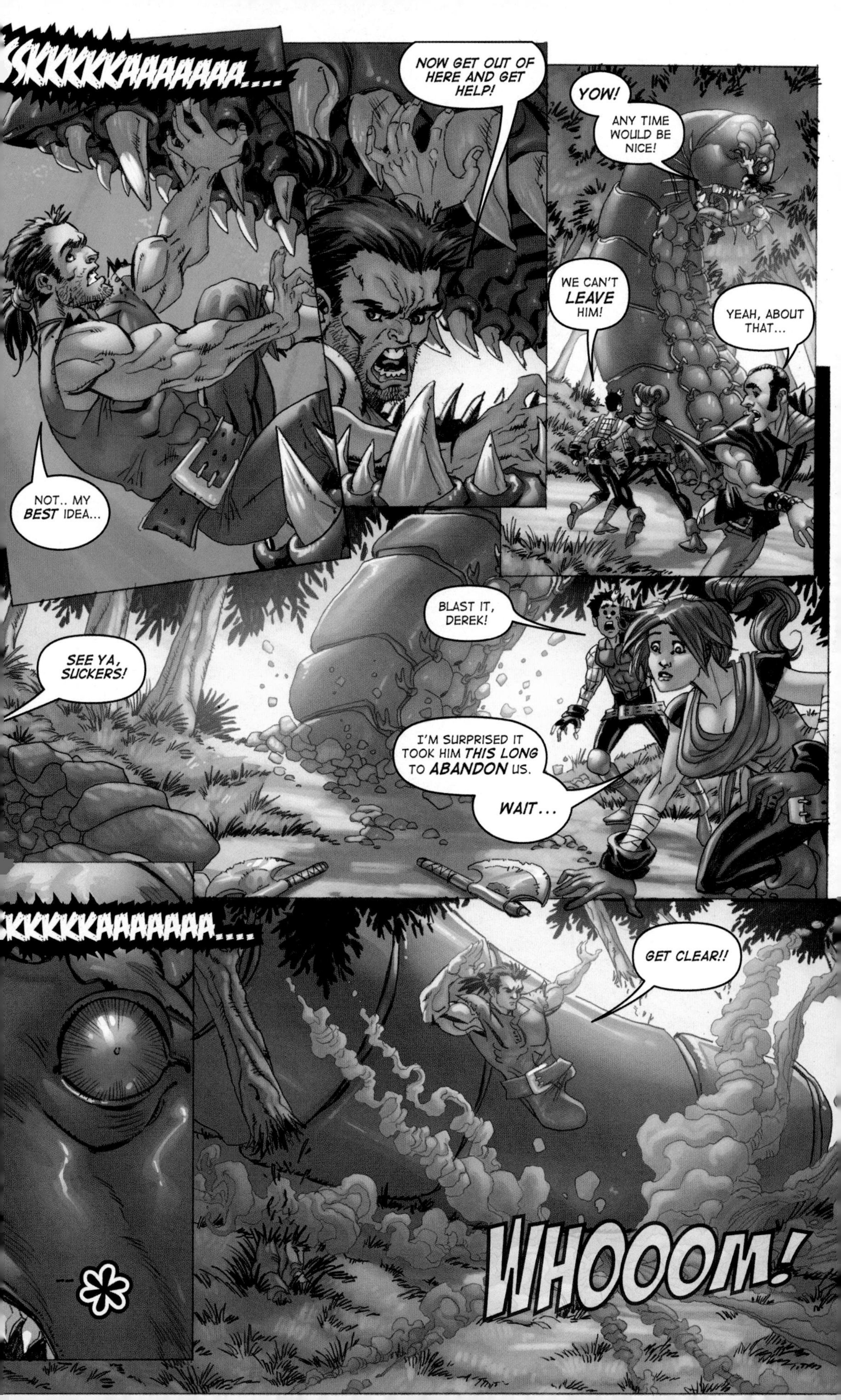
SKKKKKAAAAAAA....
NOT.. MY BEST IDEA...
NOW GET OUT OF HERE AND GET HELP!
YOW!
ANY TIME WOULD BE NICE!
WE CAN'T LEAVE HIM!
YEAH, ABOUT THAT...
SEE YA, SUCKERS!
BLAST IT, DEREK!
I'M SURPRISED IT TOOK HIM THIS LONG TO ABANDON US.
WAIT...
SKKKKKAAAAAAA....
GET CLEAR!!
WHOOOM!

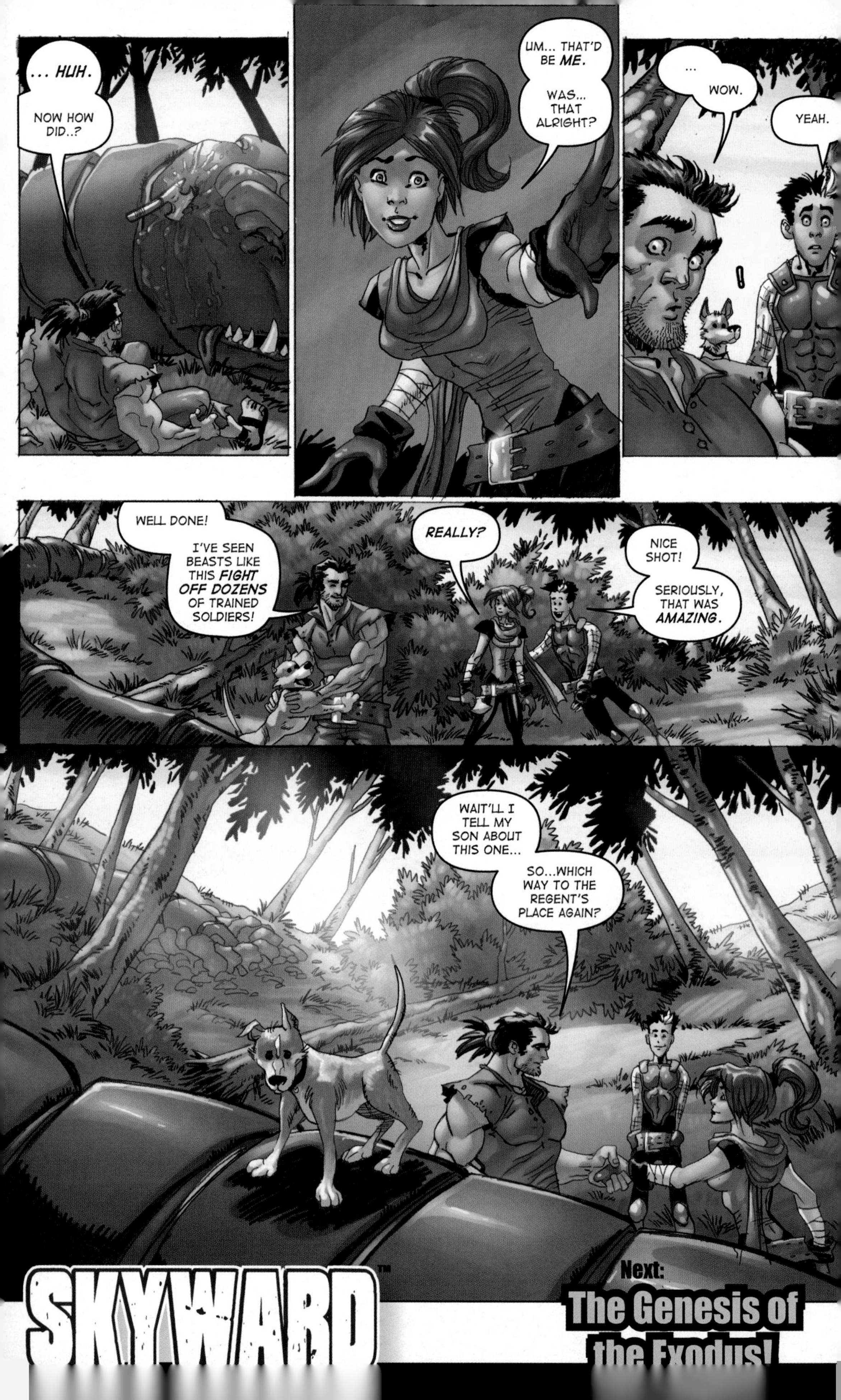

... HUH.
NOW HOW DID..?
UM... THAT'D BE ME.
WAS... THAT ALRIGHT?
...
WOW.
YEAH.
!
WELL DONE!
I'VE SEEN BEASTS LIKE THIS FIGHT OFF DOZENS OF TRAINED SOLDIERS!
REALLY?
NICE SHOT!
SERIOUSLY, THAT WAS AMAZING.
WAIT'LL I TELL MY SON ABOUT THIS ONE...
SO...WHICH WAY TO THE REGENT'S PLACE AGAIN?
SKYWARD™
Next:
The Genesis of the Exodus!

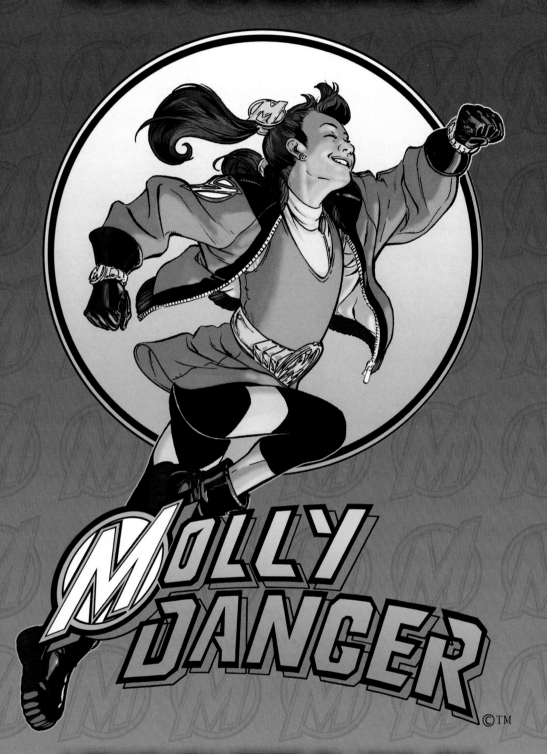

THE HERO YOU'VE BEEN WAITING FOR

MOLLY DANGER
©TM

A BRAND NEW SERIES BY JAMAL IGLE

ACTIONLABCOMICS.COM
GOMOLLYDANGER.BLOGSPOT.COM

JAMAL IGLE.COM

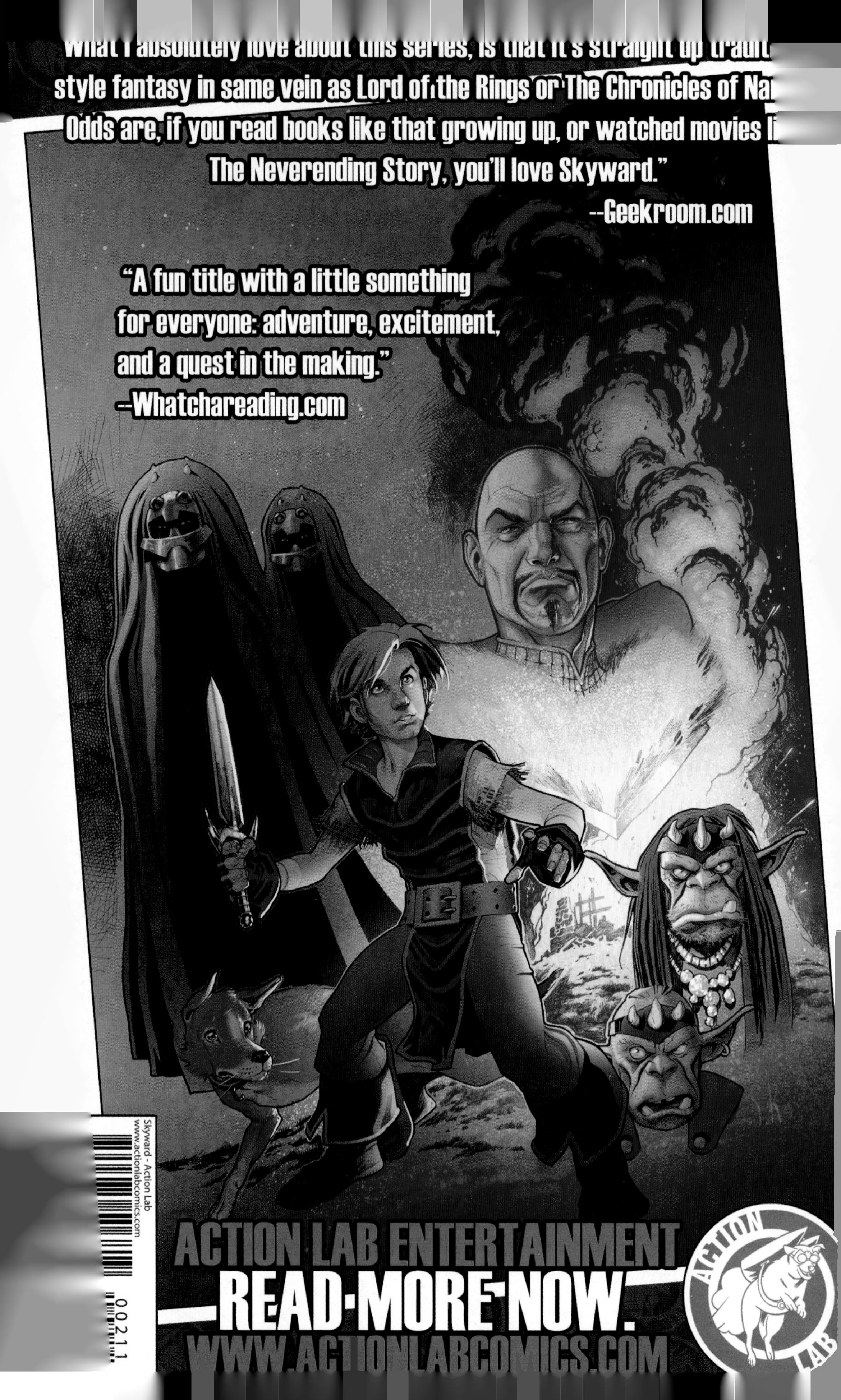
What I absolutely love about this series, is that it's straight up tradit
style fantasy in same vein as Lord of the Rings or The Chronicles of Na
Odds are, if you read books like that growing up, or watched movies li
The Neverending Story, you'll love Skyward."
--Geekroom.com
"A fun title with a little something for everyone: adventure, excitement, and a quest in the making."
--Whatchareading.com
Skyward - Action Lab
www.actionlabcomics.com
0 0 2 1 1
ACTION LAB ENTERTAINMENT
READ·MORE·NOW.
WWW.ACTIONLABCOMICS.COM
ACTION LAB

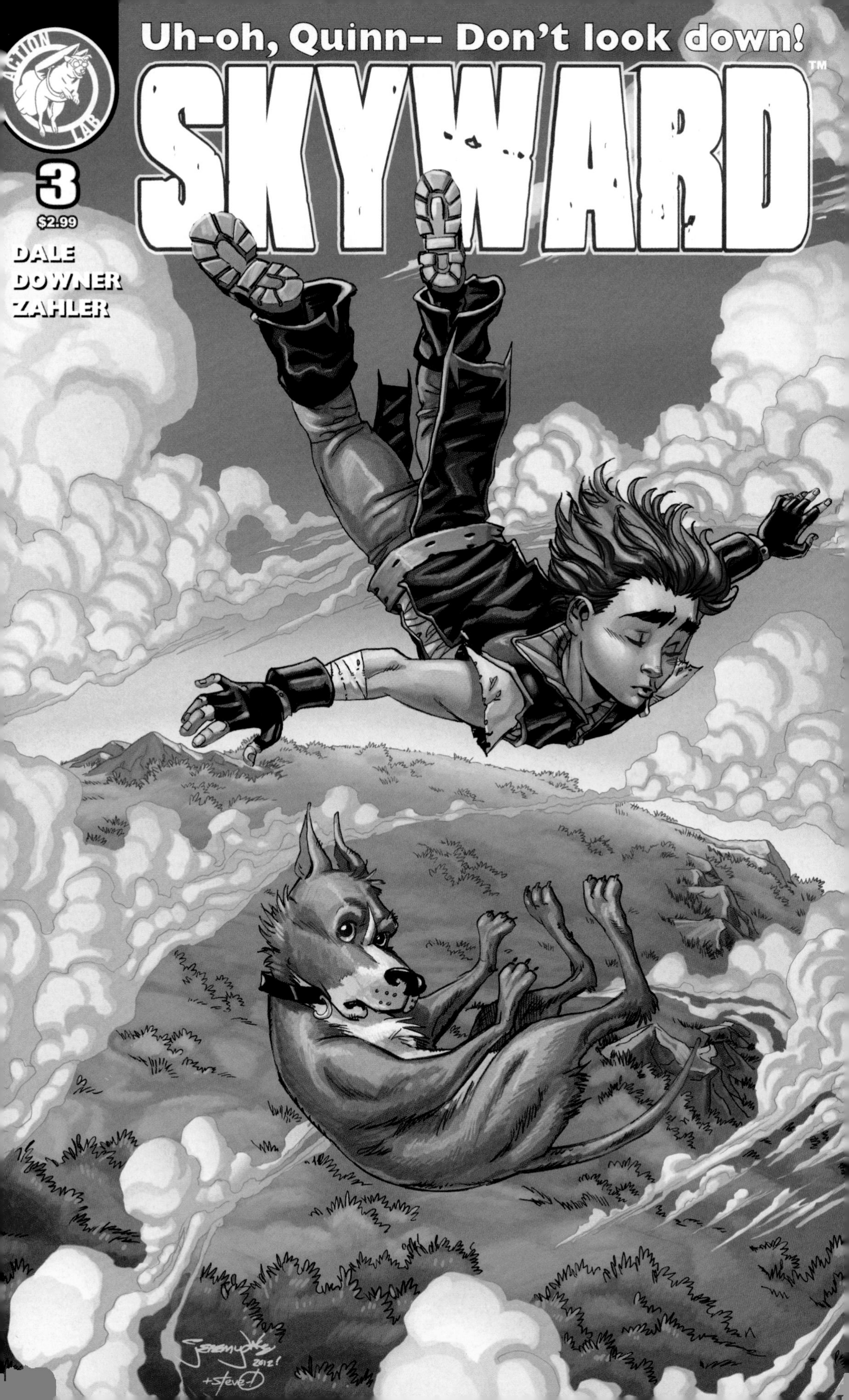
Uh-oh, Quinn-- Don't look down!
SKYWARD™
3
$2.99
DALE
DOWNER
ZAHLER

3

SKYWARD

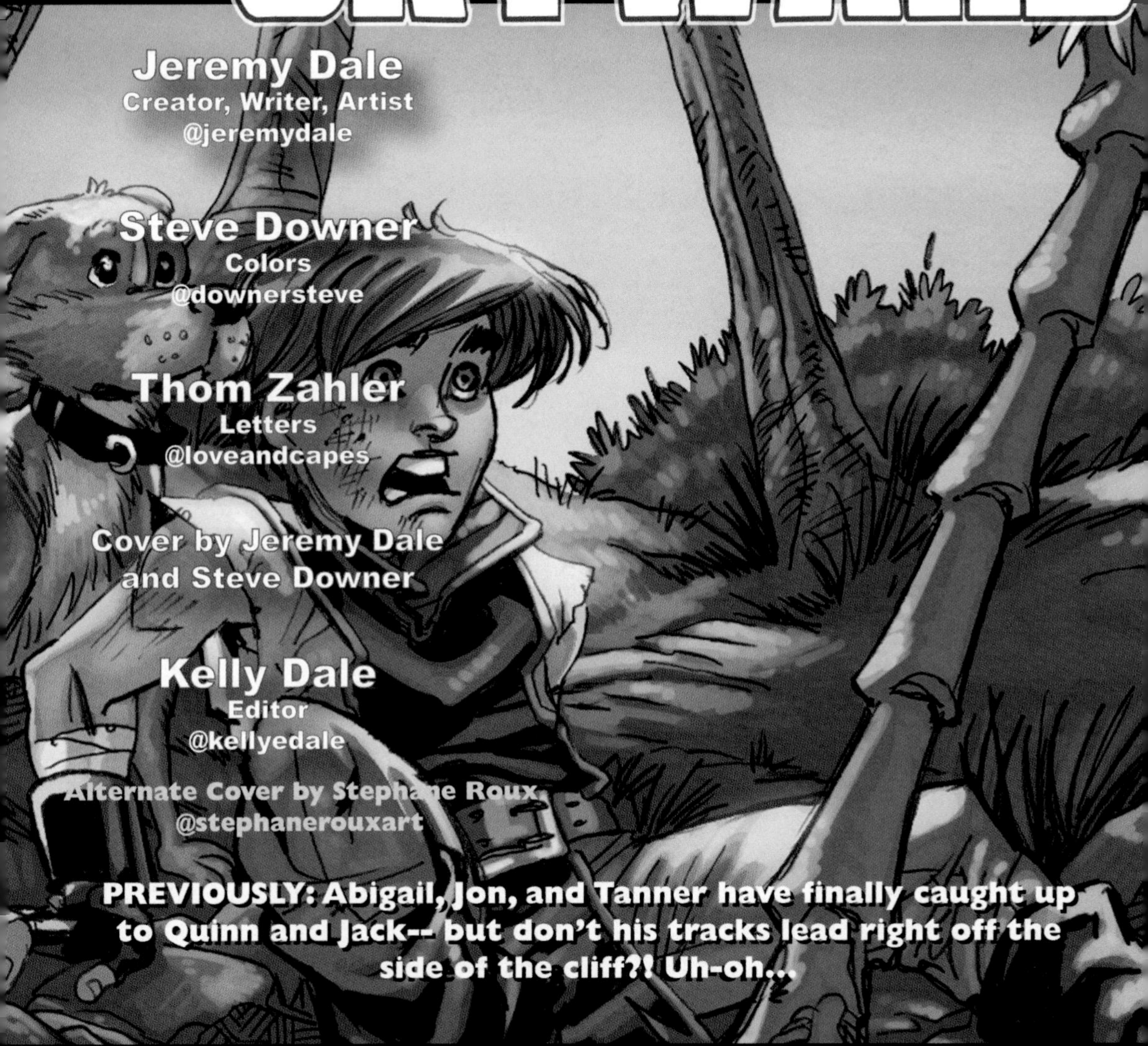

Jeremy Dale
Creator, Writer, Artist
@jeremydale

Steve Downer
Colors
@downersteve

Thom Zahler
Letters
@loveandcapes

Cover by Jeremy Dale
and Steve Downer

Kelly Dale
Editor
@kellyedale

Alternate Cover by Stephane Roux
@stephanerouxart

PREVIOUSLY: Abigail, Jon, and Tanner have finally caught up to Quinn and Jack-- but don't his tracks lead right off the side of the cliff?! Uh-oh...

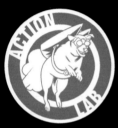

KEVIN FREEMAN- PRESIDENT
SHAWN PRYOR- VP DIGITAL MEDIA
DAVE DWONCH- CREATIVE DIRECTOR
SHAWN GABBORIN- EDITOR IN CHIEF
JASON MARTIN- EDITOR
JEREMY WHITLEY- DIRECTOR OF MARKETING
CHAD CICCONI- LOOKING FOR PEACE IN A SAVAGE LAND
COLLEEN BOYD- ASSOCIATE EDITOR

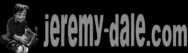

jeremy-dale.com

Jeremy Dale
the talent

Kelly Dale
editor

Kirby
Canine Relations

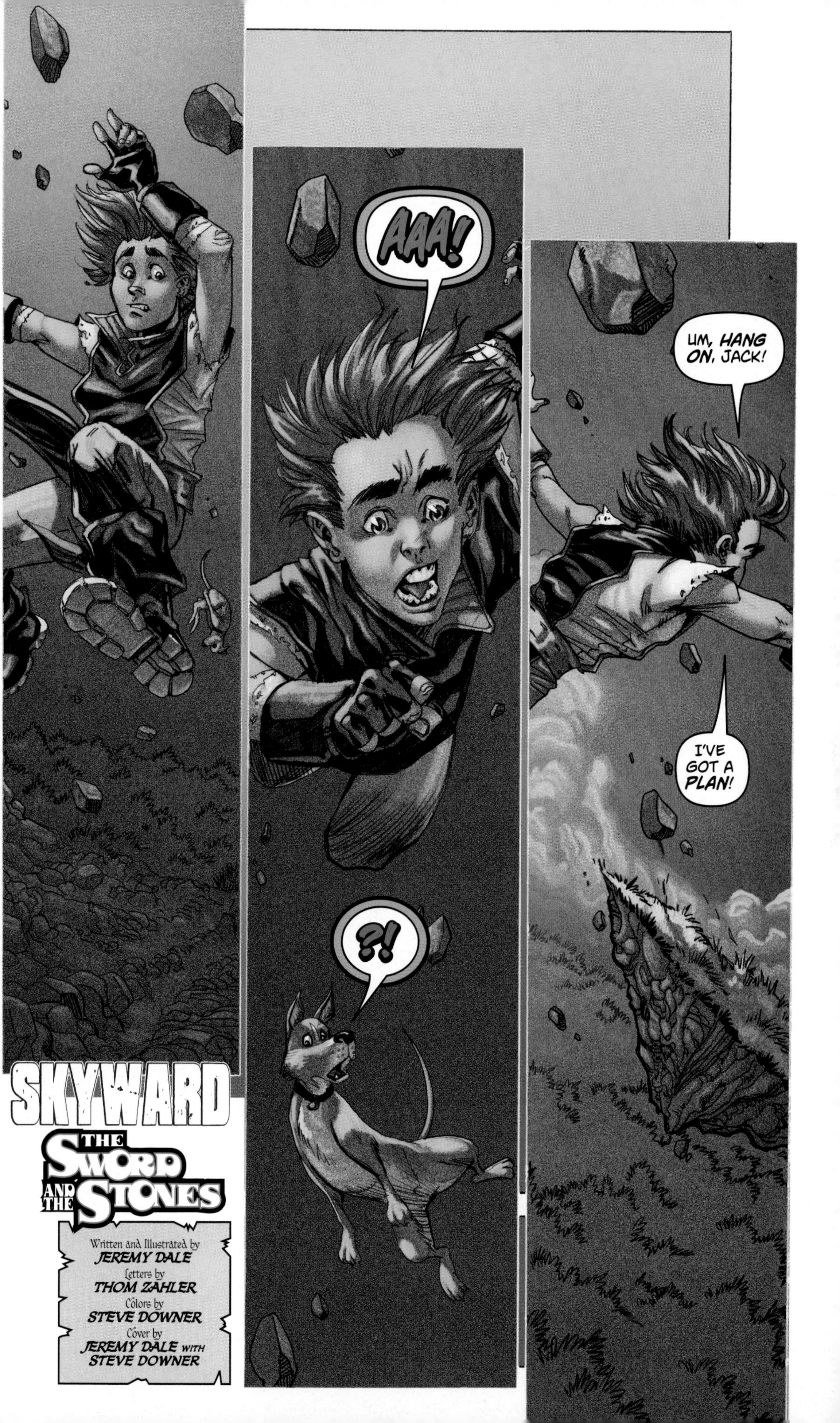
AAA!
?!
UM, HANG ON, JACK!
I'VE GOT A PLAN!
SKYWARD
THE SWORD AND THE STONES
Written and Illustrated by
JEREMY DALE
Letters by
THOM ZAHLER
Colors by
STEVE DOWNER
Cover by
JEREMY DALE WITH
STEVE DOWNER

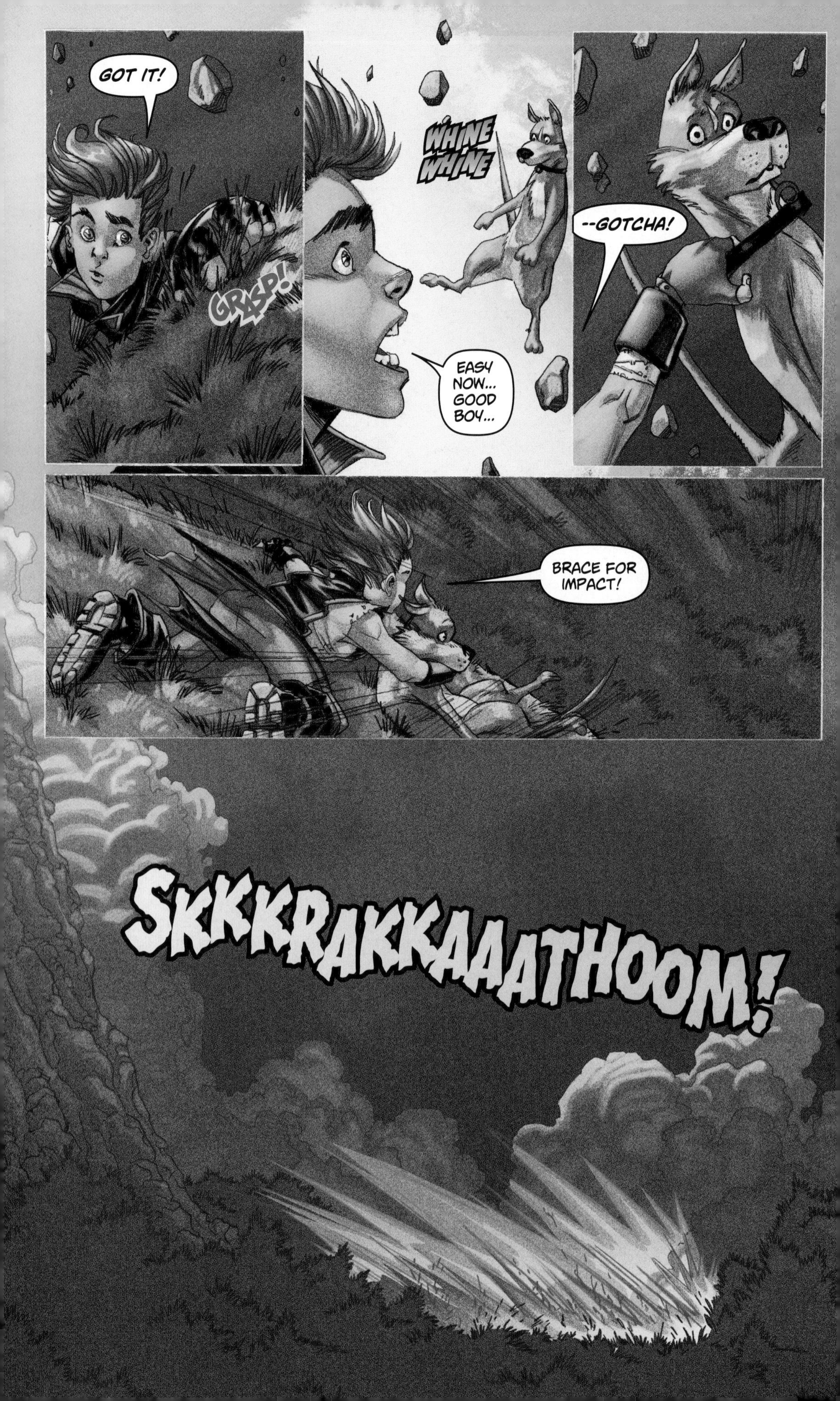
GOT IT!
GRASP!
WHINE WHINE
EASY NOW... GOOD BOY...
--GOTCHA!
BRACE FOR IMPACT!
SKKKRAKKAAATHOOM!

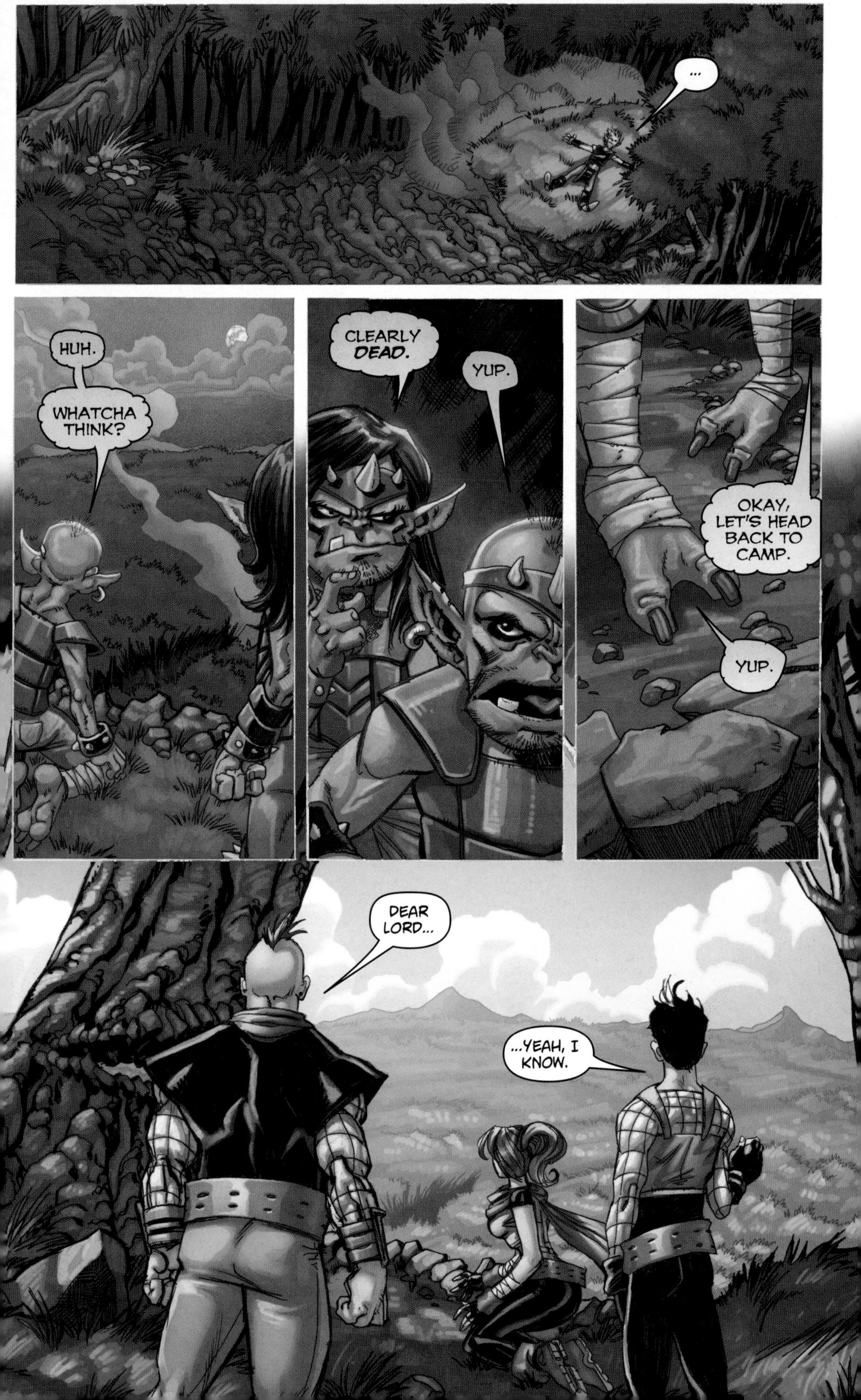
...
HUH.
WHATCHA THINK?
CLEARLY DEAD.
YUP.
OKAY, LET'S HEAD BACK TO CAMP.
YUP.
DEAR LORD...
...YEAH, I KNOW.

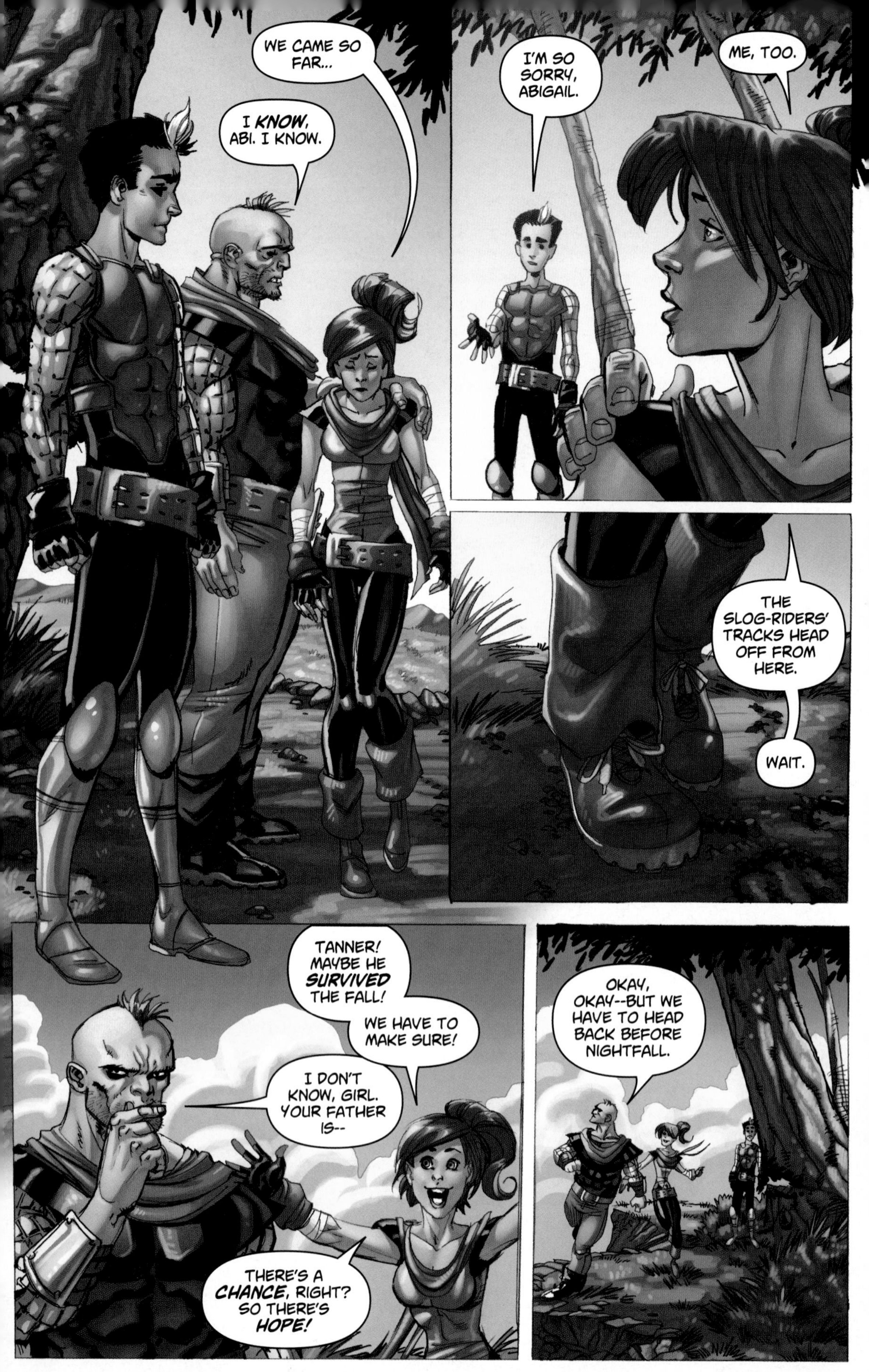
WE CAME SO FAR...
I KNOW, ABI. I KNOW.
I'M SO SORRY, ABIGAIL.
ME, TOO.
THE SLOG-RIDERS' TRACKS HEAD OFF FROM HERE.
WAIT.
TANNER! MAYBE HE SURVIVED THE FALL!
WE HAVE TO MAKE SURE!
I DON'T KNOW, GIRL. YOUR FATHER IS--
THERE'S A CHANCE, RIGHT? SO THERE'S HOPE!
OKAY, OKAY--BUT WE HAVE TO HEAD BACK BEFORE NIGHTFALL.

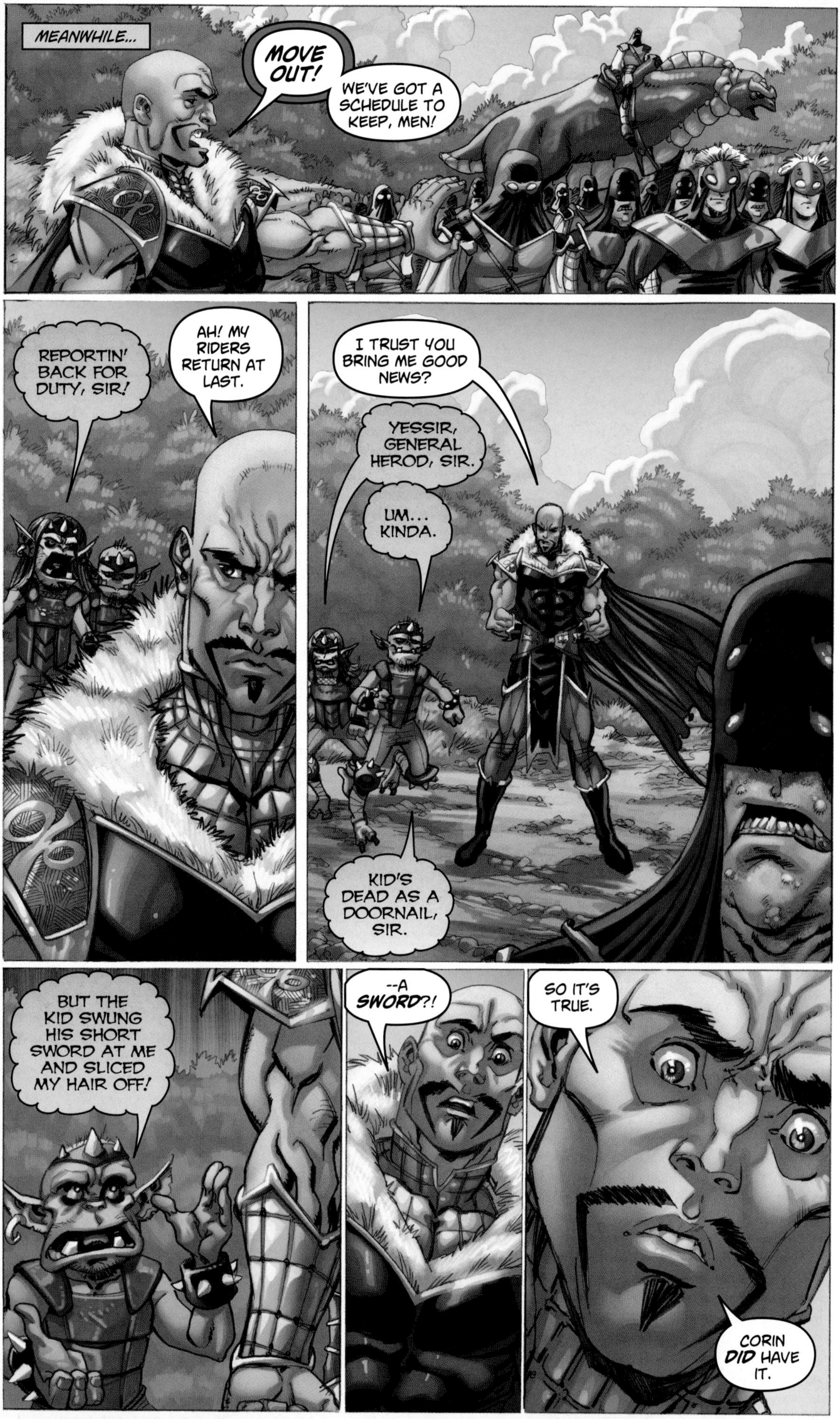
MEANWHILE...
MOVE OUT!
WE'VE GOT A SCHEDULE TO KEEP, MEN!
REPORTIN' BACK FOR DUTY, SIR!
AH! MY RIDERS RETURN AT LAST.
I TRUST YOU BRING ME GOOD NEWS?
YESSIR, GENERAL HEROD, SIR.
UM... KINDA.
KID'S DEAD AS A DOORNAIL, SIR.
BUT THE KID SWUNG HIS SHORT SWORD AT ME AND SLICED MY HAIR OFF!
--A SWORD?!
SO IT'S TRUE.
CORIN DID HAVE IT.

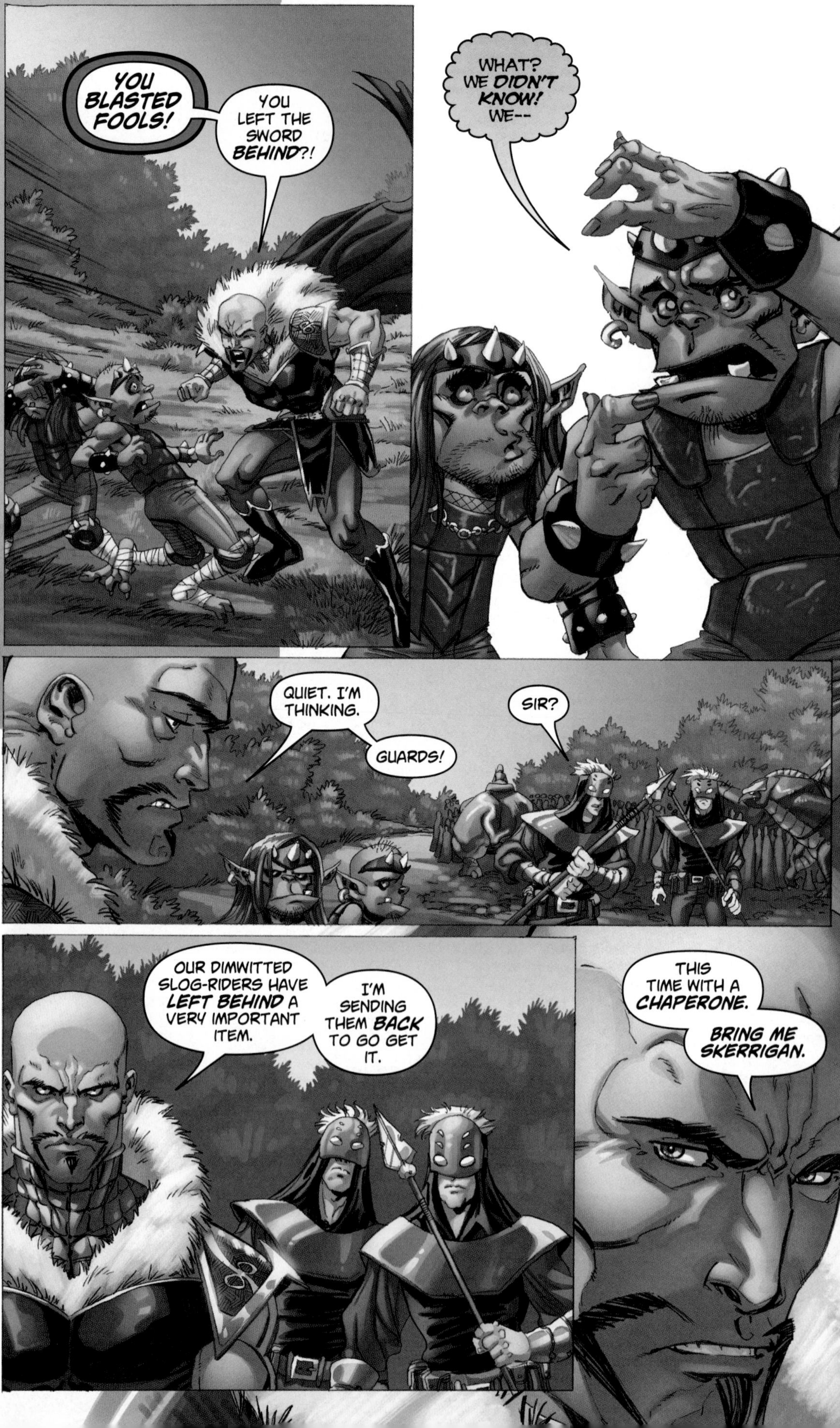
YOU BLASTED FOOLS!
YOU LEFT THE SWORD BEHIND?!
WHAT? WE DIDN'T KNOW! WE--
QUIET. I'M THINKING.
GUARDS!
SIR?
OUR DIMWITTED SLOG-RIDERS HAVE LEFT BEHIND A VERY IMPORTANT ITEM.
I'M SENDING THEM BACK TO GO GET IT.
THIS TIME WITH A CHAPERONE.
BRING ME SKERRIGAN.

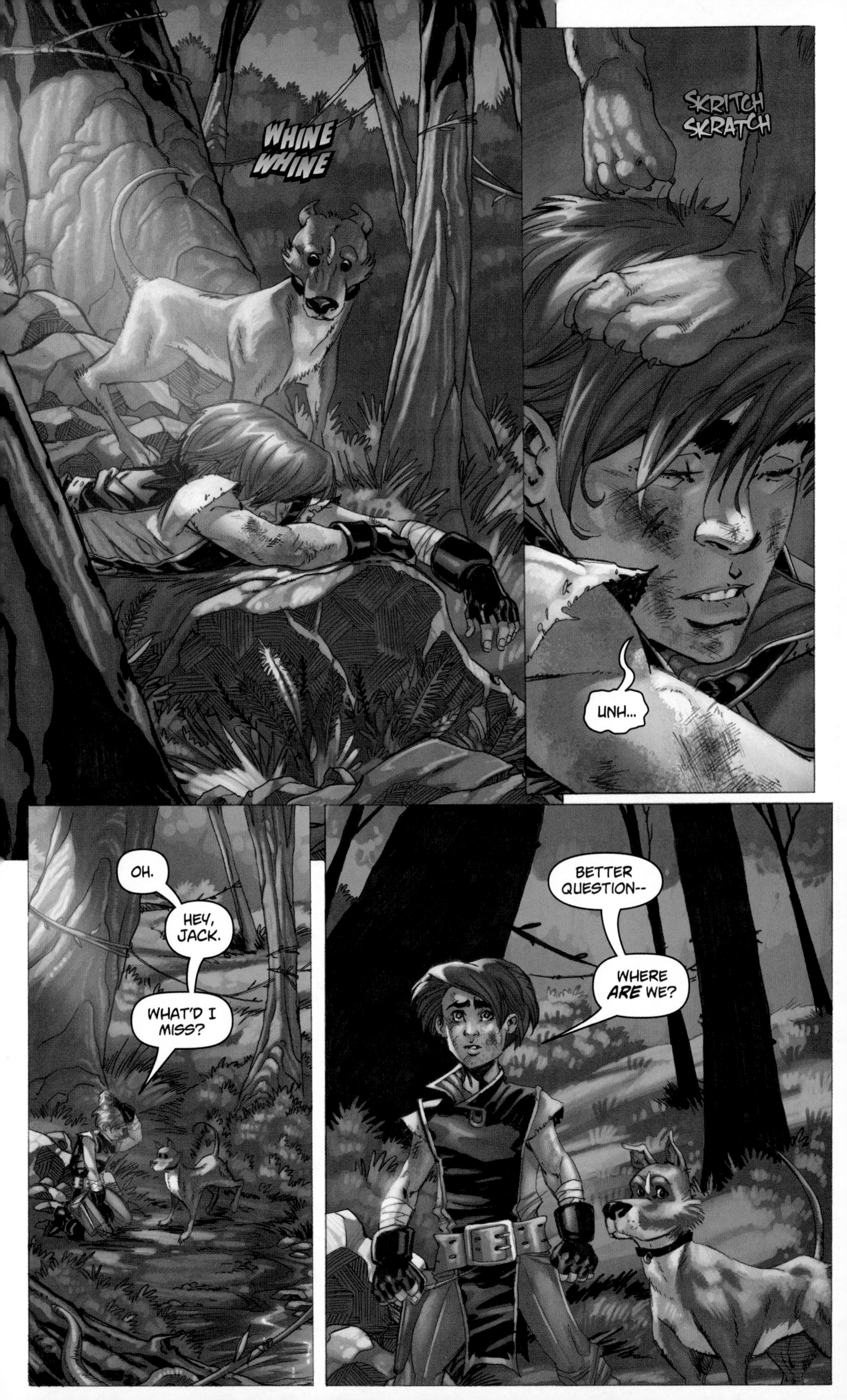
WHINE
WHINE
SKRITCH
SKRATCH
UNH...
OH.
HEY, JACK.
WHAT'D I MISS?
BETTER QUESTION--
WHERE *ARE* WE?

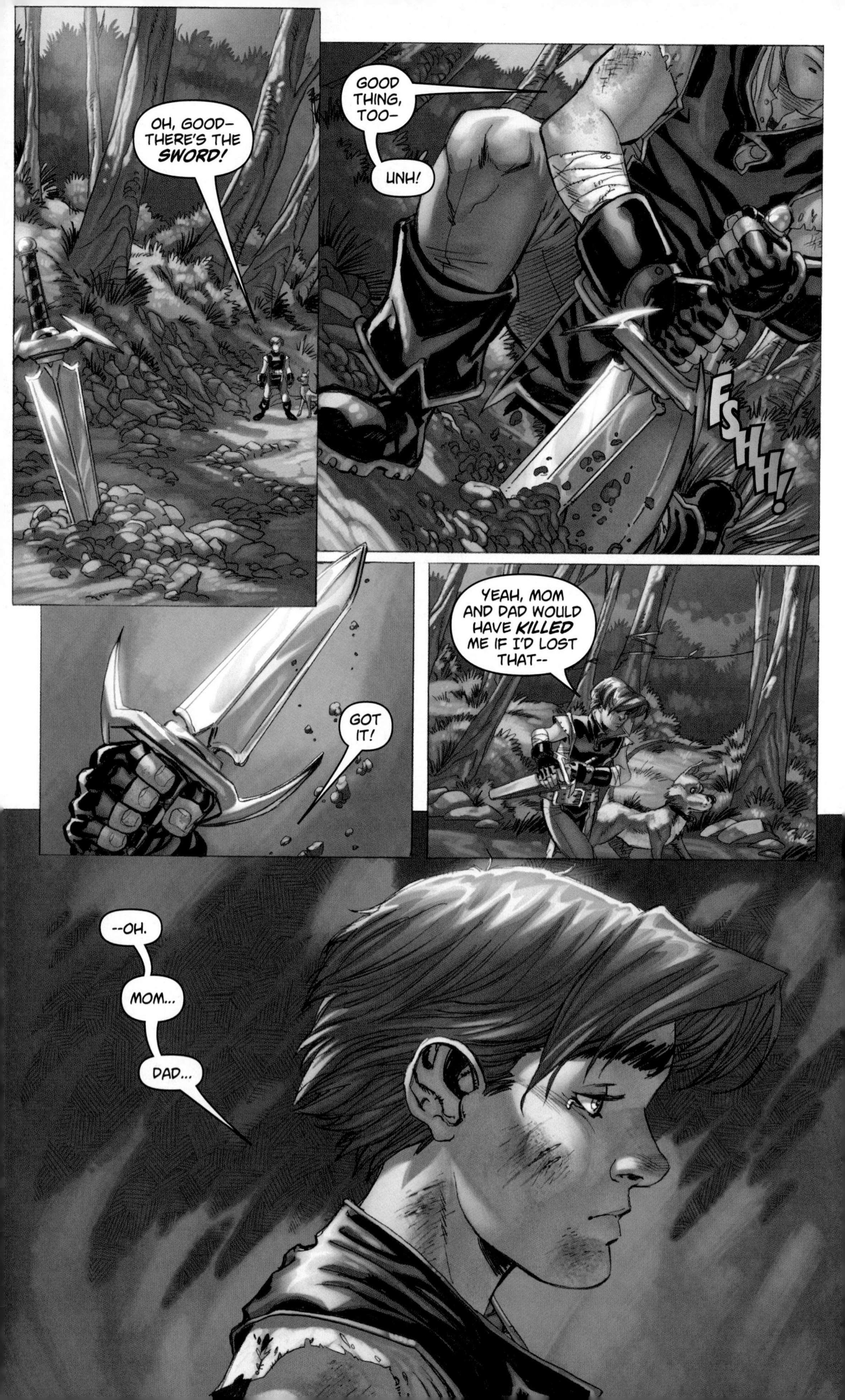
OH, GOOD-- THERE'S THE **SWORD!**
GOOD THING, TOO--
UNH!
FSHHH!
GOT IT!
YEAH, MOM AND DAD WOULD HAVE **KILLED** ME IF I'D LOST THAT--
--OH.
MOM...
DAD...

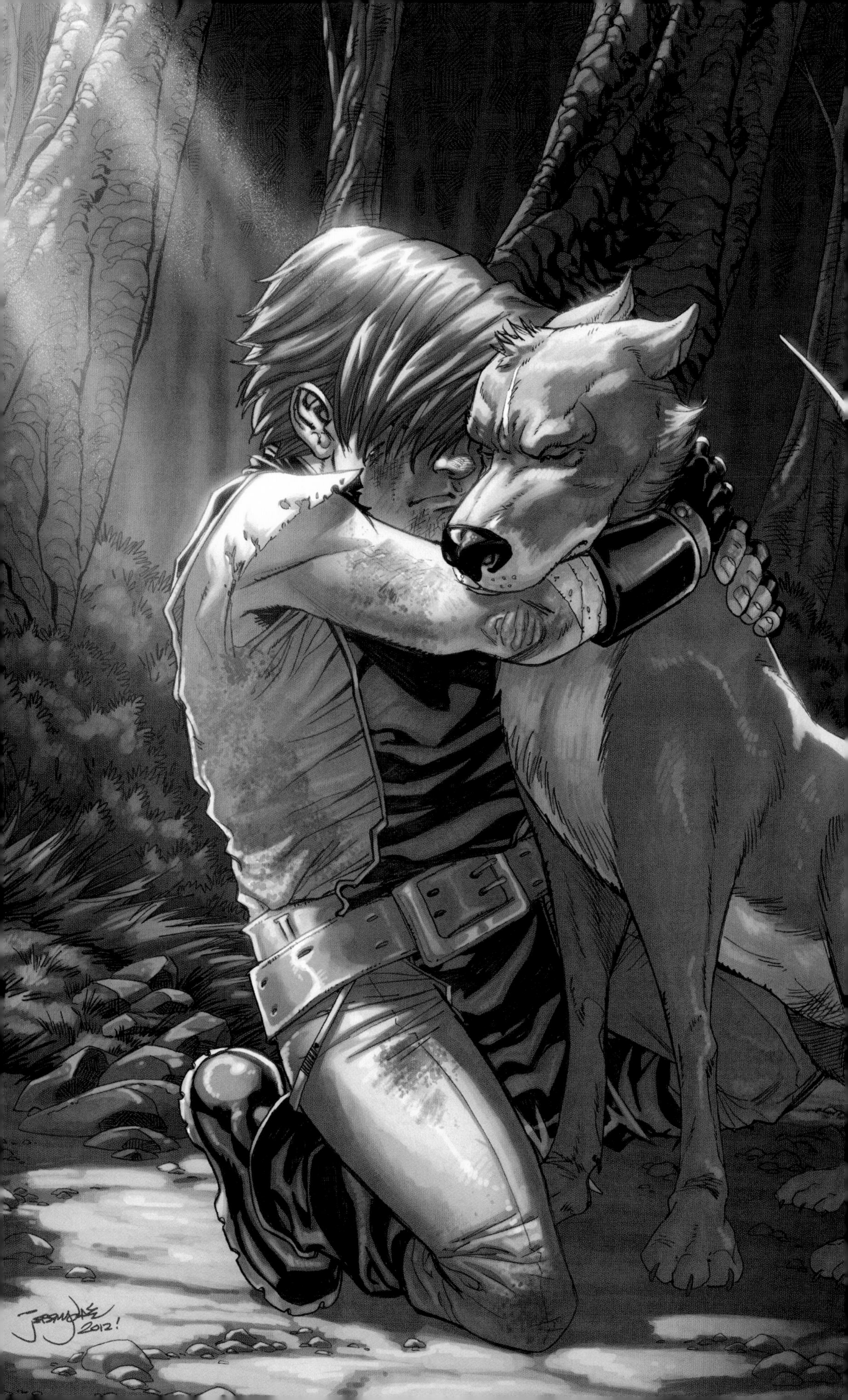

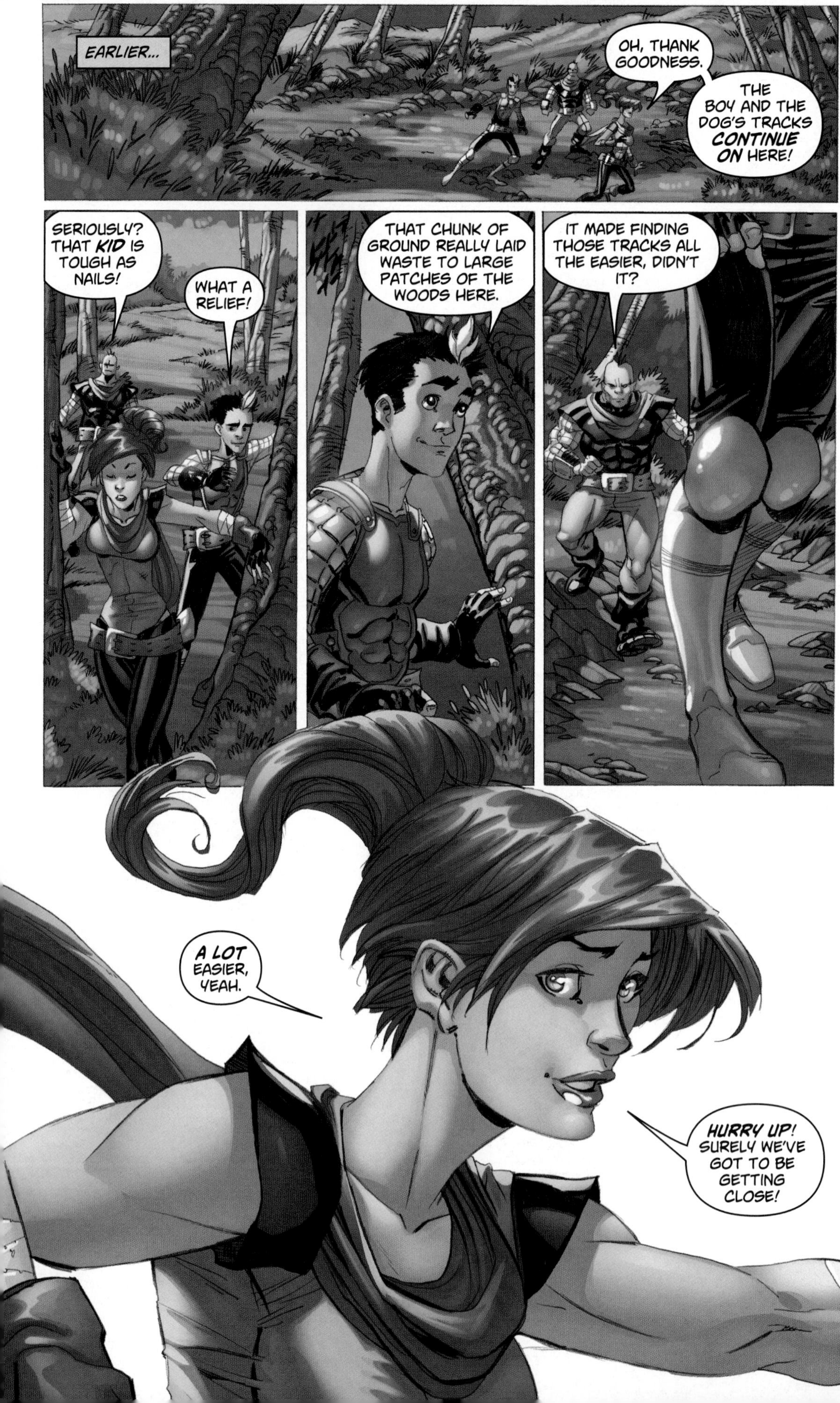
EARLIER...
OH, THANK GOODNESS.
THE BOY AND THE DOG'S TRACKS *CONTINUE ON* HERE!
SERIOUSLY? THAT *KID* IS TOUGH AS NAILS!
WHAT A RELIEF!
THAT CHUNK OF GROUND REALLY LAID WASTE TO LARGE PATCHES OF THE WOODS HERE.
IT MADE FINDING THOSE TRACKS ALL THE EASIER, DIDN'T IT?
A LOT EASIER, YEAH.
HURRY UP! SURELY WE'VE GOT TO BE GETTING CLOSE!

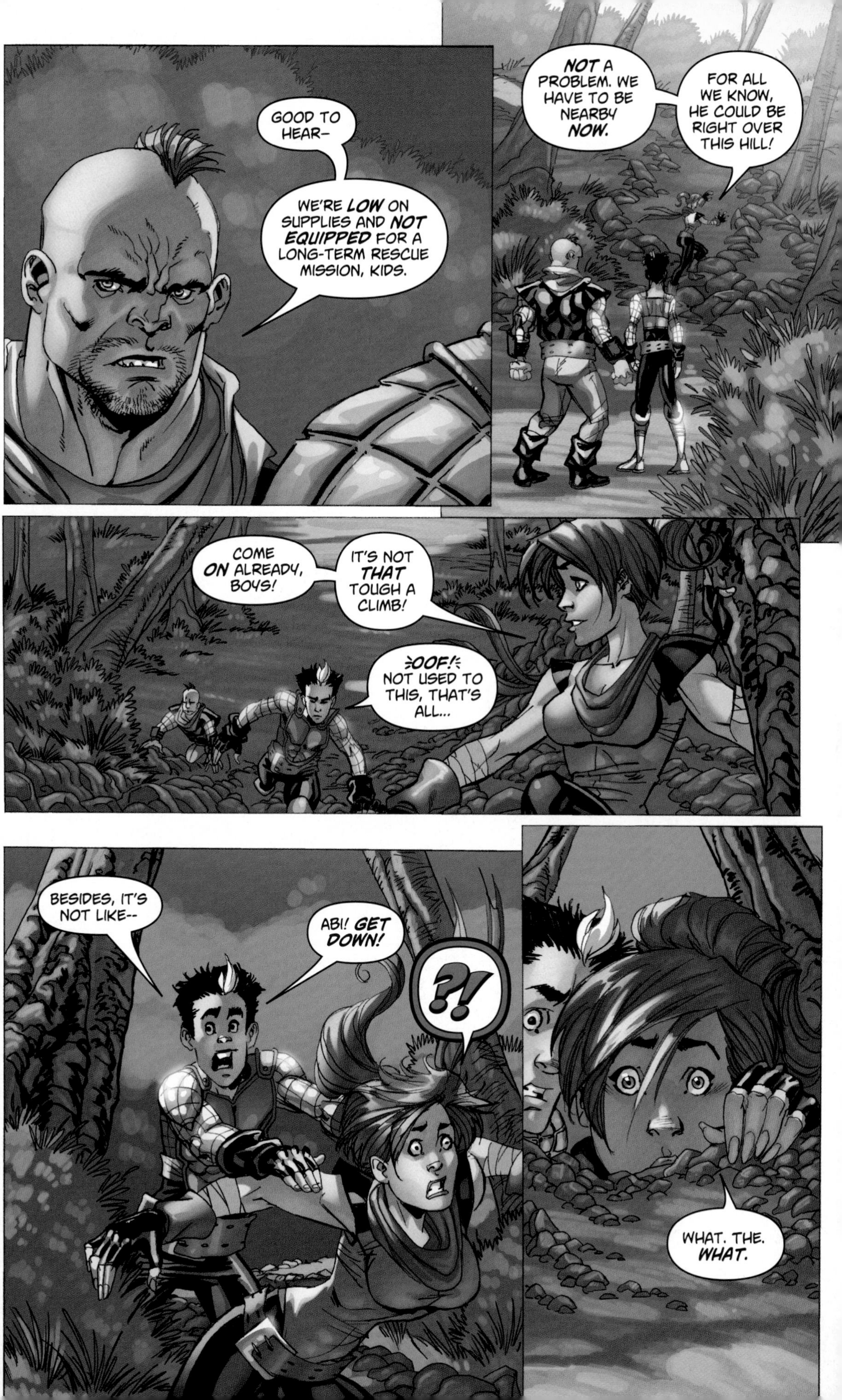
GOOD TO HEAR-
WE'RE LOW ON SUPPLIES AND NOT EQUIPPED FOR A LONG-TERM RESCUE MISSION, KIDS.
NOT A PROBLEM. WE HAVE TO BE NEARBY NOW.
FOR ALL WE KNOW, HE COULD BE RIGHT OVER THIS HILL!
COME ON ALREADY, BOYS!
IT'S NOT THAT TOUGH A CLIMB!
OOF!
NOT USED TO THIS, THAT'S ALL...
BESIDES, IT'S NOT LIKE--
ABI! GET DOWN!
?!
WHAT. THE. WHAT.

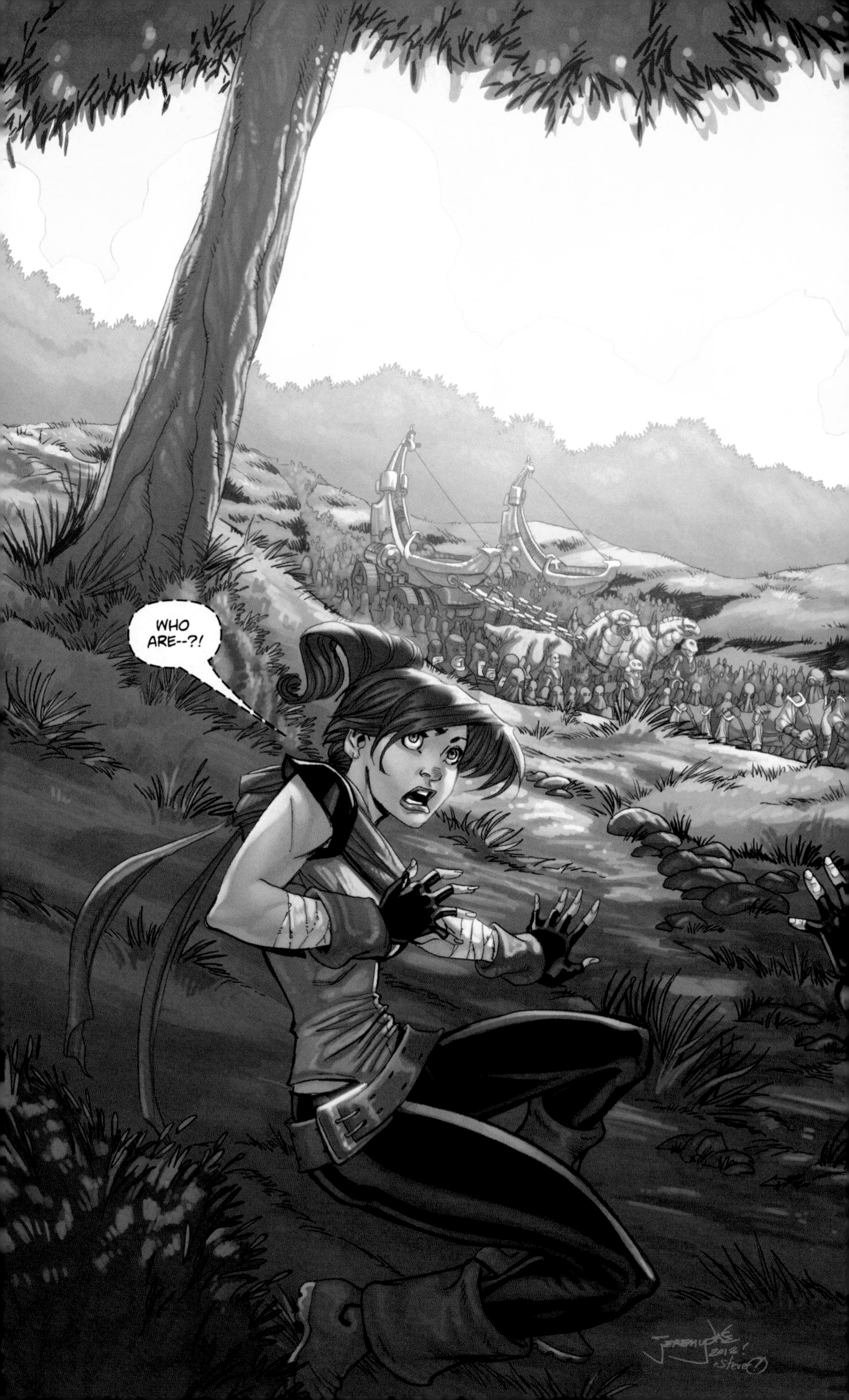
WHO ARE--?!

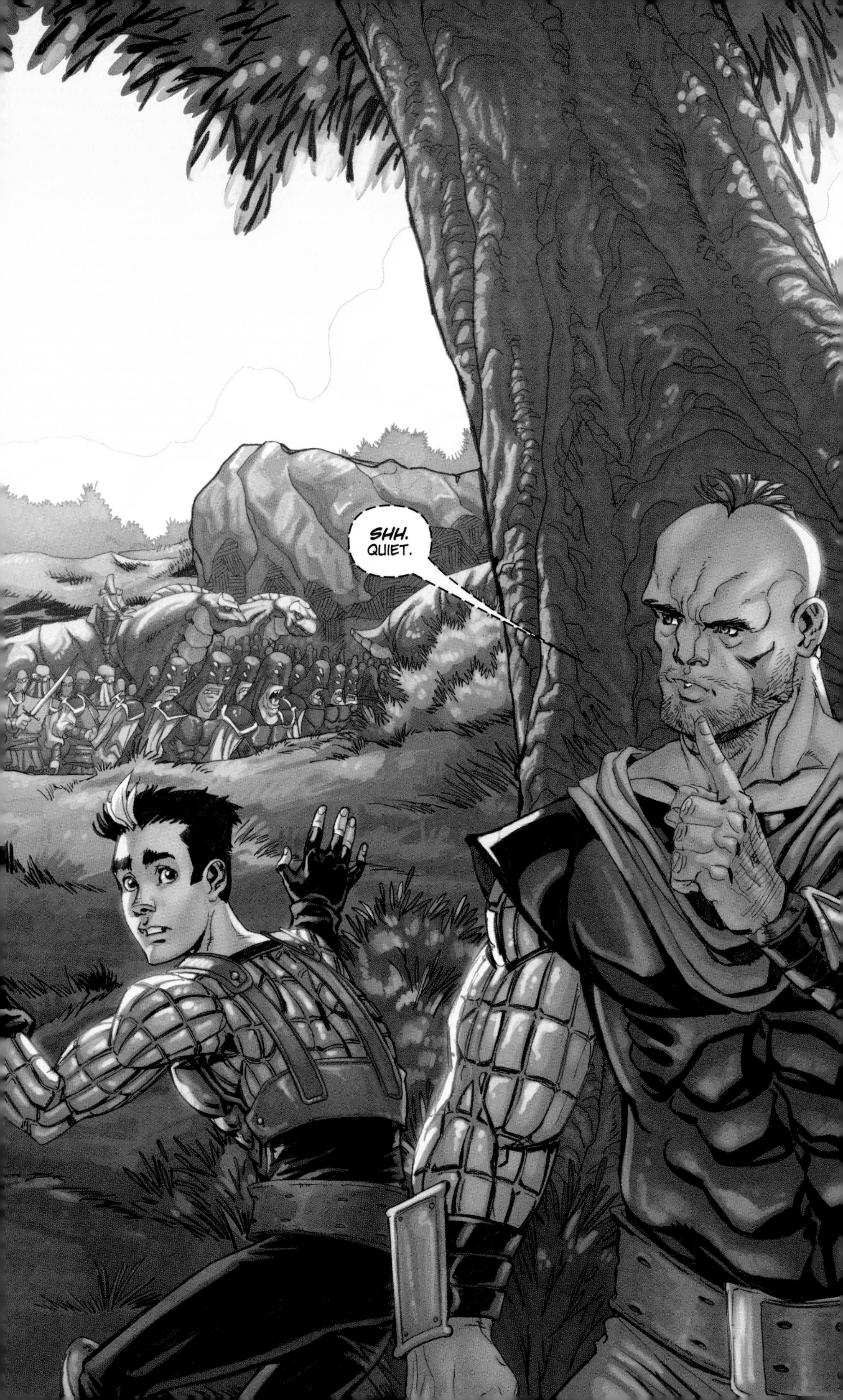
SHH.
QUIET.

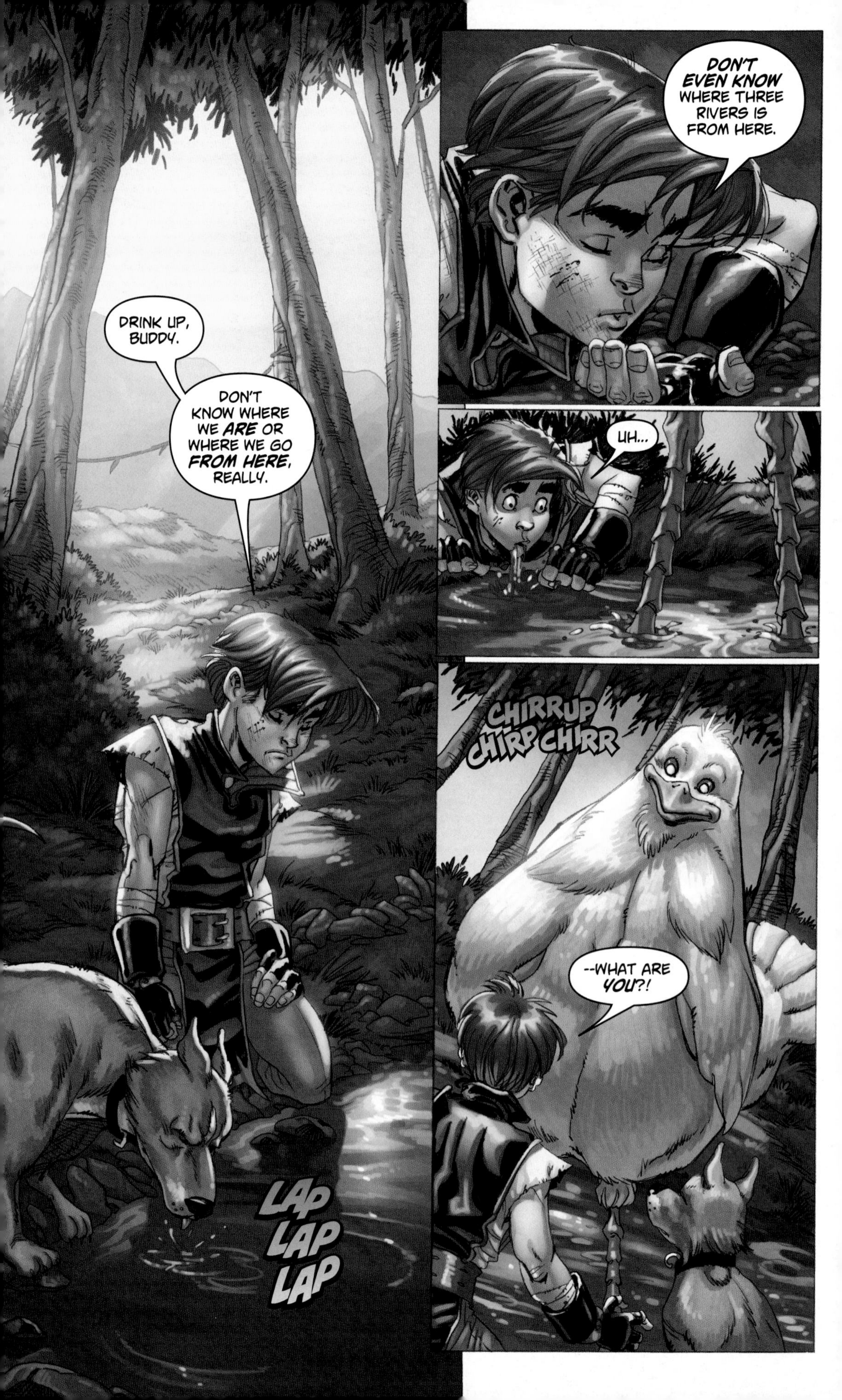
DRINK UP, BUDDY.
DON'T KNOW WHERE WE *ARE* OR WHERE WE GO *FROM HERE*, REALLY.
LAP LAP LAP
DON'T EVEN KNOW WHERE THREE RIVERS IS FROM HERE.
UH...
CHIRRUP CHIRP CHIRR
--WHAT ARE *YOU*?!

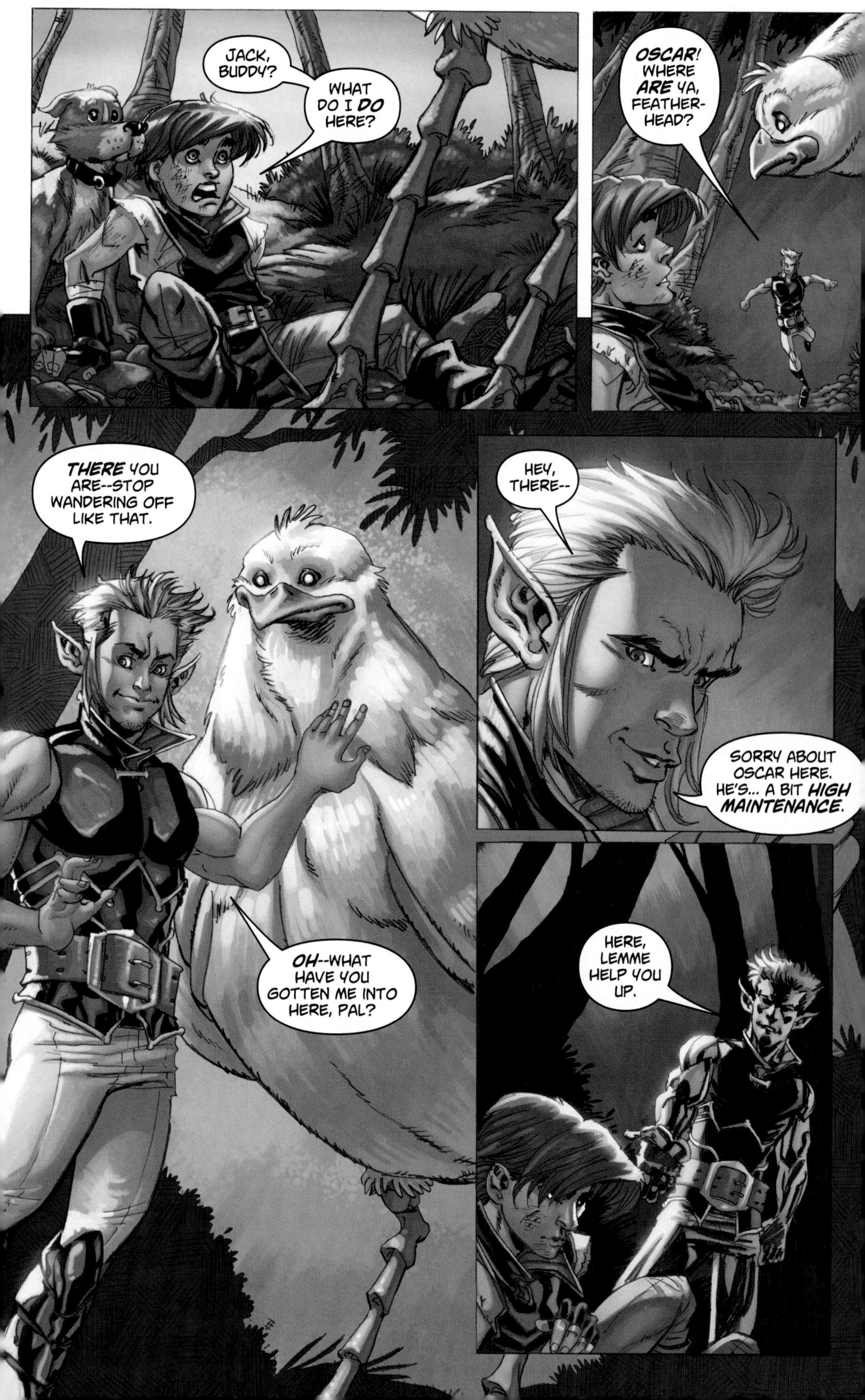
JACK, BUDDY?
WHAT DO I *DO* HERE?
OSCAR! WHERE *ARE* YA, FEATHER-HEAD?
THERE YOU ARE--STOP WANDERING OFF LIKE THAT.
OH--WHAT HAVE YOU GOTTEN ME INTO HERE, PAL?
HEY, THERE--
SORRY ABOUT OSCAR HERE. HE'S... A BIT *HIGH MAINTENANCE*.
HERE, LEMME HELP YOU UP.

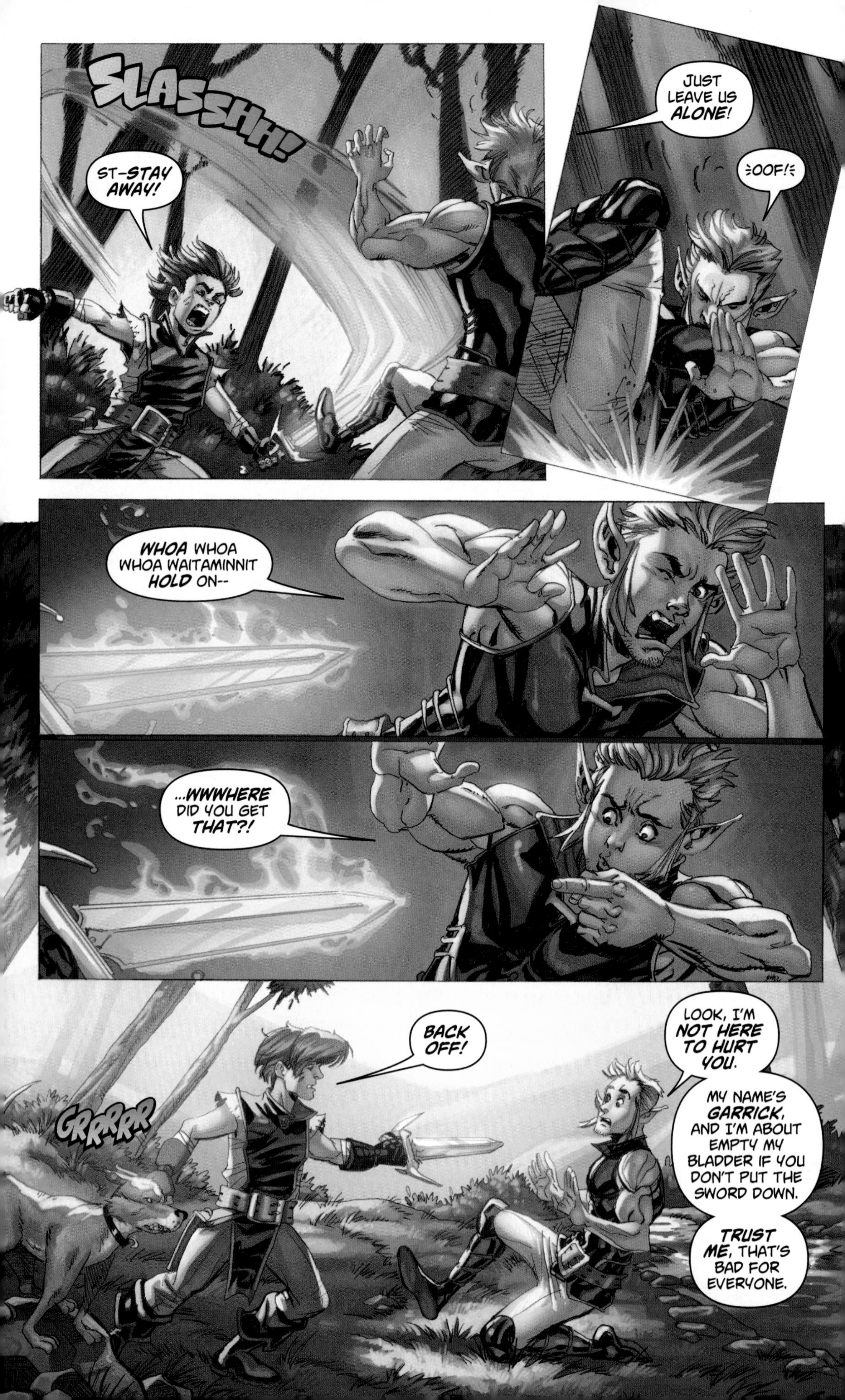
SLASSHH!
ST-STAY AWAY!
JUST LEAVE US ALONE!
OOF!
WHOA WHOA WHOA WAITAMINNIT HOLD ON--
...WWWHERE DID YOU GET THAT?!
GRRRRR
BACK OFF!
LOOK, I'M NOT HERE TO HURT YOU.
MY NAME'S GARRICK, AND I'M ABOUT EMPTY MY BLADDER IF YOU DON'T PUT THE SWORD DOWN.
TRUST ME, THAT'S BAD FOR EVERYONE.

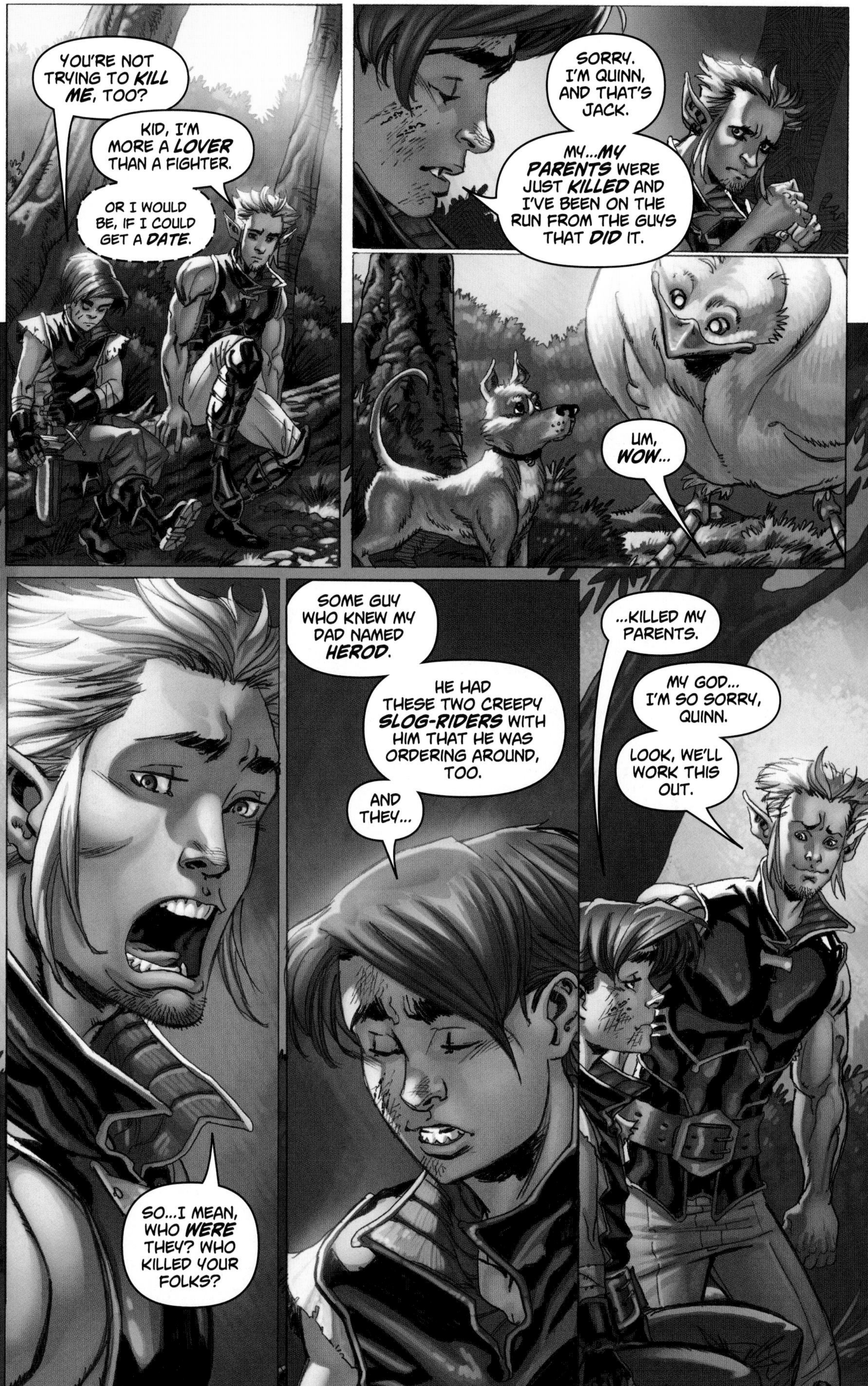
YOU'RE NOT TRYING TO KILL ME, TOO?
KID, I'M MORE A LOVER THAN A FIGHTER.
OR I WOULD BE, IF I COULD GET A DATE.
SORRY. I'M QUINN, AND THAT'S JACK.
MY...MY PARENTS WERE JUST KILLED AND I'VE BEEN ON THE RUN FROM THE GUYS THAT DID IT.
UM, WOW...
SO...I MEAN, WHO WERE THEY? WHO KILLED YOUR FOLKS?
SOME GUY WHO KNEW MY DAD NAMED HEROD.
HE HAD THESE TWO CREEPY SLOG-RIDERS WITH HIM THAT HE WAS ORDERING AROUND, TOO.
AND THEY...
...KILLED MY PARENTS.
MY GOD... I'M SO SORRY, QUINN.
LOOK, WE'LL WORK THIS OUT.

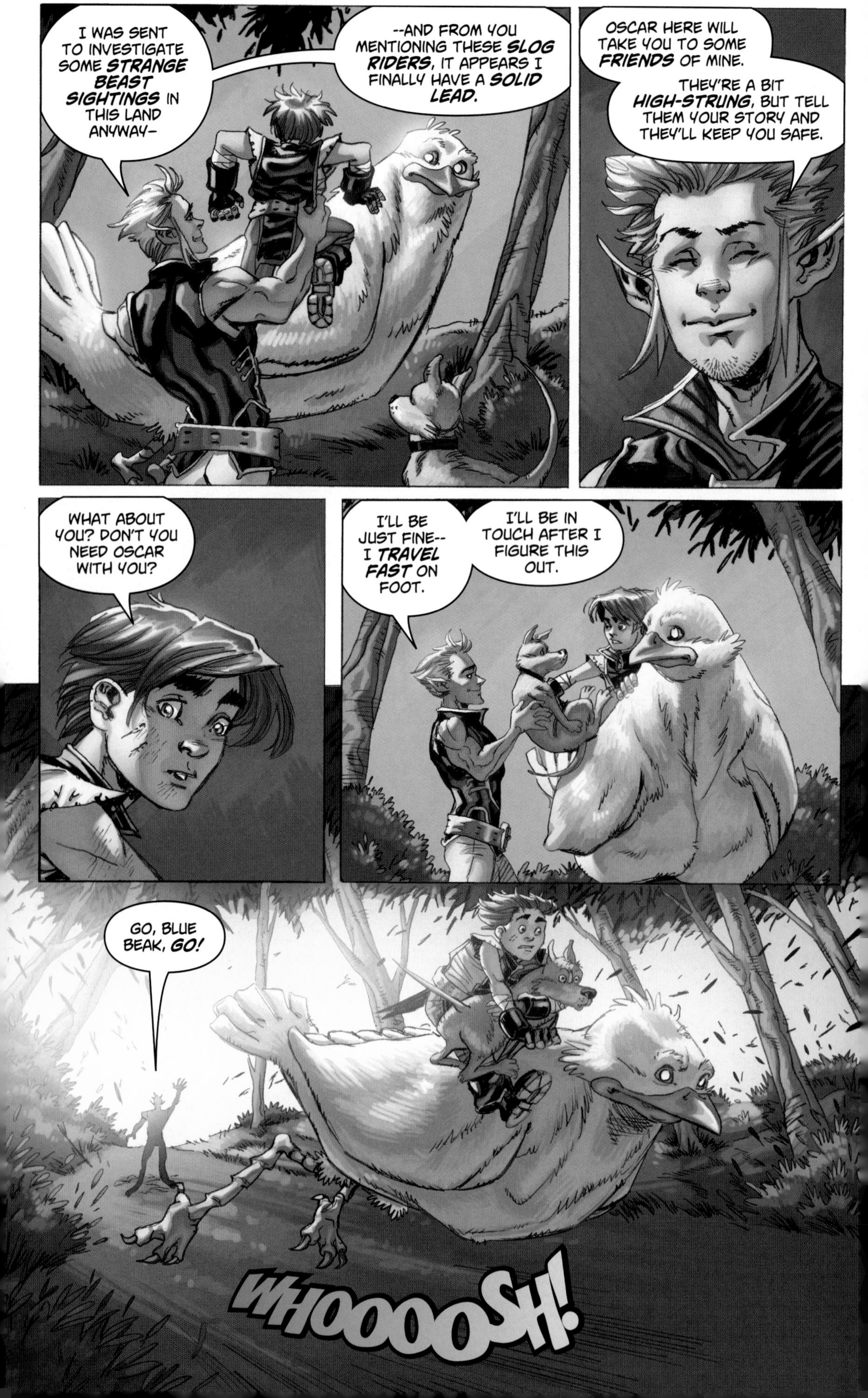
I WAS SENT TO INVESTIGATE SOME STRANGE BEAST SIGHTINGS IN THIS LAND ANYWAY–
--AND FROM YOU MENTIONING THESE SLOG RIDERS, IT APPEARS I FINALLY HAVE A SOLID LEAD.
OSCAR HERE WILL TAKE YOU TO SOME FRIENDS OF MINE.
THEY'RE A BIT HIGH-STRUNG, BUT TELL THEM YOUR STORY AND THEY'LL KEEP YOU SAFE.
WHAT ABOUT YOU? DON'T YOU NEED OSCAR WITH YOU?
I'LL BE JUST FINE-- I TRAVEL FAST ON FOOT.
I'LL BE IN TOUCH AFTER I FIGURE THIS OUT.
GO, BLUE BEAK, GO!
WHOOOOSH!

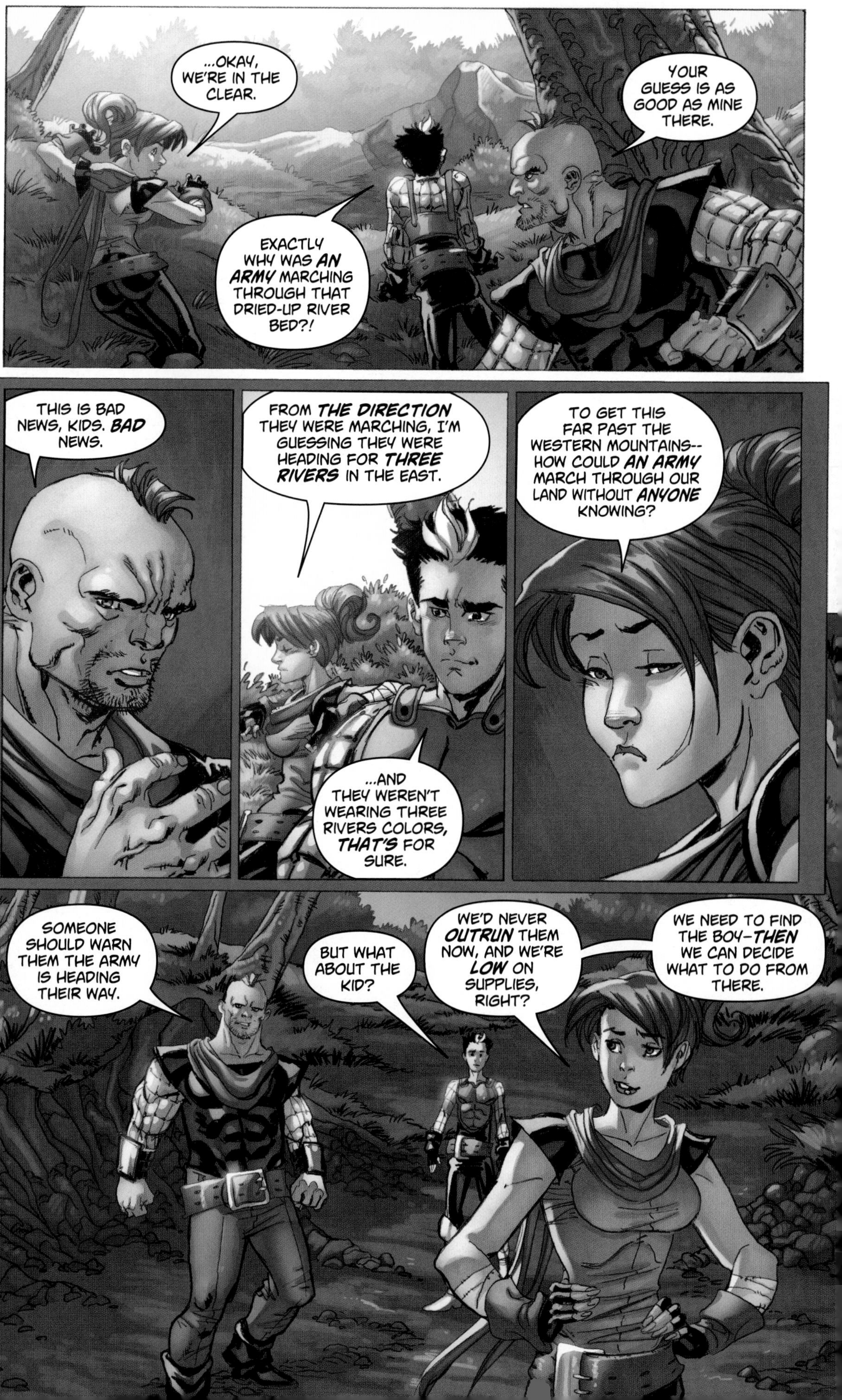
...OKAY, WE'RE IN THE CLEAR.
EXACTLY WHY WAS AN ARMY MARCHING THROUGH THAT DRIED-UP RIVER BED?!
YOUR GUESS IS AS GOOD AS MINE THERE.
THIS IS BAD NEWS, KIDS. BAD NEWS.
FROM THE DIRECTION THEY WERE MARCHING, I'M GUESSING THEY WERE HEADING FOR THREE RIVERS IN THE EAST.
...AND THEY WEREN'T WEARING THREE RIVERS COLORS, THAT'S FOR SURE.
TO GET THIS FAR PAST THE WESTERN MOUNTAINS-- HOW COULD AN ARMY MARCH THROUGH OUR LAND WITHOUT ANYONE KNOWING?
SOMEONE SHOULD WARN THEM THE ARMY IS HEADING THEIR WAY.
BUT WHAT ABOUT THE KID?
WE'D NEVER OUTRUN THEM NOW, AND WE'RE LOW ON SUPPLIES, RIGHT?
WE NEED TO FIND THE BOY—THEN WE CAN DECIDE WHAT TO DO FROM THERE.

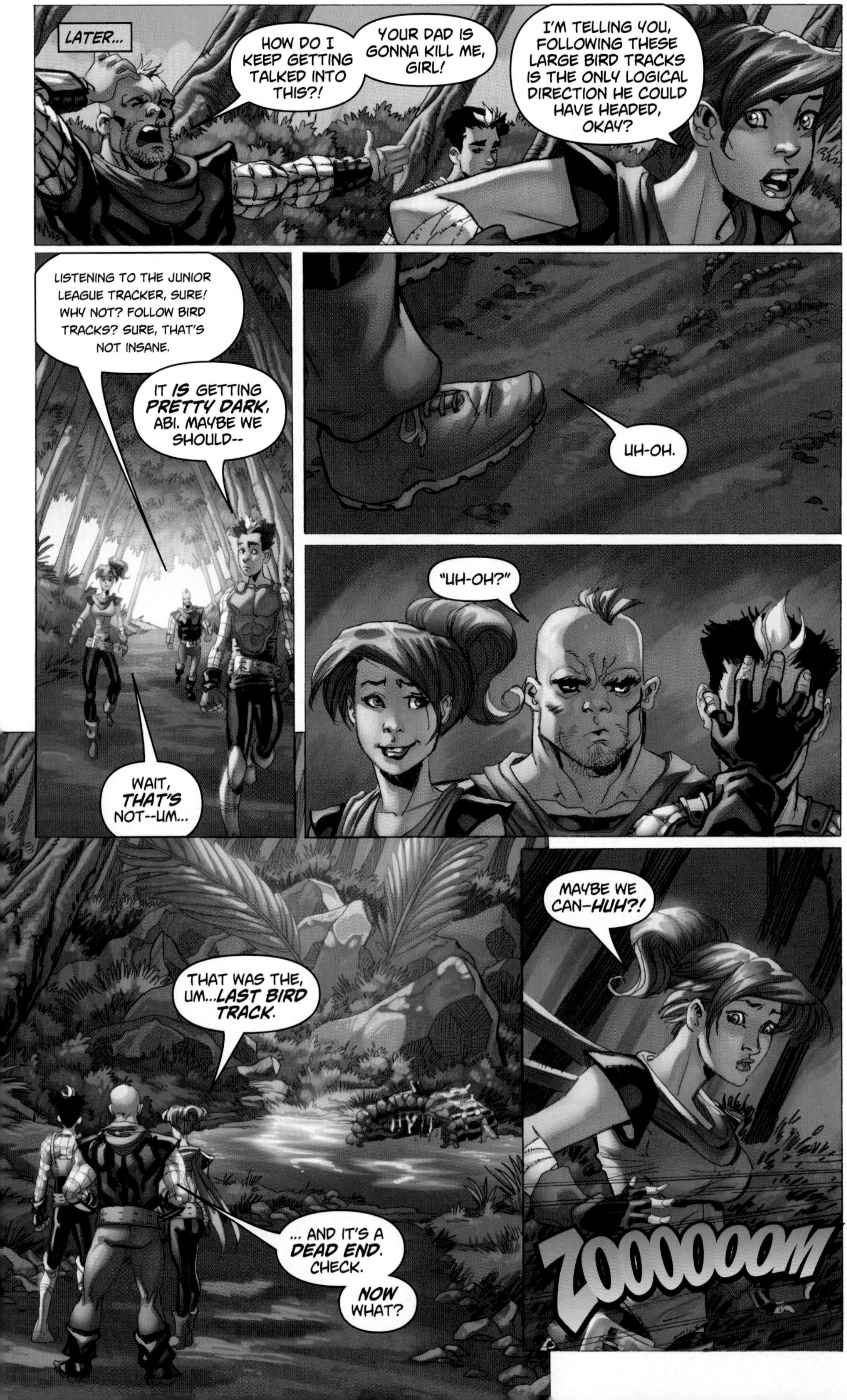
LATER...
HOW DO I KEEP GETTING TALKED INTO THIS?!
YOUR DAD IS GONNA KILL ME, GIRL!
I'M TELLING YOU, FOLLOWING THESE LARGE BIRD TRACKS IS THE ONLY LOGICAL DIRECTION HE COULD HAVE HEADED, OKAY?
LISTENING TO THE JUNIOR LEAGUE TRACKER, SURE! WHY NOT? FOLLOW BIRD TRACKS? SURE, THAT'S NOT INSANE.
IT IS GETTING PRETTY DARK, ABI. MAYBE WE SHOULD--
WAIT, THAT'S NOT--UM...
UH-OH.
"UH-OH?"
THAT WAS THE, UM...LAST BIRD TRACK.
... AND IT'S A DEAD END. CHECK.
NOW WHAT?
MAYBE WE CAN--HUH?!
ZOOOOOOM

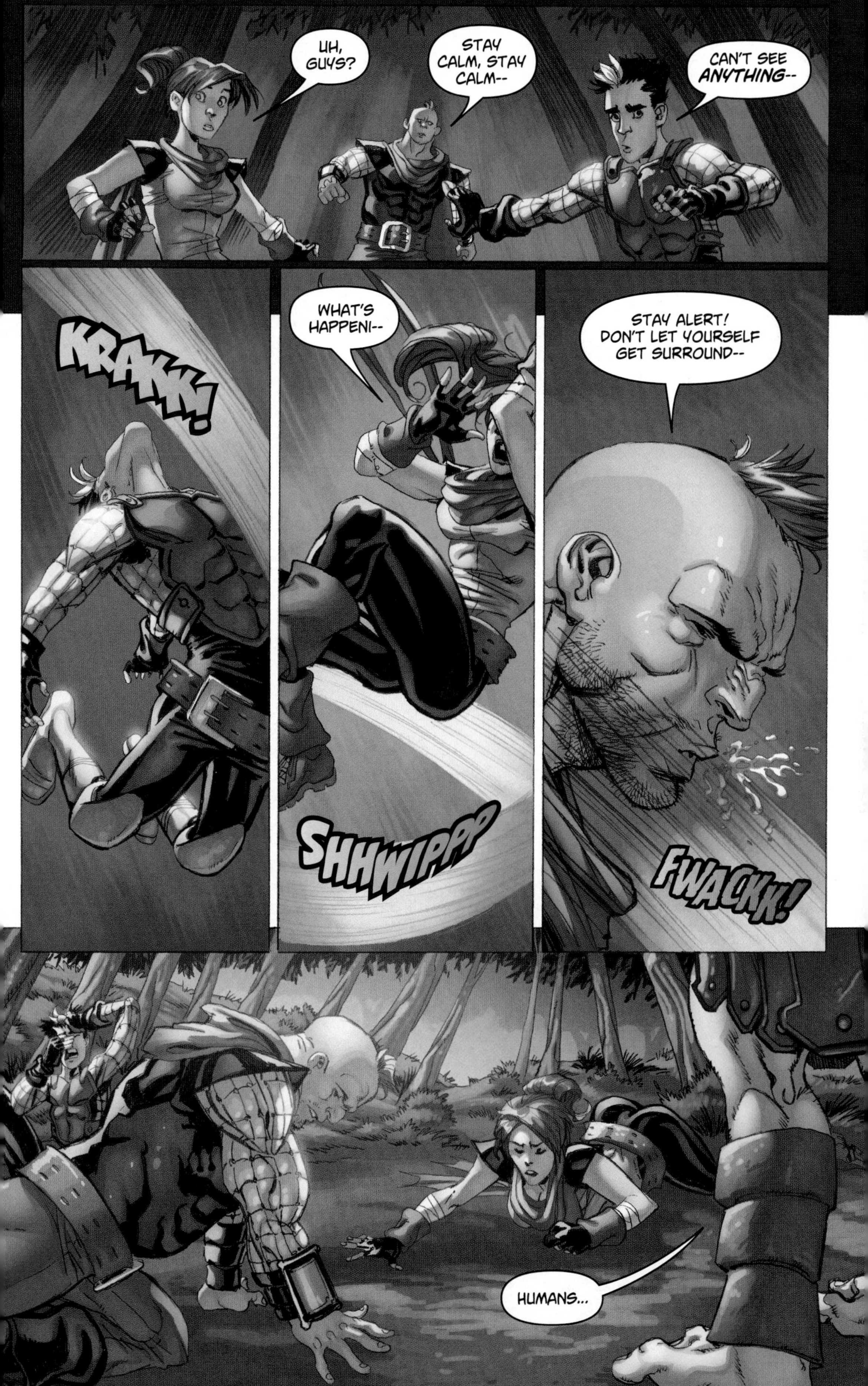

UH, GUYS?
STAY CALM, STAY CALM--
CAN'T SEE ANYTHING--
KRAKK!
WHAT'S HAPPENI--
SHHWIPPP
STAY ALERT! DON'T LET YOURSELF GET SURROUND--
FWACKK!
HUMANS...

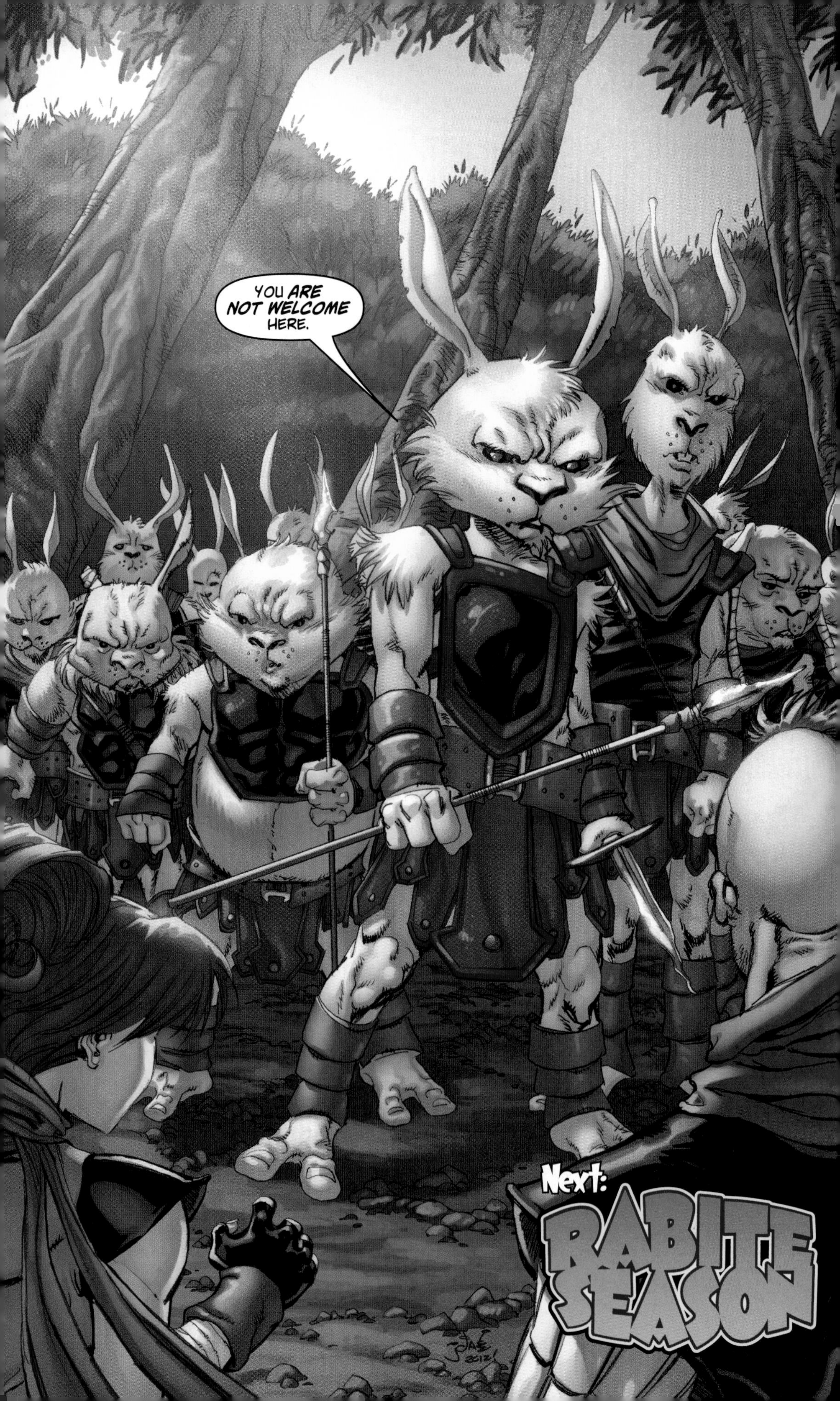

YOU ARE NOT WELCOME HERE.
Next:
RABITE SEASON

SKYWORDS

Got thoughts?
Fan art?
Ransom notes?

WRITE US @
skywardfans@gmail.com

Issue 3!

Can you believe it?! Seriously, we're having a great time with Action Lab at the moment-- those guys are great. I don't know if you Google "Skyward Comic Review" as much as I do, but wow-- the reaction to this book so far has been 1,000% stellar. I'm so humbled, all. Thanks!

On to the letters!

Hey Jeremy,

It was very cool to talk to you and Kelly this weekend at C2E2. I will definitely let Fantasy Shop know that they should order Skyward! Consider me your St. Louis ambassador. It's awesome how much you've stuck with the project. I will definitely be buying it.

I stopped by the Action Lab booth and talked to them after you spoke so highly of them. They encouraged me to submit the proposal for my own project, Tyrants. If you had any advice before I submitted it, I would greatly appreciate it. Would you recommend following their submission guidelines to the letter, or should I simply submit my full publishing proposal? The proposal has all that they ask for and more, but I wanted to get your thoughts first.

Anyway, I hope you had as much fun at the con as I did!

- Josh
joshbarbeau@gmail.com

Josh-- please do! I have far too many stories to tell with these characters (plotted well into the issue 30+ range as I write this), so your support and enthusiasm is greatly, greatly appreciated!

Tell the world! Skyward is here to stay, baby!

Hello,

We just met at HeroesCon a couple weeks ago. I hadn't heard of Skyward before then, but I am glad I came across your booth and your new comic. Skyward is amazing! We really don't get enough books that kids can read (although I have to admit, I stole my daughter's copy to read a few nights this week! Don't tell her).

Thank you for making this comic! I look forward to the new series in July.

- Devin Mackey
Address witheld at request

Devin, this is the kind of letter I really love. Not only are adults and established fans really enjoying this book, but kids, too! It almost brings a tear to the eye.

This goes for all of you out there-- if you enjoy what I'm doing with this book, drop me a line at the email address at the top of this page and let me know! You see, we comic book creators are a cowardly and superstitious lot, and we don't get a lot of feedback outside of the occasional glance at a Google vanity search or internet news article, interview, or review.

Love your creators! We're all huggable and stuff.

Hi Jeremy Dale and Team Skyward,

I heard about Skyward online and read some of them thanks to torrents and WOW AWESOME! When will there be more?

PS - Are these comix fanfics of the Zelda games?

- Barack0lypse

Aaaand...sigh. Well, Barack0lypse, putting out a creator-owned series is a tough road. I really wish you'd have picked up your copy in print -- or through Comixology or ComixPlus! There are tons of reasons why one should pay for their entertainment, but let's take a step back and realize this:

I'M NOT MARVEL OR DC. I'M NOT DRAWING A LICENSED BOOK, THIS IS A CREATOR-OWNED VENTURE. It kinda hurts getting emails like this. As much as I'm thrilled you enjoyed the book and all that, I gotta make a living.

So all of you reading the book through less-than-legal means via torrenting or whatever? If you liked it, consider dropping some $ in a comic or digital comic sometime.

That's all I ask. Thanks for your enthusiasm!

Also: No relation to the Zelda series in any manner. This is all-original, friends! :)

NEXT! The Rabites! vs Jon, Abi, and Tanner! Quinn's fate! Skerrigan vs Garrick! Three Rivers revealed! It's too much comic excitement for one book! In your face in 30 days! GET EXCITED!

- jeremy

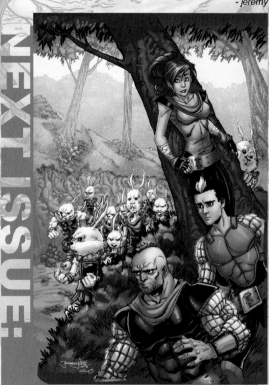

NEXT ISSUE!

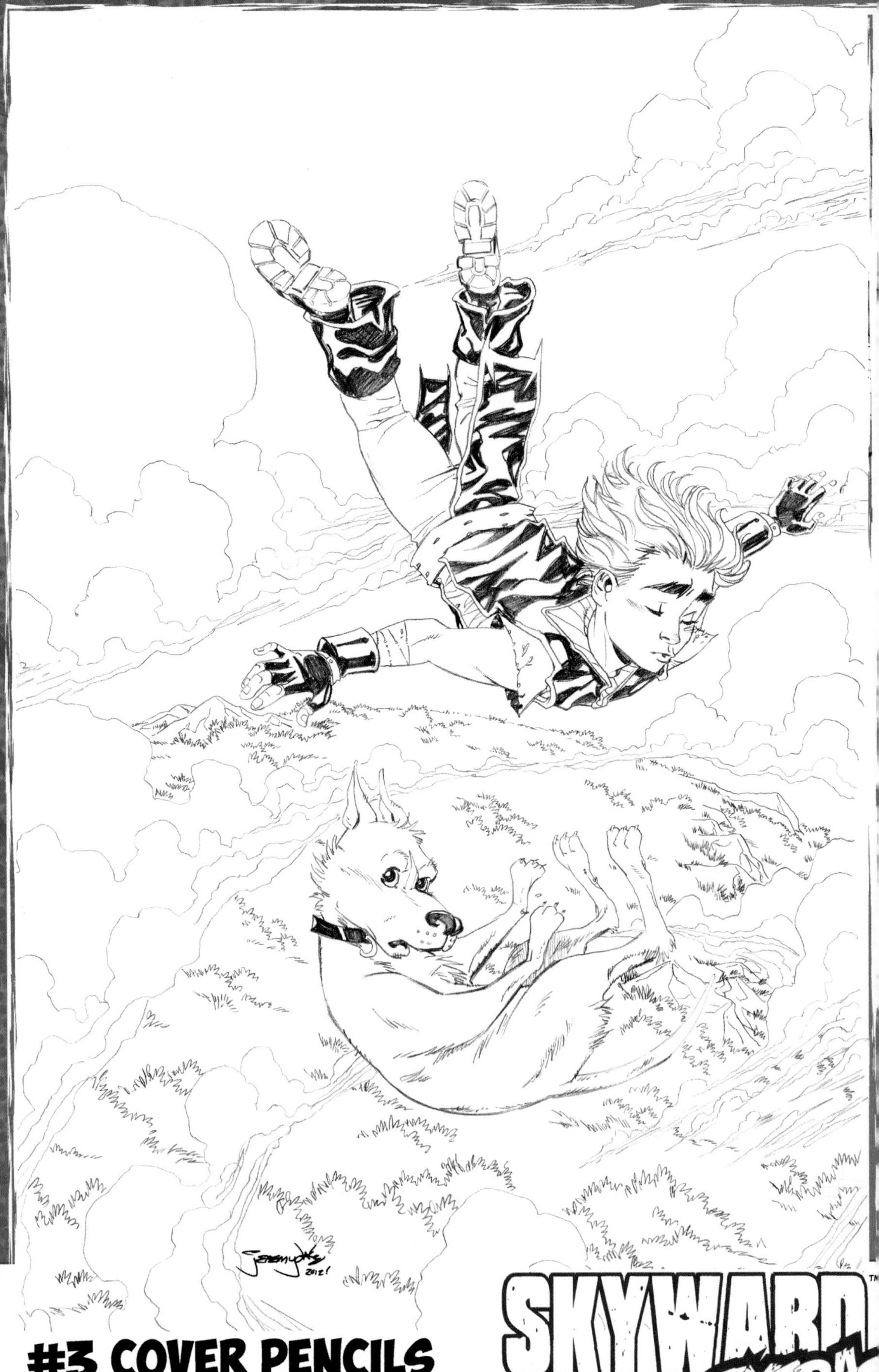

#3 COVER PENCILS
BY JEREMY DALE

SKYWARD™ EXTRAS

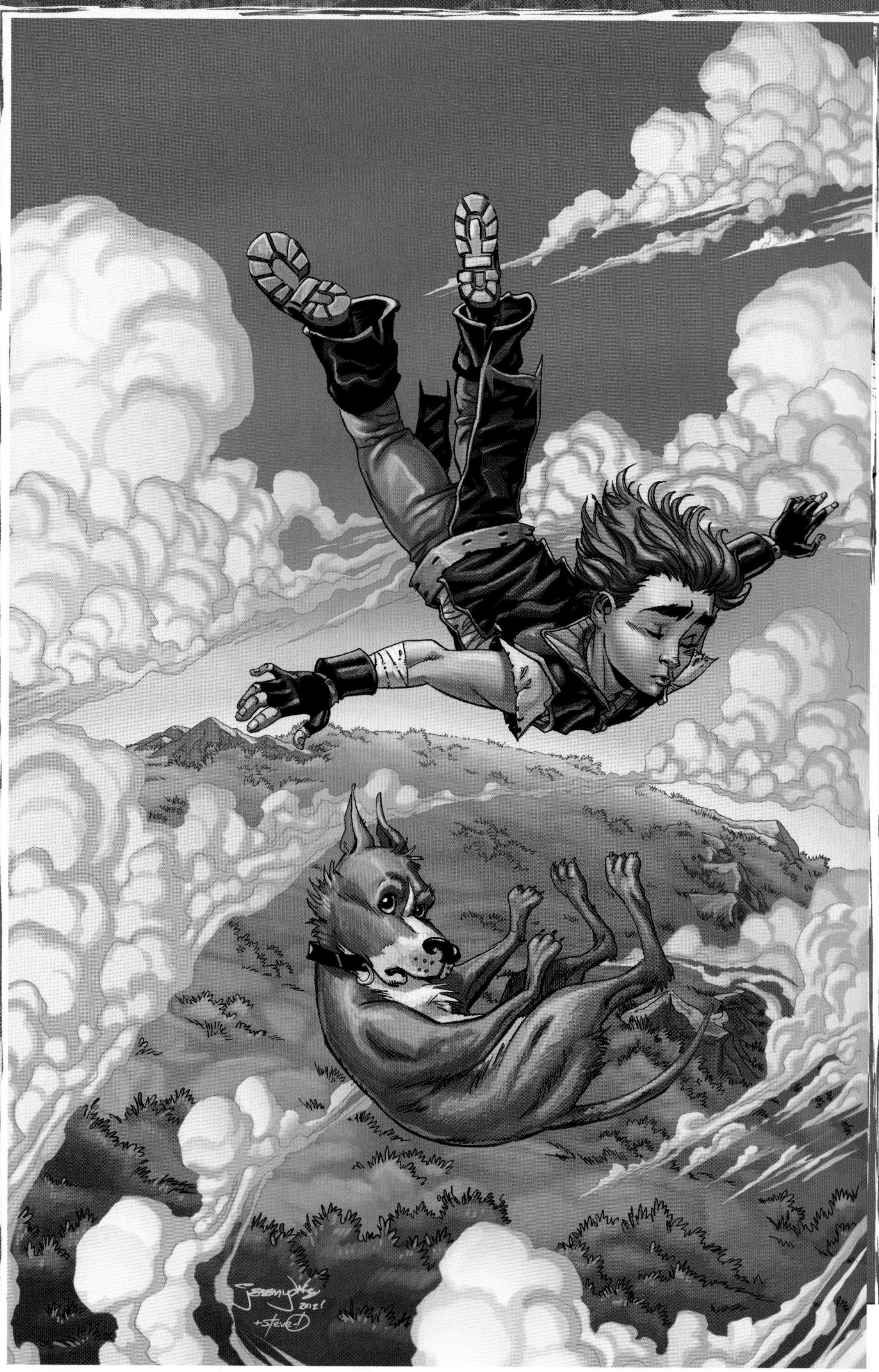

#3 COVER
BY JEREMY DALE & STEPHEN DOWNER

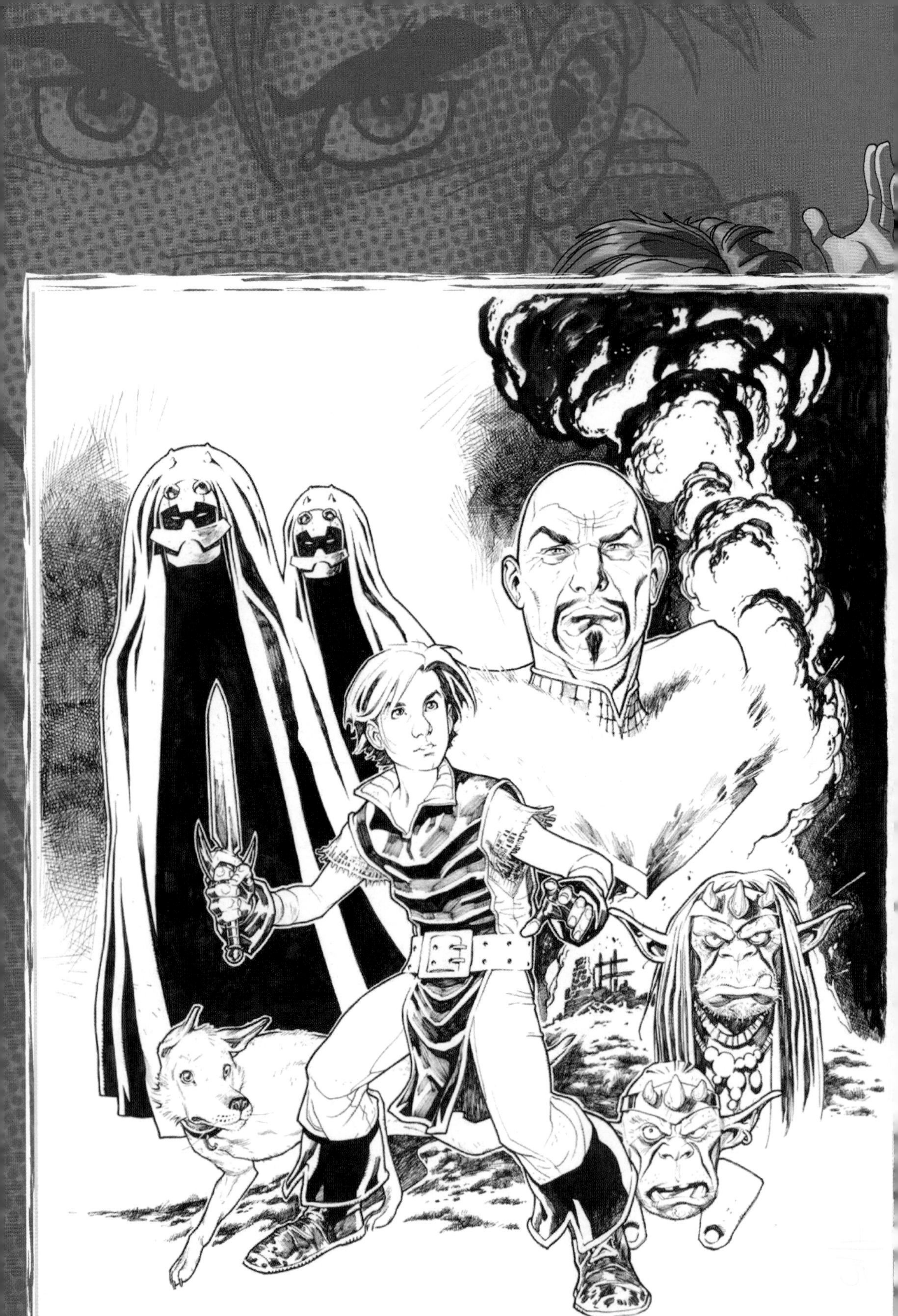

#3 VARIANT ART
BY STÉPHANE ROUX

SKYWARD™ EXTRAS

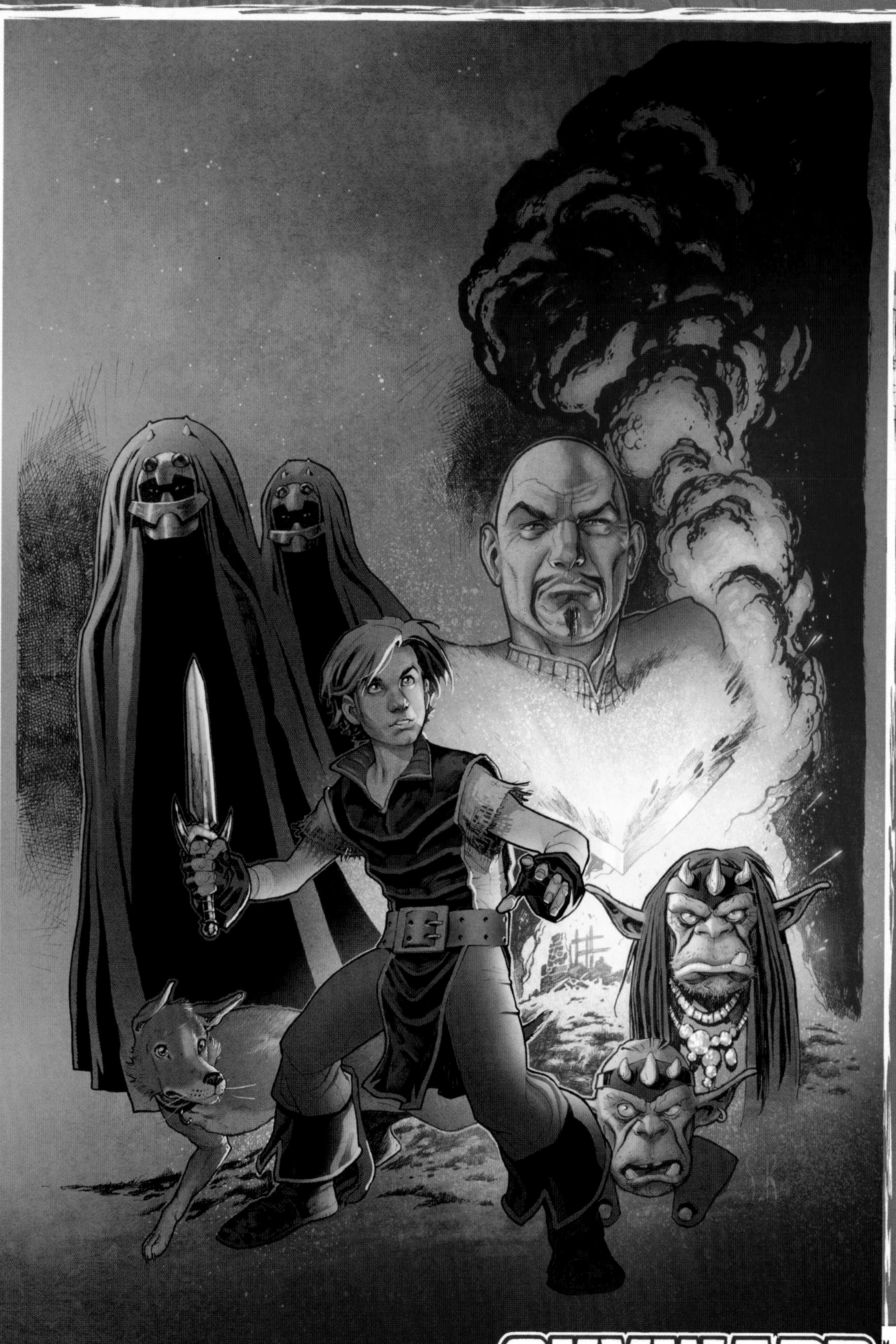

#3 VARIANT COVER
BY STÉPHANE ROUX

SKYWARD™ EXTRAS

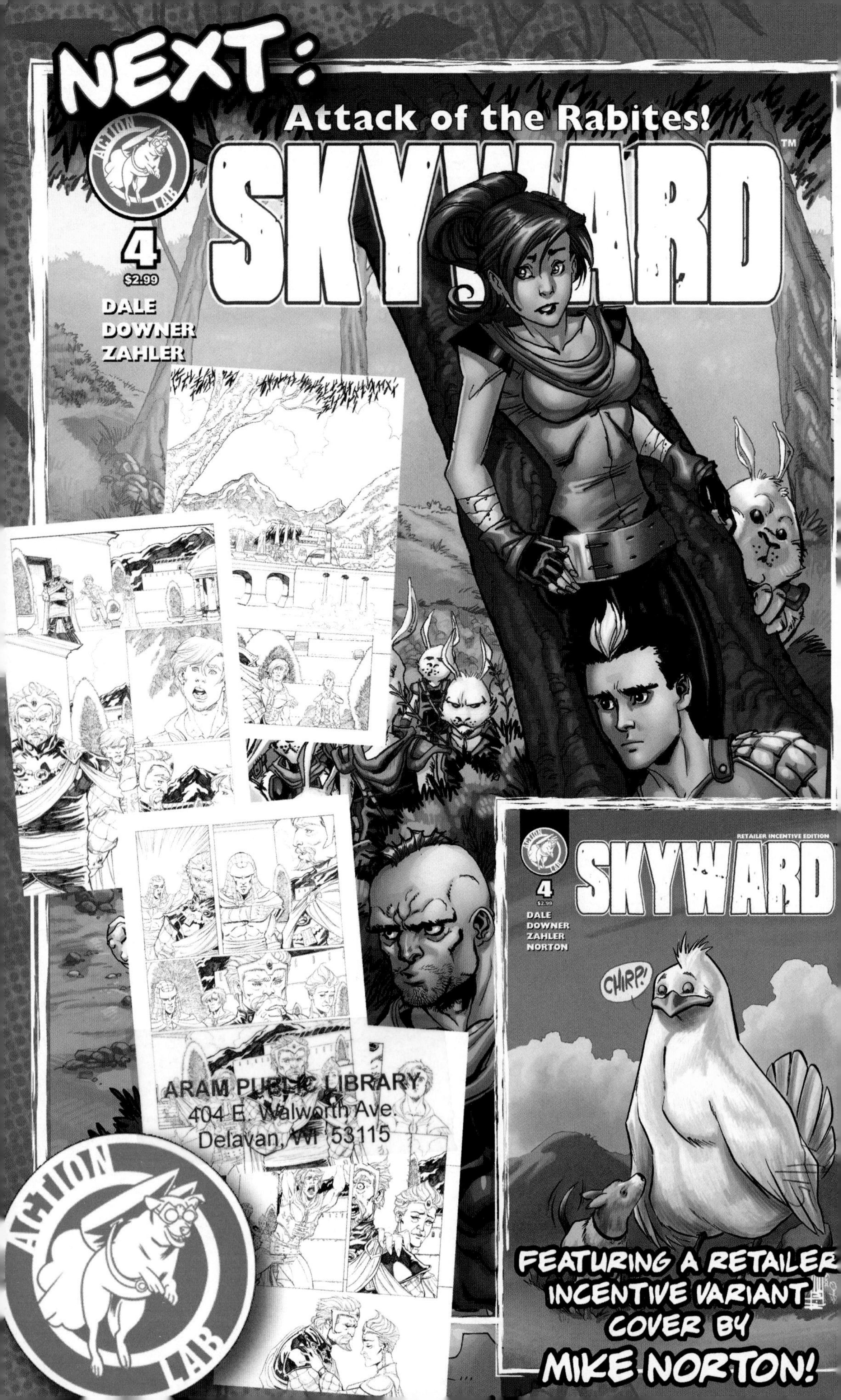
NEXT:
Attack of the Rabites!
SKYWARD
4
$2.99
DALE
DOWNER
ZAHLER
RETAILER INCENTIVE EDITION
SKYWARD
4
$2.99
DALE
DOWNER
ZAHLER
NORTON
CHIRP!
ARAM PUBLIC LIBRARY
404 E. Walworth Ave.
Delavan, WI 53115
ACTION LAB
FEATURING A RETAILER INCENTIVE VARIANT COVER BY
MIKE NORTON!